THE LIBRARIAN OF CROOKED LANE

THE GLASS LIBRARY, BOOK #1

C.J. ARCHER

WWW.CJARCHER.COM

CHAPTER 1

LONDON, SPRING 1920

*T*he woman crouching under the desk near my feet expelled an unladylike snort of derision.

I stilled. I didn't dare urge her to keep quiet with a nudge of my boot for fear that Mr. Parmiter, the head librarian, would notice. At the sound of the snort, he'd turned back and scrutinized me yet again. He had a way of making me feel like a speck under a microscope. Moments ago, he'd pressed both palms on the desk, leaned in until his face was close to mine, and inspected me with all the rigor of a detective searching for evidence at a crime scene.

Indeed, Mr. Parmiter's initial scrutiny had come about because he did suspect me of a crime. The crime of wearing makeup. According to the library charter, which I'd never seen, female staff were forbidden from adding so much as a smudge of color to their cheeks. Although I was sure the rule never existed since I was the first female employee, I didn't question him. I simply informed him I was not wearing makeup. He'd sniffed, as if trying to smell a lie, then turned away.

1

Until Daisy had gone and snorted like a bull at a red rag.

Mr. Parmiter scrutinized me again, but this time he stood a foot back from the desk. "Are you unwell, Miss Ashe?"

"No," I said. "I was just clearing my throat."

Those beady eyes of his narrowed further. He moistened his lips with a lizard-like flicker of his tongue, dampening the overhanging gray moustache. I wouldn't have been surprised if he reached across the desk to touch my forehead, checking for a fever, but the fear of getting too close held him back. I couldn't blame him for that. The Spanish flu had recently wreaked devastation and we all worried it would return.

"You should go home if you feel unwell," he said.

"I feel fine."

He waved a hand at my face. "And remove that vile stuff. This is a respectable institution where gentlemen of learning come for quiet study. Attractive women are a distraction. If it were up to me, I wouldn't have employed someone like you, but needs must." This last sentence he muttered as he walked off.

Thankfully Daisy didn't emit another snort. She was probably too shocked and angry to speak. I was just as angry but not shocked. In the two months since I'd taken the position of assistant librarian at the London Philosophical Society's library, I'd been exposed to Mr. Parmiter's misogynism on a regular basis. He blamed young women for just about every ill that had ever befallen him—or the world in general. I'm sure he could find a way to blame us for the war if he put his mind to it.

"It's safe," I whispered.

Daisy crawled out from the desk's footwell and cast a disdainful look in the direction in which Mr. Parmiter had departed. She hadn't seen him leave; it was the only exit from the reading nook. I was using the empty desk to inspect some old books for signs of disrepair. Tucked away on the first floor, between the stacks, it was the perfect place for quiet research—or hiding from one's manager while chatting to a friend who shouldn't be in the library at all. Daisy was not a member of the London Philosophical Society. She wasn't at all philosophical, not even after drinking too many cocktails. A drunk Daisy was a giggling Daisy, not terribly unlike a sober Daisy.

But she wasn't giggling now as she perched herself on the edge of the desk and regarded me with a frown. "What did he mean when he said he wouldn't have employed 'someone like you, but needs must?'"

I balanced the book on pragmatism on both my hands then closed it with a satisfying *thunk* of its thick pages and heavy leather cover. The smell of old paper wafted up, causing Daisy to cover her nose. I breathed the scent deeply into my lungs. "There were no other suitable applicants for the position of assistant librarian," I told her. "He had to resort to hiring a *female*." I rolled my eyes and gave a wry laugh.

"Really? Even with all the returned soldiers looking for work?"

"There were other applicants, but according to Mr. Parmiter, none were *suitable*. There were three others, in fact, all returned from the war. One was blind in one eye, another was missing a leg, and the third had shattered nerves that saw him jump at any loud noise. Mr. Parmiter claimed he couldn't employ them because they are a distressing reminder of the war and will put off the Society's members."

"He truly said that?"

I nodded.

"After everything those poor souls have been through, and now they have to endure the sneers of people like Priggy

Parmiter. And to imply you're only attractive when you're wearing makeup! The nerve of him." The heat with which she said it was on par with her defense of the returned soldiers. To Daisy, the two wrongs were equally abhorrent. "You're pretty, Sylvia, and don't let a dusty old bore like him tell you otherwise."

I thanked her for the compliment, but to be quite honest, I was no beauty. Not like Daisy, with her blue eyes and strawberry-blonde hair cut into a wavy bob that framed her face. The style was very modern, but in the few short months I'd known her, I'd come to realize Daisy followed trends like winter follows autumn—inevitably. She never settled for very long before moving on to the next thing that caught her eye. Her desire to try new things was understandable. I didn't blame her for shrugging off the heavy blanket that had shrouded the nation after four years of war and another one and a half of the flu. Sometimes the bleakness had seemed as though it would never end. But despite their personal losses, some people were ready to move on. Daisy *needed* to move forward with her life.

I hadn't quite reached that point yet.

"Speaking of dusty..." Daisy wrinkled her nose as she pushed away the book I'd been about to inspect for damage. One of the pages had come loose and the corners of several others had been turned over to act as a bookmark. The thin layer of dust on it bothered Daisy more.

It had been on the desk for some time, waiting for a librarian to tend to it. Years ago, someone had collected all the books in the library that looked as though they might need to be sent away for repairs and piled them up on this desk in the remotest reading nook in the building. Then war had broken out, the assistant librarian had died on the battlefields of France, and no one had been employed in his stead until I started work in March. Filling a dead man's shoes wasn't easy, particularly when Mr. Parmiter made it clear my gender meant my work was inferior to my predecessor's, but I enjoyed it when he wasn't bothering me.

It was quiet. Few members came into the library and when they did, they preferred to speak to Mr. Parmiter rather than me. The job didn't pay particularly well, but I could walk to work, saving myself the cost of transport. I also got to chat to Daisy, when she wasn't in her flat painting—which seemed to be most afternoons—and when she wasn't hiding from Mr. Parmiter who came upstairs to check on me from time to time.

Daisy watched me as I gently opened the book she'd pushed away. "If you must work in a library, why not work in a modern one with novels?"

"With all the returning soldiers resuming their previous employment, there are few jobs for women. I was fortunate to get this one."

She sighed. "It's a pity you have to work at all, really."

I looked up, frowning. She looked back at me with sympathy. "Don't *you* have to?" I asked.

"Oh yes, but we artists don't have a schedule like regular people. We work when the muse strikes. Besides, I was left a little money by my grandparents. It keeps me going."

It was the first time she'd mentioned an inheritance. Daisy's parents lived in Wiltshire and didn't approve of their middle child moving to London. She had an older sister who'd lost her husband in the war and a younger brother who'd signed up upon turning eighteen in 1918. Thankfully he survived.

"I actually like working," I said, and I meant it.

Whether Daisy believed me or not, I never found out. She became distracted by a newspaper discarded on a small table beside the armchair. She flounced into the chair and began to read.

I sat too and made notes on the damage to the books, sorting them into different piles according to the type of repairs required. For the many pages with dog-eared corners, I smoothed out the creases with my thumb. It was easy and relaxing work. Although the topics didn't particularly interest me, it was satisfying to know these books would once again be read and valued by the society's members thanks to my efforts today.

"He is the prime article," Daisy murmured from the armchair. She folded the newspaper in half and turned it to show me what she'd been reading. I couldn't make out much from this distance, however, just a dark-haired man standing on the deck of a yacht. "Handsome, rich, the heir to a title *and* a war hero. So many virtues in one man."

"None of those are virtues, Daisy, except for perhaps being a war hero. He could be selfish and vain for all we know."

"You're so unromantic, Sylvia."

I picked up the book on pragmatism and waved it at her. "Perhaps I've worked here too long." I smiled but she took me seriously.

"I'm glad you finally agree."

"I was referring to this title. I've only been here two months."

"Long enough." She glanced around, worried our conversation was being overheard. "If it weren't for me, your days would drag."

I laughed. Daisy's unfailing self-confidence had won me over when we met. If I could bottle it, I would take a sip whenever I felt my own confidence waning.

She studied the newspaper article again. "I wonder if he's married."

"If not, he soon will be. A paragon like that won't be single for long. The unmarried women of England won't allow it." One of the saddest outcomes of war was that it took young men. Now that we were emerging from the fog, women my age were bemoaning the lack of eligible bachelors.

I was not among them. I was still shrouded by the fog. I'd not only lost my brother in the war, but my mother had succumbed to the flu pandemic that had struck down so many in the war's aftermath. They'd been my only family. I'd also left behind friends when I moved to London. Not that I had many friends to lose. We'd moved too often to put down deep roots anywhere.

But I was determined to make a go of it in London. In the two and a half months since my arrival, I'd made a friend in Daisy and found gainful employment. It was a foundation I could build on to help me climb out of the fog, in time.

"What has the paragon done to warrant an article written about him?" I asked.

"He attempted to rescue a fisherman and his teenage son while out sailing off the coast of the Isle of Wight. Apparently he saw their boat capsize and didn't hesitate to dive in and risk his life to save them. They were tangled up in their net under water and he had to cut it to free them. The son survived but the father didn't."

"How awful."

"The article says it was a miracle Mr. Glass didn't drown too. It then goes on to list all the medals he won in the war. Good lord."

I peered over her shoulder. "What is it?"

"He joined up at the start of the war and survived the entire four years on the front lines. He was there for every major battle, and he didn't once get seriously injured."

"Then he couldn't have been in *every* major battle for the entire duration. Besides, the heir to a title would be given something safe to do well away from the enemy."

"Not according to this. Gallipoli, the Somme, Ypres, Amiens...he fought in them all. His parents must have been beside themselves with worry. It says here he is the only child of Lord and Lady Rycroft."

I read over her shoulder. "'Mr. Gabriel Glass, Baron and Baroness of Rycroft. Lady Rycroft is the famed magician, India Glass, nee Steele.'"

"Where can a girl meet such a man?"

"The Isle of Wight, apparently." I returned to the desk but instead of picking up a book, I stared out of the window. The view wasn't interesting, just the dark gray buildings opposite and a thin layer of cloudy sky above the roofline. I hardly registered any of it. My mind was elsewhere. "Daisy, does the name India Glass mean anything to you?"

She shook her head. "No, but I'm not a magician, nor can I afford to buy magical objects. I'm trying to make the inheritance last, and I'm yet to sell a painting."

"Does the article say anything else about her?"

"Just that she gave up practicing watchmaking magic to marry Lord Rycroft and has been an advisor to the government on magician policies for years. Why? Have you heard of her?"

"The name rings a bell." I just couldn't remember why. The memory was there in my mind, just out of reach, buried in the fog.

* * *

I LAY on my back on the narrow bed in the room I rented at the lodging house and stared at the water stain on the ceiling. I felt tired but pushed against it, wading through the fog as I searched for the name.

India Glass.

Where had I seen it? I knew I'd *seen* it, not heard it. That meant it had appeared in a letter or an article, but I rarely read the newspaper, so it must be private correspondence. There was only one person who ever wrote to me. One person whose letters I'd kept.

I pushed the chair up against the wardrobe and stood on it, rising onto my toes to reach, cursing my short stature. Fortunately, the suitcase was light. I managed to grasp it without pulling the entire thing down on my head. It was a child's suitcase made of tan leather, small enough for a young girl to drag around the country. And drag it I had. Frequent moves accounted for the scratches and patchwork of dents. I opened it on the bed and stared at the remaining contents of my mother's and brother's lives.

I'd kept her favorite shawl, made of emerald green silk with Japanese motifs embroidered throughout, as well as a plain silver ring, two enamel hair combs and some old photographs of James and me as children. James's belongings were just as meager. I'd not seen any point bringing his old clothes with me so I'd sold them before leaving for London. I'd needed the money. I set aside his pocket watch, war medal, and notebook. I plucked out the two packets of letters, both tied with string. One packet was thick and contained dozens of letters written by my mother and me to James. He'd kept them all, and they'd been returned to us after his death. The other packet contained letters he'd sent to us. I untied the string around them and lightly caressed the topmost envelope.

The sight of his neat, precise handwriting brought a fierce ache to my chest.

I read each letter but didn't find any reference to India Glass. Perhaps I'd misremembered or I'd seen the name elsewhere.

I retied the string and, with a heavy sigh, placed the letters back into the suitcase, wedged between the notebook and the back.

I removed the notebook and flipped it open. It had been with James a long time. The leather cover was scratched and faded from its original forest green to the color of a muddy puddle. The pages were crinkled from being damp and drying out, making the whole book fatter than it would have been when new. My brother's dirty fingerprints appeared on almost every page, and the once white paper was now brown from the mud of the Western Front. I'd read the notebook cover to cover after it was returned to us before storing it in the suitcase with his other belongings. With Mother becoming ill and dying, then contracting the flu myself, I'd forgotten about it and not looked at it since. Reading James's words had been painful then, so soon after losing him. It was still painful now, but the initial sharp ache dulled to a throb as I became lost in my search for the name.

India Glass.

I scanned the pages, not wanting to read every word. That would only make the ache in my chest swell again. The pages were filled with James's thoughts, some forming complete sentences, others merely fragments of ideas in the form of single words or a sketch. He'd been a good artist.

I found the name near the end. It was on a line of its own and didn't form part of a sentence. It was just those two words, India Glass, which I'd thought meant glass from India when I first read it, perhaps referring to a vase or trinket. I'd not wondered why my brother would be making notes on glassware from a country he'd never been to, but back then, I'd been too grief stricken to think clearly about anything.

Knowing the words were in fact a name gave the notes above and below it new meaning. When I'd first read them, I'd been shocked to learn my brother thought he was a silver-smith magician, simply because he liked silver things. Who didn't like silver things? I was partial to jewelry set in silver, but I preferred gold. I owned neither, unless I counted the silver band of my mother's. Magic couldn't possibly run in our blood. We were unremarkable. Mother had been a seamstress, James a teacher, and I'd written articles for several local newspapers and journals before that work dried up when the soldiers returned in large numbers. Female journalists were once again relegated to the sections on cookery, housekeeping and fashion, none being topics in which I could claim any expertise or flair. The Ashes weren't craftspeople. We were just a family with dissimilar interests.

I fought back tears as I removed Mother's ring from the suitcase and slipped it on my finger. It fit my middle one. It was simple, plain and thin, not a special item at all. I felt nothing as I touched it. Wasn't I supposed to feel something if it had silver magic in it? Or did only other magicians feel magic?

I didn't know how it worked. I couldn't afford magician-made things, so I'd never bothered to learn about magic.

I returned to the notebook. According to James's notes, he'd asked Mother about silver magic, and she'd told him he was mistaken and to not bring it up again.

Below the name India Glass he'd written the word "Answers" followed by a question mark. Answers to what? To the question of whether the Ashe family could perform silver magic?

I closed the book and returned it and the suitcase to the space above the wardrobe. I fell asleep and thought no more about India Glass, silver magic, or my brother until the following morning when I returned to the reading nook on the first floor of the library and spotted the newspaper Daisy had been reading.

"War hero saves boy in miraculous underwater rescue" the attention-grabbing headline read.

The image of the brave rescuer stared back at the camera. Gabriel Glass looked a little annoyed by the attention, as if he wanted to shout at the journalists to leave him alone. As a former journalist, I'd been told to go away many times. I'd lacked the confidence to insist where my colleagues had persisted. It was probably why I was one of the first women to lose their jobs when the journalists-turned-soldiers returned from the war.

I placed the newspaper in the desk drawer and worked until Daisy snuck into the library. When she flopped into the armchair with a dramatic sigh of boredom, I handed it to her.

She frowned. "Are you trying to tell me something?"

"I want to meet his mother, India Glass—Lady Rycroft."

She sat up straight. "If you think the way to a man is through his mother, you know even less about men than I thought you did."

I bristled. "I know as much about men as you, Daisy."

She battled with a smile. "Dear, sweet Sylvia, have you exchanged more than a 'good afternoon' with a single man since arriving in London?" I opened my mouth to answer her, but she put up a finger to stop me. "Priggy Parmiter doesn't count."

I snatched the newspaper from her. "I'm not interested in meeting Gabriel Glass. I'm interested in his mother."

"Lady Rycroft? Why?"

Footsteps on the staircase cut off my answer. "Blast. Hide, Daisy, quickly."

She dove into the cavity under the desk, tucking her legs into her body. I stood behind the desk, blocking the view to the cavity as best as I could in case Mr. Parmiter decided to come around to my side.

I smiled and pretended to listen as the head librarian complained about a particular member who hadn't returned a book that was now well overdue. I was actually thinking about my brother's claim that he might be a silver magician and our mother's denial. Although I agreed with my mother, I felt as though I owed it to James's memory to find out, once and for all. If he believed India Glass could provide answers then I would do everything I could to speak with her.

But first I had to find her.

CHAPTER 2

*A*fter Mr. Parmiter departed and Daisy once again crawled out from beneath the desk, I told her about my brother's notebook and his notion that we were silver magicians. She didn't laugh or think him peculiar. She took it in her stride. I was beginning to think nothing fazed her.

She became enthused by the idea of finding Lady Rycroft and immediately put her mind to how we could engineer a meeting. Daisy was naturally excitable. The first time she snuck into the library she looked as though she'd stumbled upon a pot of money when she joined me in the stacks. But she was simply thrilled to have correctly guessed the number of steps leading up to the society's front door.

She sat in the armchair and stared down at the photograph of Gabriel Glass in the newspaper, her brow furrowed in concentration. "It may be easier to find Lady Rycroft through her son. After all, he probably attends society parties, dinners, that sort of thing."

"Yes, but we *don't* attend society parties and dinners. I'm a librarian and you're an artist." I almost added that she was an artist of no repute, but that was a little mean. Just because she

14

didn't make a living off her art didn't mean she wasn't very good. Many famous artists had been virtually unknown in their lifetime. For all I knew, Daisy was the same. Since I was no art expert, I would refrain from voicing an opinion on her style, although secretly I'd vowed not to hang anything of hers in a prominent place. They weren't to my taste.

Daisy continued to frown at the newspaper.

"Do you think it's odd that James wrote India Glass in his notebook and not Lady Rycroft?" I asked. "It's not like him to be disrespectful."

"Perhaps he knew her personally." Daisy gasped. "Perhaps they were having an affair!"

"That's highly unlikely, considering she must be at least fifty and he was only twenty-six when he died."

"There's nothing wrong with an older woman being with a younger man."

"No, but my brother was not in the habit of having affairs with married women."

"Perhaps the husband is dead."

"If he was, your war hero would be Lord Rycroft now, but he's simply reported as Gabriel Glass."

"Good point. Nothing gets past you, Sylvia. It must be your journalist's keen eye for detail." When I'd told her I'd been a journalist during the war, she'd thought it a most interesting career. She'd continued to scour the employment advertisements for journalism positions for me, even after I'd given up and taken the job at the library. It wouldn't surprise me if she continued to check even now.

"Anyway, where would James have met a baroness?" I continued.

"I don't know where *he* met her, but I think I know where *we* can meet her." She slipped off her Oxfords and curled her feet under her on the armchair. "Do you remember my painter friend, Horatio? He's exhibiting at the Royal Academy's summer exhibition this year, and I believe the private viewing starts tomorrow." She gave a pert little twitch of her shoulders and grinned at me in triumph.

I gave her a blank look. "I don't understand the connection to Lady Rycroft. Does the exhibition have something to do with magic?"

"The private viewing of the Royal Academy's summer exhibition is a key event on the London social calendar. Lords and ladies will be in attendance." She waved the newspaper at me. "If we get in, we can find her and ask her if she knew James."

It would require diplomacy, but I'd manufactured introductions before in my work as a journalist. This time it was more important. It was personal. And I found I wanted to know more about James and his thoughts in his final weeks and months. It was a way of honoring him.

And a way of climbing out of the fog.

"Do you think Horatio will agree to help us get into the private viewing?"

She smiled a secret smile. "Oh yes. He owes me a favor." Her smile suddenly vanished as her gaze focused on something behind me. "Bloody hell."

"I knew it!" Mr. Parmiter charged up to the desk, a finger pointed at me like a weapon. "I knew you were hiding someone up here."

I stepped back. "I—I'm sorry, Mr. Parmiter. Daisy was just leaving. She only came to show me a newspaper article about…um…"

"Her brother's friend." Daisy flashed the newspaper at him. "Sylvia has been searching for him ever since the war ended. It's why she came to London, but she hasn't managed to find any sign of him. She'll think she's getting close then WHAM!" She smacked the newspaper down on the desk causing both Mr. Parmiter and me to jump in fright. "He disappears. Until now." She pointed at the photograph of Gabriel Glass. "You wouldn't deny her the opportunity to find out more about her poor departed brother's friend, would you?"

Mr. Parmiter grasped the lapels of his jacket as if they were the edges of an academic gown and peered down his nose at her. "I am not denying her anything, young lady. Your discovery could have waited until she finished work."

"Why should she wait a moment longer?"

He glared pointedly at her shoes, positioned by the chair. "Kindly get dressed and leave."

Daisy straightened and threw her shoulders back, ready for battle. I intervened before she engaged and cost me my job.

"I'll speak to you later," I said quickly.

Her lips flattened, but she gave in. She slipped on her shoes, retied the laces, and marched off, casting a final glare over her shoulder at Mr. Parmiter.

Once she was gone, he turned to me. He regarded me like a strict school master, with a mixture of self-righteousness and authoritarianism. It was maddening but I couldn't walk away like Daisy had. "Are you aware how fortunate you are to have a job here at all, Miss Ashe?"

"Yes, sir."

"I run a tight ship. I don't abide having my rules broken. They are there for a reason. First the makeup, and now allowing your friend to wander about the library unsupervised." He paused, perhaps waiting for me to utter an apology. I simply picked up a book that was missing its front cover and inspected it for further damage. I might not dare try to defend myself, but I could simply not speak. It was a protest, of sorts.

It didn't deter him. "Our noble institution cannot be treated so cavalierly. It must be respected. The charter rules must be obeyed. If everyone disobeyed the rules, where would we be?"

I couldn't stay silent any longer. "May I see the charter, please?"

He stretched his neck out of his collar and cleared his throat. "This is your final warning, Miss Ashe. Overstep again and I'll have no choice but to dismiss you." He strode off.

I watched him go then sat with a sigh. I should have insisted on seeing the so-called charter. I'd wager he couldn't provide it.

"Chin up, old girl."

I swallowed my gasp, which only caused me to cough.

Daisy grinned at me. She must have hidden in the stacks instead of leaving. "I wanted to make sure you were all right before I go."

"I'm fine, thank you."

"I think he believed the story about your brother's friend." She indicated the newspaper. "I'll speak to Horatio now. See you later, Sylvia." She tiptoed off, wiggling her fingers at me in a wave.

I smiled. The more I got to know her, the more I liked her.

I COULD CURSE DAISY. If I'd wanted to work in service, I would have applied for jobs as a maid when I came to London. Offering platters of food to well-heeled guests at the Royal Academy of Art's private viewing had not been my plan for Saturday. I'd hoped to mingle with them, not be ignored by them. I suppose I shouldn't have expected Daisy's friend to just hand me an invitation to the exclusive event. I'd never blend in, anyway. The ladies were dressed in the latest styles and dripped with jewels; they sparkled more than the chandeliers overhead. My best dress and Mother's ring were too plain.

To add insult to injury, Daisy spent more time flirting with one of the waiters than working, while I did my best to do the job I was employed to do and still search for Lady Rycroft. I offered the pastries to a cluster of ladies and gentlemen positioned in front of the wall of landscapes. The framed paintings depicted bucolic scenes with country cottages, rolling green hills and grazing cattle. Some were quite beautiful. I could stare at them all day and imagine myself enjoying a picnic beneath a shady oak. There wasn't a single reminder of the war in any of them.

The group ignored me and continued chatting about their estates and people they knew. They sounded as though they hadn't seen one another in months. I ought not to feel slighted. I was dressed in black, designed to disappear into the background, and no one wanted hors d'oeuvres at this hour. Most would have just come from lunch.

At least I was in good company—the paintings and artists were ignored too. I spotted Horatio chatting to two other fellows he'd introduced me to earlier as friends who were also exhibiting. With hair meeting their collars instead of cut short, and wearing cravats rather than ties, they looked like fish out of water as they studied an oil painting. When a middle-aged woman dressed all in black joined them, they were all smiles. They seemed to know her, and even revere her. She must be an art lover and potential customer, going by the way they fell over themselves to talk to her.

She touched Horatio's chest with the flat of her hand, so perhaps she was a lover of artists as well as their work. It would seem older women and younger men weren't such an unusual combination after all. I wondered if Daisy knew. She seemed quite keen on Horatio. Her eyes lit up when she spoke about him, and she was eager to include him in our search for Lady Rycroft.

I attempted to offload more pastries but had little luck. Nor did I have any luck finding Lady Rycroft, although it was too soon to give up. I'd begun my search in the main room, but there were many more galleries, each filled with invited guests. The one good thing about being ignored was that it meant I could move between groups and listen for Lady Rycroft's name. I didn't know what she looked like. Horatio hadn't met her either, but he'd promised to let me know if he heard she was here. Unlike the service staff, the artists could mingle, and he had a greater opportunity to meet her than Daisy or me.

Daisy approached, a tray of oysters balanced on her hand. "He's here," she whispered.

"He who? We're looking for Lady Rycroft, not a man."

"Her son, the paragon. I recognized him from his photograph in the newspaper." Her lips curled into a smile. "He's even better looking in real life."

"I suppose we could ask him which one is his mother." I glanced around at the ladies nearby, one of which was looking down her nose at us. "You'd better go," I hissed at Daisy.

"Come with me to the basement where we can talk."

"I can't leave yet. I have to finish serving these."

She walked off, bumping me hard in the shoulder. I lost my balance and the tray tumbled to the floor with a clatter, sending pastries scattering. Nearby conversations stopped. Everyone turned to look.

With my face flaming, I bent to gather up the pastries. The waiter who'd been flirting with Daisy in the basement earlier crouched next to me and helped. Daisy was suddenly nowhere to be seen.

"Are you all right?" he asked quietly.

"Yes. Thank you for helping. I appreciate it."

"First time?"

"Is it that obvious?"

He flashed me a grin. It softened his strong features, turning him from a rather fierce looking man into a friendly one. He had brown skin and, when he stood up, I realized how tall he was. He towered over me. He was well-built too, with a frame that strained against the stiff, formal livery. The collar looked as though it were strangling him, but he continued to smile at me as if nothing bothered him.

The butler, Mr. Ludlow, appeared out of the crowd, his nostrils flaring like a raging bull's. No smile would soften *his* fierce looks. "Get back to work," he growled, his voice guttural. "You! New girl! Take those back to the kitchen and fetch fresh ones."

I shot a smile of thanks to the waiter who'd helped me and hurried away, wending my way through the crowd and exiting the main gallery into a smaller gallery with more oil paintings, and after that an even smaller room showcasing watercolors and miniatures. This led to the stairs down to the basement service area where the staff bustled to and from the kitchen, carrying platters of food and glasses of champagne.

Daisy was waiting for me. "Don't glare at me, Sylvia, I did you a favor. We need to talk."

"It was embarrassing!"

She waved off my concern. "You'll never see those people again. Anyway, you're forgetting why we're here. It's to find Lady Rycroft, not serve snobs with nothing better to do than gossip when they should be admiring the art. I don't think a single one of them cares about the paintings."

I shoved the tray at her. She put it down on a side table. We were in the long corridor that led to the kitchen and other service rooms where staff assembled hors d'oeuvres on platters and ushered the waiters and waitresses off with a flap of their aprons. No one paid us any attention, but it wouldn't be long before the butler came down the stairs. After the debacle upstairs, he might dismiss me altogether.

"Do you have a plan?" I asked Daisy.

"I do, as it happens. You should speak to Gabriel Glass. Ask him where to find his mother, since she doesn't appear to be here."

"I can't approach a stranger and ask him where his mother lives."

"If you don't, you'll lose your only opportunity to find her. Do you want to find her or not?"

"Of course."

She nodded at the stairs leading back up to the galleries. "Then go. He was in the sculpture room, the one at the back not the central one. You'll recognize him when you see him." She handed me the tray and gave me a little shove toward the stairs.

"I can't serve these. They fell on the floor."

"No one will notice. Anyway, it'll be amusing to see those snobs eating them."

"They're not eating at all."

She clicked her tongue. "Typical. Now go or I'll do it instead, except I'll forget to ask him about his mother because I'll be too busy flirting."

I headed back up the stairs only to be accosted by the nostril-flaring butler, hand up to halt me like a traffic policeman. "Did you get fresh ones?"

"Of course." I quickly side-stepped around him and hurried off, ignoring his hissed command for me to wait. As Daisy said, I wouldn't see these people again after today, and I was quite fed up with waitressing. I wanted to speak to Mr. Glass and get out as quickly as possible.

The exhibition was held across several rooms of Burlington House, the home of the Royal Academy of Arts.

Before the invited attendees arrived, I'd been given a brief tour, along with the other new staff, so I knew where to find the sculpture room at the back. Being small and the crowd thick, I had to occasionally ask guests to step out of my way. The disdainful looks I received for my impertinence were the most attention I'd received all day.

I looked all around the sculpture room, but Mr. Glass was not there. I moved through the adjoining rooms, no longer bothering to ask guests if they wanted an hors d'oeuvre. Finally, I found my quarry in the large room with the oil paintings where I'd made a spectacle of myself.

He was easy to spot, not merely because he was tall enough to be seen over the heads of the rest of the crowd, but also because a collection of young ladies hovered in his vicinity, no doubt drawn by his magnetism. He was undeniably handsome, but it was more than his height and good looks that drew the gazes of both men and women. He nodded as his companions talked, genuinely interested in what they had to say. He never interrupted, only answering when they appeared to ask for his opinion on a painting. His bearing was erect but not stiff, his gaze direct but without judgement. And his smile! It made everyone else smile in response.

He stood with Horatio and the other people I'd seen Horatio talking to earlier, two artist friends and the elegant woman dressed in black. The gaggle of young ladies did not intrude, but they were clearly orbiting the small group in an attempt to catch Mr. Glass's attention. Their attempts failed.

The woman in black took Mr. Glass's arm and steered him to a gilt-framed seascape of an ocean liner powering through the silver-crested waves. The artists followed, and the young ladies edged along too, pretending to admire the same painting. The middle-aged woman claimed his entire attention as she indicated the steam billowing from the ship's funnels, blending into the clouds until it was impossible to tell where steam ended and sky began.

Mr. Glass nodded along. I couldn't tell if he was merely being polite or if he genuinely liked the painting. It seemed well executed to me, and I would happily hang it on my wall if I could afford it.

With so many people around him, I had no hope of speaking to Mr. Glass in private. I was considering how to proceed when Horatio signaled for me to approach with a jerk of his head.

Daisy's friend was an intriguing fellow. When I'd first met him, I'd thought him to be in his early twenties like me. He was always dressed in his artist's overalls, with a dash of paint on either his forehead or cheek, his slender frame in need of feeding. But now that I saw him dressed in a formal suit, his brown hair slicked back instead of sticking up as if he'd not combed it for days, I wondered if he was closer to thirty or even older. He wasn't handsome. In fact, his sharp nose made him look somewhat mousy, but his big eyes saved him. That and his friendly nature. If he wanted to take a lover, he probably wouldn't have much difficulty finding one. I just wasn't entirely sure if the lovers would be men or women.

As I drew closer, Horatio stole Mr. Glass from the woman's side and steered him towards me. It was done so quickly and deftly that she took a moment to realize. That moment was long enough for me to introduce myself.

The focus with which Mr. Glass had given the painting was now turned entirely onto me. Daisy was right. He was more handsome in person than in the newspaper photograph. It was difficult to pinpoint the reason why. His features were unremarkable, when considered separately, but put together, he was perfectly arranged. The sculptures in the other galleries were bland in comparison, and I doubted a portrait artist could capture the precise shade of green for his eyes.

The woman dressed in black, whom he'd been talking to, wore an emerald necklace almost the right color, but Mr. Glass's eyes had flecks of a lighter shade in them that made his gaze compelling.

Everything about him was compelling; so much so that I froze. The more I realized I had only moments in which to speak to him before the glowering woman joined us, the more my mouth refused to work.

I was pathetic.

Thankfully Horatio saved me. "Forgive us for the ambush, Mr. Glass, but it's important. Miss Ashe here needs to speak to your mother."

"My mother?" Even his voice was lovely, dark and velvety like his hair. He waited for me to speak. When I didn't, he arched his brows and a small smile tugged at his lips.

He found my awkwardness amusing. I found that rather infuriating. With my anger directed outward instead of in, I was able to finally find my voice.

"My brother thought our family might be silver magicians and seemed to believe Lady Rycroft could help him discover if we are or not." It sounded somewhat foolish now that I voiced it to this stranger in the middle of a crowded room as his companions bore down on us.

Mr. Glass didn't look at me as though he thought me foolish. He looked as though I'd piqued his curiosity. "Why does he think that?"

"I don't know."

"There must be a reason." His voice held a hint of urgency.

I blinked, taken aback by his sudden steeliness. "I suppose there must."

He glanced over my shoulder and gave a slight shake of his head at whoever stood there. I turned to look, but I only saw the tall waiter who'd assisted me earlier. I ought to leave before the butler noticed I'd accosted one of the guests and dismissed me on the spot.

"You should ask him," Mr. Glass said.

It took me a moment to realize he meant my brother. "I can't. He died in the war."

Mr. Glass stilled. He regarded me with those eyes of his, full of sympathy and something deeper and darker. Something troubling. "I'm sorry."

Horatio cleared his throat. "Sylvia, you should go."

I followed his gaze to the butler storming toward us, parting the crowd like the prow of the ship in the painting, nostrils expanding with every heaving breath.

"I'm afraid you can't speak to my mother," Mr. Glass said to me.

"But I must!" It was fortunate that I was still holding the tray or I might have grabbed him with both hands. "Sir, please, I believe Lady Rycroft can help. My brother certainly thought so, and he was very smart. He wouldn't have written her name down if it wasn't important. Sir, I *need* to understand where I come from."

Mr. Glass grasped my arms, but it wasn't his firm grip that stopped my prattling. It was the shock at my own words.

I need to understand where I come from.

I had never known my father. My mother never spoke about him. I knew from a very young age not to ask questions. I didn't even know his first name. I thought I'd not wanted to know him, but now I realized I did—and very much. And so had my brother. Perhaps James had found a clue that indicated our father was a silver magician and that somehow India Glass, Lady Rycroft, could help locate him. She was, after all, a famous magician. It wasn't unreasonable to assume she knew other magicians.

"Please let me speak to your mother, sir," I whispered through trembling lips.

Mr. Glass regarded me with an intense gaze that made my heart quicken and my face heat. "I would, but she's gone."

Oh no. "I'm so sorry."

His brows drew together in a small frown before clearing. He gave me that smile again, the one that hinted at his amusement at my expense. "She's gone to America. She and my father left yesterday."

"Oh." Gone only yesterday. I'd been so close. If only I'd learned about India Glass earlier. If only I'd been more interested in my brother's notebook. If only, if only... "When will she return?"

It wasn't until he let me go that I realized Mr. Glass had held onto me the entire time. His grip had been steadying and now I felt myself weaken. The tray was too heavy. I was going to drop it and make a fool of myself again, but this time it would be so much worse because the compelling Mr. Glass was watching.

"Excuse me, sir, I am sorry she's bothering you," said the butler, Mr. Ludlow, with a disapproving pinch of his lips.

"She's no bother," Mr. Glass said.

"Miss, if you would come with me."

Mr. Ludlow couldn't even remember my name. I might be employed on a temporary basis, but he could at least bother to learn my name. "Ashe," I said automatically. "My name is Sylvia Ashe."

The butler bristled. "I said *come with me.*"

I looked from him to Horatio to Daisy, who'd joined us, her tray of hors d'oeuvres nowhere in sight. She arched her brows, asking me if I was all right. She looked worried.

"What's going on here?" the woman wearing the black dress and emerald necklace asked. "Why are you not working, girl?" She sounded like Daisy when she aped the upper classes, pronouncing girl as "gel."

"We were just having a conversation," Mr. Glass said. "No harm done."

"On the contrary! She shouldn't be talking to you. The only word that girl should say is 'pastry' as she offers them around." She indicated the platter in my hands. The thing hadn't weighed much when I first picked it up, but now it seemed as heavy as a stack of books. "Ludlow!"

The butler drew in his chin, weakening it even further. "My apologies, Lady Stanhope. I'll see that she's escorted from the premises immediately." He stepped aside and indicated I should walk ahead of him.

"This isn't necessary," Mr. Glass said. "Please allow Miss Ashe to continue to work. The blame is mine alone."

It was gallant of him to say so, but it was too late. Neither Lady Stanhope nor Mr. Ludlow could back down now. Everyone was looking, including the other staff. Mr. Ludlow had to maintain his authority, and Lady Stanhope wouldn't want her friends to see her pandering to a servant.

"*Now*, Miss Ashe," Mr. Ludlow ground out between unmoving lips.

Mr. Glass opened his mouth to protest again so I got in first. "It's all right, I'm going." I handed the platter to Daisy and walked off.

"Do try a pastry," I heard Daisy say ever-so-sweetly. "They're delicious."

I glanced over my shoulder to see Lady Stanhope pluck a pastry off the platter. She popped it in her mouth and Daisy snickered, spun on her heel, and followed me.

We returned to the basement to change out of the maids' uniforms. I wanted to go directly to the exit, but Daisy wanted to be paid. She went in search of Mr. Ludlow.

"The wage wasn't the point of the exercise," I said, trying to keep up with her long strides.

"We ought to be compensated for our time." She asked

one of the cooks if she'd seen Mr. Ludlow but received a shrug in response and a smirk.

We received a lot of smirks and odd looks as we searched for the butler. It would seem our confrontation upstairs was fodder for gossip downstairs.

"Miss Ashe!"

My heart skipped a beat. Mr. Ludlow may not be my regular employer, and I may never see him again, but his bark still managed to shred my nerves. "What are you still doing here?"

Daisy marched up to him. "Looking for you. We'd like to be paid."

"You're lucky I don't call the police on you. Get out." He opened the door that led to a set of steps.

Daisy planted her hands on her hips. "Pay us or I'll make an even bigger commotion."

Mr. Ludlow's lips went white from pursing.

Daisy grabbed my hand. "Come on, Sylvia. I think the main gallery had the most people, don't you?" She dragged me off along the corridor.

"Wait! Very well, I'll pay you for the hours you worked, not a penny more." Mr. Ludlow disappeared into his office and returned with an envelope for each of us. "Now get out!"

I slunk toward the door. I just wanted to leave. For someone who loathed attention, the day had been exhausting. There was only so much public humiliation one could take.

Daisy checked the contents of her envelope before following me. At the door, she turned back to Mr. Ludlow, gestured rudely, and slammed the door behind her. "Bully," she said as we climbed the stairs.

"He's only doing his job, Daisy."

"I blame that woman. If it weren't for her carrying on like the Queen of Sheba, Mr. Ludlow would never have noticed you talking to Mr. Glass. She was rude, not to mention a dreadful snob. She got what she deserved, though. I hope she choked on a dirty pastry."

She pushed open the door and we emerged onto the courtyard. It was still busy with ladies and gentlemen arriving for the exhibition while others departed after getting their fill of art and gossip.

"You spat in those pastries, didn't you?" The deep voice startled a gasp out of me.

I pressed a hand to my rapidly beating heart. "Mr. Glass! Er, no, of course not! There was nothing wrong with the pastries. They were perfectly acceptable."

"So, if Lady Stanhope thought they had an unusual flavor, it's not your fault?" He was smiling again.

I found it unnerving. Was he trying to catch us out? Was he going to report to Mr. Ludlow that we'd served food that had fallen on the floor?

Daisy had no such qualms. She put out her hand which he shook. "Daisy Carmichael, at your service. This is my friend, Sylvia Ashe."

"How do you do?" He shook my hand too then indicated we should walk with him across the courtyard. "Ordinarily I'd introduce myself, but you seem to already know me. May I ask how?"

He addressed the question to me, so I answered. "We read about you in the newspaper."

He rolled his eyes to the sky. "That damned article. I didn't want any part of it, but before I knew what was happening the photographer was shoving his camera in my face and the journalist was noting down everything I said. Don't believe what you read. He got a lot wrong. So how did that lead you here?"

"Daisy heard that the private viewing is one of the main events on the social calendar and that people like you and your mother are invited."

"People like us?" He huffed a humorless laugh. I think I'd offended him. "My parents try to come every year. They're great patrons of the arts. When my mother couldn't make it this year, she asked me to attend in her stead." I'd definitely offended him, going by his tone.

"Daisy's friend Horatio is one of the exhibiting artists and he managed to secure us employment."

"We don't usually work in service," Daisy said.

His wry smirk reappeared. "Is that so?"

"That Lady Stanhope is horrid. Is she a friend of yours?"

"We'd never met before today. She's married to one of the Academy's honorary members, Sir Richard Stanhope. She arranges the private viewing, extending invitations, making sure the artists show up, that sort of thing."

"No wonder she wants everything to run smoothly," I said. "She must put in a lot of effort."

"That doesn't give her a license to be rude to the staff," Daisy said.

Mr. Glass agreed. "It does not."

"You didn't have to leave the exhibition in protest over the way she treated us," I said.

"I didn't."

"Oh." Of course he hadn't. I was a fool for thinking his departure had anything to do with that confrontation. He'd simply happened to leave the exhibition at the same time as us. This meeting was purely coincidental. The only reason it was so lengthy was because he hadn't thought of a way to politely disengage.

We passed through the arched gateway onto Piccadilly, where a motorcar pulled up and two well-dressed passengers stepped out. "How long will it be before Lady Rycroft returns to England?" I asked.

"I don't know." Mr. Glass glanced along Piccadilly at the steady stream of automobiles and wagons being held up by a single horse-drawn cart. The honks of horns made no impact on either horse or driver. Mr. Glass raised a hand, signaling to one of the motorcars in the queue.

I indicated to Daisy that we should leave, but she wasn't ready. "Mr. Glass, will you ask your mother to write to Sylvia? Her address is—"

"I'm afraid not."

"Why not?"

"Daisy," I urged. "Leave Mr. Glass alone. It doesn't matter."

"It does matter."

"My mother doesn't know any silver magicians," Mr. Glass said.

Daisy frowned. "How can you possibly know that?"

"Miss Ashe, I suggest you try the Silversmiths' Guild. They'll know if your family were ever silversmiths, even if they can't tell you definitively if they were magicians."

It was a logical step, but not one that had occurred to either Daisy or me. We'd become fixated on India Glass. "Yes, of course. I'm sorry to have bothered you."

"You're no bother."

Daisy seemed intent on proving him wrong, however. "If it was as simple as calling on the guild, her brother wouldn't have written down the name India Glass in his notebook, would he?"

Mr. Glass smiled tightly. "I'm sorry I can't be of help. If you'll excuse me, my motor is here."

A large black automobile suddenly moved out from behind the horse-drawn cart, cut in front of it, then veered toward us. It halted with a screech of tires.

Mr. Glass frowned at it. "Dodson, what the—"

A heavy-set man sprang out of the motorcar and roughly grabbed Mr. Glass's arms, twisting them behind his back. He tried to fight the man off, but he was a solid brute and had a firm hold. He wrestled Mr. Glass toward the open door of the car as the driver revved the engine.

It all happened so quickly that it took those of us in the vicinity a second or two to realize Mr. Glass was being kidnapped.

When the horror finally registered, I did what came naturally. I screamed.

CHAPTER 3

*D*aisy screamed too. The piercing sound was like a slap to the face, jolting me into action. I kicked the kidnapper in the back of the knee.

His leg buckled. He did not let Mr. Glass go, but his grip must have loosened enough for Mr. Glass to free himself, because all of a sudden, the tables were turned. Mr. Glass had the thug in a headlock.

"Let him go or I'll shoot!" growled a man from inside the motorcar.

With a curse, Mr. Glass released the brute and watched helplessly as he dove into the back seat. With a roar of its engine, the motorcar sped away.

"Gabe!" The tall, dark waiter who'd been kind to me ran up to us, surprisingly fast considering he was built like a heavyweight pugilist. He grasped Mr. Glass's shoulders and inspected him. "Thank God you're all right."

Mr. Glass sucked in deep breaths of air and nodded. "They got away."

"They?"

"The driver and a third man in the back seat. All I saw

was the barrel of a gun pointed at me. I couldn't see his face."
Mr. Glass glared in the direction it had fled, the motor already
disappeared from view. He drew in another deep breath,
which seemed to refill his emptied lungs. "I thought it was
Dodson."

Another large black motorcar stopped at the curb. It
looked very similar to the kidnappers' motor. Mr. Glass
greeted his chauffeur.

"The kidnapper's car wasn't a Hudson," the waiter
pointed out.

Mr. Glass dragged a hand through his hair and sighed.
He'd lost his hat during the scuffle. "And mine is. Thank you
for stating the obvious, Alex."

The waiter glared at Daisy and me. "I see you were
distracted."

"Don't, Alex."

But the waiter ignored him and powered on. "You're not
regular staff." It was said with an accusatory glare and a
crossing of his arms over his chest. "Today was your first
day."

"Have you been spying on us?" When he didn't respond,
Daisy scoffed. "I should have known there was another
motive for your kindness earlier. I mean, you obviously
weren't flirting with me. You're absolutely dreadful at it. I've
had less wooden conversations with a railway sleeper."

Alex's jaw firmed. "Who are you? What are you doing
here?"

Daisy planted a hand on her hip. "We're not answering
that."

Alex stepped closer until Mr. Glass put a hand to his arm.
"Not answering makes you look suspicious, so I advise you
to speak up," Alex snarled.

"You think *we're* suspicious!" She scoffed again. "If
anyone is suspicious here, it's you two. You seem to know

one another very well, considering one of you is a lord and the other a mere waiter."

Alex blinked at her. He opened his mouth to say something but closed it, as onlookers who'd not dared intervene in the kidnapping approached now that it was safe. The women fussed over Mr. Glass while the men exchanged witness accounts. He ignored them all.

"Are you all right?" he asked Daisy and me.

"Fine, thank you," I said.

"Thank *you* for what you did. It was good of you to try to save me."

"Try?" Daisy echoed. She was still irritated with the waiter named Alex. "Sylvia did more than try. If she hadn't kicked that man, he would have succeeded in bundling you into the motor."

Alex gave a derisive snort.

Mr. Glass shot him a glare, more severe than the last. Alex rubbed a hand across his mouth, somewhat chastised.

The exchange set me on edge. Alex seemed to think we had something to hide. Perhaps he even thought we were linked to the kidnappers. Mr. Glass was harder to read, but it was possible he was silencing his friend so as not to give away their suspicions.

My nerves were still on edge, my heart racing, and I had a sudden urge to get as far away from Mr. Glass as possible. Not only did he attract danger, but he either blamed me for distracting him with my questions about his mother, or he suspected me of being directly involved with the kidnappers. My saving him meant nothing.

I had saved him, hadn't I?

I was no longer sure. It had all happened so fast. Perhaps my kick had connected *after* Mr. Glass managed to free himself. No wonder he thought us silly fools for claiming his freedom was all because of me. It was likely I'd done nothing but give the kidnapper a bruise.

"You ought to report the incident," said one of the gentlemen who'd rushed up after the danger had passed.

"There are never any constables nearby when you need one," his wife said.

"You ought to be thanking my friend," Daisy cut in, her voice rising over the top of them.

Mr. Glass hesitated then gave me a little bow. "Thank you, Miss Ashe."

"Properly, not with a condescending tone."

"That *was* proper," Alex ground out.

Daisy straightened to her full height, which was considerably less than his. Mr. Glass was tall, but Alex was a giant. "I beg to differ," she said, simply.

"Neither of you have answered my questions." Alex turned to me, the muscles on his face were tight, his body rigid. There was no evidence of the kind man who'd helped me pick up the fallen pastries. He wanted answers, and he looked as though he'd do anything to get them. "Who are you and what are you doing here?"

I suddenly felt very hot and a little faint. I glanced from him to Daisy to Mr. Glass. Then I turned on my heel and walked away.

"Miss Ashe!" Mr. Glass called out.

"Gabe, no." That was Alex speaking. "Your motor is here. Get in. The only place you're going now is home."

Gabe? Daisy was right. These two knew each other well. She was right about Mr. Glass's tone being condescending too, which only confirmed that I hadn't helped free him. At least he didn't try to stop us leaving, despite his suspicions that we were involved in the kidnapping.

Daisy fell into step alongside me. "That man is not at all what I hoped he'd be like."

"Oh?"

"I blame his wealth, title, and good looks—not to mention all the fuss made over him being a war hero and saving that boy from drowning. I'm not denying that he is a hero, but the praise has gone to his head. That's the problem with men like Mr. Glass. They don't have to strive for what they want because people just give them everything. I bet he's never worked a day in his life, never had to struggle for anything, including recognition."

"So, you no longer consider his many attributes to be virtues?"

"I do not."

We walked on, only to turn when my name was called out again.

Mr. Glass hailed us from the front passenger seat of his motorcar. "Miss Ashe, please may I have a word?"

"Interrogate, more like," Daisy muttered.

Mr. Glass went to open the door, but Alex, sitting behind, clamped a hand on his shoulder. "No, Gabe. The kidnappers could still be in the vicinity."

We didn't wait to see what Mr. Glass did next. Daisy steered me down one lane then another, and another, until I was quite lost. London was still new to me, and this wasn't a part I visited often. We were in the heart of the high-end shopping precinct, judging by the boutique shops on both sides of the street. We passed the entrance to a luxury hotel where a doorman nodded a greeting and a porter collected parcels from a waiting carriage. This wasn't an area of the city where hawkers pushed rickety old carts filled with odds and ends, or shop-keepers stood out the front and shouted the daily special. The ladies were genteel, the gentlemen upright and proper. Some of the younger men wore officers' uniforms.

Neither of us mentioned Mr. Glass again. Daisy had gone quiet, however, and a small furrow dented her brow.

"What is it?" I asked.

"I thought I'd have more presence of mind than to stand there and just scream."

"Screaming is an excellent response to danger. It alerted those nearby."

"Who would have thought that of the two of us, you'd be the one to act?"

It surprised me too, at first, but when I thought about it, it was understandable. Daisy had confidence in abundance, but it was of the verbal rather than physical kind. She was an artist at heart. From her accent and manner, I could tell she was well brought up, educated, and most likely came from a loving household where her greatest fear was whether her younger brother would eat her helping of breakfast.

While I wouldn't say my life was hard, it wasn't as soft as hers had probably been. I'd also been taught to defend myself by my mother. From a young age, she'd shown me ways and means to get out of a man's grip if I were being attacked. Today was the first time I'd put those lessons into practice. My mother would have been proud of me. Proud and terrified, although she would have found comfort in the knowledge that I was helping someone else and not the target myself. Not that I was entirely sure I had helped Mr. Glass.

"So what will you do now?" Daisy asked.

"Call on the Silversmiths' Guild."

"I'll come with you. What will you ask them?"

"I have no idea."

* * *

SILVERSMITHS' Hall, the headquarters of The Worshipful Company of Silversmiths, was not open at the weekend. We'd walked all the way from Piccadilly to the city center for nothing. We should have waited for the bus.

With a hand clamped to her navy felt hat, to stop it falling off, Daisy tipped her head back and swore softly at the two rearing dragons carved in stone above the first-floor balcony door. "You would think a company wealthy enough to be housed in such a grand building as this would be able to afford a porter to answer questions at the weekend."

I leaned against the high pedestal at the base of one of the enormous columns holding up the portico and sighed. "A porter may not be able to answer our questions. We need to check their archives for families named Ashe."

The silver magic connection—if there was one—might not be to the Ashes. James may have suspected it was my mother's family or another branch of the family tree; I didn't know any of those names, including her maiden name. I was diving blindly into the research, and it could end up being an impossible task. That's why I'd wanted to start with Lady Rycroft. If James had written her name down in his notebook, I was certain that meant he suspected she could provide us with a shortcut to answers.

Daisy hooked her arm through mine. "Come on. Let's find a teashop then go home."

"Do you mind if I skip the teashop? It's been quite a day."

"Very well. I want to start a new painting anyway. One of the oils at the exhibition inspired me. Did you notice it? The one with the steam ship. Not usually my sort of thing, but there was something quite lovely about it. The way the artist captured the sunlight on the crests of the waves was pure genius, and the smoke spewing from the funnels... If I could paint half as well as him, I could die happy."

"Don't be so macabre, Daisy."

She squeezed my arm. "Don't fret, my sweet little friend. I'm not dying anytime soon. You're stuck with me, now."

I would have given her a smile in return, but I didn't want her to see the tears filling my eyes. She'd think me pathetic. But I couldn't help it. I'd somehow found myself a real friend without even trying. I'd not had a good friend in…well, perhaps ever. Moving every year or two as a child had made it difficult to maintain friendships. My mother and I had stayed put for the entire four years of war but had once again moved to a new city after my brother died. We'd both been too busy working in her final months to make friends there. I'd thought myself beyond the age when new friends were easily made anyway, but Daisy had proved me wrong. Having arrived in London a few months before me, she was also looking for female companionship. It seemed we'd both found each other when we needed someone the most.

* * *

MY ROOM in the lodging house may not have a bathroom, kitchen or sitting room, but there was enough space for a small table, a chair, and shelves on which to store some books, personal items and cans of peaches for when I didn't feel like joining the other lodgers in the basement dining room at mealtimes. I'd made myself a cup of tea and brought it up to my room and had just sat down to enjoy it when Daisy burst in without knocking.

"They're coming," she said, breathless.

"Who?"

"Mr. Glass and that friend of his, Alexander Bailey. We'll pretend you're not here. Hopefully that dragon of a matron can convince them you're out."

"She won't lie for me."

She glanced around the room. "You could hide."

"Daisy, stop!" She was going too fast and left me far behind at the station. "How do you know Mr. Glass and Mr.

Bailey are coming here? And how did you learn the waiter's last name?"

"They came to my flat and asked me where to find you."

"And you just told them?"

She chewed on her lower lip. "I'm afraid I just gave in. They were all very official and somewhat authoritative. I blame Alex Bailey. Mr. Glass is nice, but his friend is quite rude. He *demanded* I tell them where you live."

I squeezed the bridge of my nose and tried to make sense of her words. "Official?"

"I cycled here as fast as I could, taking the shortcut, but I'm afraid they're not far behind me."

Mrs. Whitten the matron arrived. "You have visitors, Miss Ashe. Two men." Her disapproving scowl emphasized her thick features and double chins. "They're in the main sitting room."

Daisy clasped my hand between both of hers, attempting to hold me back. Her wide eyes implored me not to meet with them.

"Come *along*, Miss Ashe, I haven't got all day."

I didn't see that I had any choice. Besides, it would give me an opportunity to tell them we were not in any way involved in the kidnapping. "We ought to set them straight, Daisy. They're under the false impression that we are somehow to blame for that incident."

"Miss Ashe!"

Daisy sighed. "Lead on."

We followed Mrs. Whitten along the corridor, past the sign on the wall reminding us to KEEP INNOCENCE, albeit in vain. Although male guests were not allowed up to the rooms, I knew some of the girls had found inventive ways of sneaking their suitors in.

Mrs. Whitten pushed open the door to the main sitting room. I hesitated on the threshold. Mr. Glass stood near the fireplace with Mr. Bailey. They both loomed rather large and sported the same grim expressions as they stared into the clean grate. They looked up upon our entrance.

"Miss Ashe, thank you for joining us." Mr. Glass extended his hand to me. "Allow me to introduce my friend, Alex Bailey, properly." He cleared his throat. "Hopefully we can wipe the slate clean and begin again."

Mr. Bailey's sheepish nod in greeting proved he was suitably chastised. That sheepishness was replaced with coolness as he regarded Daisy. She folded her arms and regarded him with an equally frosty look.

Being late Saturday afternoon, the lodgers who worked in offices or as teachers were not at work. A small group were enjoying cups of tea and the view that had just walked in on two sets of long legs. Some openly ogled Mr. Glass and Mr. Bailey, while others attempted subtlety by peering over the rims of their teacups.

The main sitting room was the larger of the two in the building. Just because it was larger didn't mean it was more elegant. It was a utilitarian space, designed to fit the maximum number of tables, chairs and sofas. There was no space set aside for dancing near the piano, no cushions on the hard chairs or rugs on the floor, and not a shred of elegance in the heavy green brocade drapes.

"We're sorry to bother you, but—" Mr. Glass broke off mid-sentence to smile at the matron. She'd settled herself on a chair within hearing distance. "Madam, may we have some privacy, please?"

She wasn't used to having her authority questioned. She didn't put up with it from the lodgers, evicting any girl who broke the rules, but coming from a man, and a gentleman at that, she looked uncertain how to proceed.

One of the girls snickered into her teacup.

"Miss Ashe is quite safe with us," Mr. Glass went on, "but if you wish to find out more about me, take my card."

She accepted it, turning it over in her hand and rubbing her thumb and finger over it as if she could tell the quality of the man by the quality of his card.

"His father is the Baron of Rycroft," Mr. Bailey said.

Mr. Glass's smile stiffened, and I got the feeling he was trying not to glare at his friend.

Mrs. Whitten finally rose. "Come along, girls. We'll adjourn to the other sitting room."

Mr. Glass waited for them to leave before offering Daisy and I chairs at one of the tables, as if he were hosting us in his own house. "First of all, I want to apologize for coming to your home unannounced." He cleared his throat and glanced at Daisy but didn't acknowledge that she'd raced ahead to warn me. "We returned to Burlington House and asked your friend, the painter, where to find you. He gave us Miss Carmichael's address, and she directed us here. Don't be angry with her. I was insistent."

Daisy turned to me. "Mr. Bailey gave me no choice. He said they'd arrest me if I refused!"

I gasped. "Arrest? Are you policemen?"

Mr. Glass reached into his inside jacket pocket and handed me a card. "Not quite, but we work for the police from time to time."

I stared at the card. If he thought us involved with the kidnappers, we could be in awful trouble. A lump of dread formed in my chest. I ought to say something, but I found I couldn't speak.

"We consult on cases where magic is involved or suspected," Mr. Glass went on.

"I think the attempted kidnapping is related to the case we're working on," Mr. Bailey added.

"Is that what *you* think, Mr. Glass?" I asked.

Mr. Glass's thumb began to tap on his thigh. "It's the logical explanation."

"It's the only explanation," Mr. Bailey told him.

"What is the case?" Daisy asked.

"We can't discuss it with civilians."

Mr. Glass was a little more civil. "We can't reveal too much, but I can tell you we're investigating the theft of a magical painting." That explained why Mr. Bailey was working as a waiter at the exhibition.

"The artist is a paint magician?" I asked.

He nodded.

"I can see how the theft might be linked to your kidnapping if the thief is trying to stop your investigation."

"That's what I tried telling him," Mr. Bailey said wryly.

My courage returned somewhat with every passing moment. Mr. Glass wouldn't be so open with us if he suspected us. But I wanted to make sure. "And you think we had something to do with it?"

Daisy spoke before either man had the opportunity. "Why would Sylvia kick one of them if we are in league with them?"

"To make it look like she's innocent," Mr. Bailey pointed out.

Mr. Glass held up his hand. "We haven't formed an opinion one way or another. We're just trying to clear up a few points." He lowered his hand to his thigh where his thumb resumed tapping. It appeared to be a nervous habit. I wondered if he'd picked it up in the war. Some men came back with shredded nerves. Some were so bad they could no longer function in society, but others only exhibited mild symptoms like a facial tic or other involuntary physical habit. I tried not to stare.

"Can you describe the kidnappers, Miss Ashe?" he asked.

"A little. You saw them too?"

"I didn't see the man inside the car. If I'd known he was in there, I would have taken a look, but..." He clicked his tongue, annoyed with himself. It was hardly his fault, however. It had happened so quickly, and he'd been caught by surprise.

Mr. Bailey agreed. "You were distracted, Gabe."

Clearly, Mr. Bailey still blamed me for that distraction. He was right to do so. I shouldn't have continued to pester Mr. Glass about seeing his mother after his initial refusal.

I lowered my head. "I am sorry."

"Sorry?" Mr. Glass sounded confused.

"I'm afraid I didn't see the other man either." I gave them a description of the thug I'd seen, but Mr. Glass wrote none of it down. I hadn't told him anything he didn't already know. "I wish I could be more help. Daisy?"

"I have nothing more to add," she said, still glaring at Mr. Bailey.

Mr. Bailey returned it with a narrowed gaze of his own.

Mr. Glass sighed. "You've both been a great help. Thank you." He stood. "If you remember anything, please contact me using the telephone number on my card."

He and Mr. Bailey bade us goodbye then headed for the door. Mr. Bailey exited, but Mr. Glass turned back. "I wish to apologize for my tone earlier. I'm afraid I was a little brusque with you when you enquired about my mother."

"It's all right. I can see you're protective of her."

"It's not that."

"It is," Mr. Bailey cut in.

"Very well, it is, in part. My mother doesn't like the attention that comes with being known as the Mother of Magic, or whatever it is the newspapers have dubbed her this year. She prefers a quiet life and has little to do with magicians or policy making these days. The grandiose things you've heard about her are probably not true."

46

"I haven't heard anything about her. That's the point. My brother wrote her name in his notebook, suggesting she might be able to give answers about whether we're silver magicians or not. I have no idea how she could answer that. It's me who should apologize to you. You were right to direct me to the Silversmiths' Guild. If there is silver magic in our family, they will be listed in the guild's archives."

"Only if they were from London." He arched his brows.

I shrugged. I had no idea where the Ashes were from originally. "The guild is closed over the weekend. I'll return during my lunch hour on Monday and ask their archivist if he can find out anything about the Ashe name."

"Don't forget your mother's maiden name, and your grandmother's."

"Go back as far as you can," Mr. Bailey added.

"She knows that," Daisy snapped.

That was the problem. I knew nothing about my grand-mothers. I'd never met my grandparents, and my mother never mentioned them. Or, rather, she refused to tell James and me anything about them. We were scolded whenever we asked.

"What I can tell you is that silver magic is rare," Mr. Glass said. "If the guild knows of a silver magician, they're probably related to you."

"I highly doubt there's magic in my family. I feel nothing when I touch silver things." I fingered my mother's ring which I'd kept on my finger. "I should feel something, shouldn't I?"

"If you're a magician, yes. It's possible you didn't inherit the magic and your brother did. If one parent is artless and the other a magician, there's a fifty percent chance the children will be artless. Which parent or grandparent did your brother suspect of being a silver magician?"

I looked down at the ring. "I don't know. My mother

never mentioned magic, and I never met my father." I looked away, unable to meet his gaze. What must he think of me, a fatherless child of indeterminate lineage? The shame I'd felt growing up came back to haunt me. Children can be cruel. When they learned that James and I didn't know anything about our father, they'd teased us mercilessly.

It was another reason I had so few friends.

"Where do you work?" Mr. Glass suddenly asked.

"In the London Philosophical Society's library. Why?"

"In case I need to speak to you again. I'd rather not face Mrs. Whitten's wrath a second time." He touched the brim of his cap and headed out with Mr. Bailey on his heels.

I stared down at his card, cradled in the palm of my hand. It gave no address and only included a telephone number. I tucked it into my skirt pocket and tried to think of a detail about the kidnappers I may have forgotten to tell him. But no matter how hard I tried, I could think of no reason to telephone him.

"I don't like that man," Daisy said.

"Which one?"

"The big one. How dare he suspect us of aiding the kidnappers when your interference is the only thing that saved Mr. Glass?"

"He's just worried about his friend. Besides, he has a right to be suspicious. After all, we only took employment at the exhibition so we could speak to his friend, and were there when the attempted kidnapping took place."

"I still don't like him. He flirted with me *before* the kidnapping attempt. Clearly he thought us suspicious from the moment he met us, and without evidence, too. That's a violation of my rights."

I smiled. "Not quite, but I do see your point. How dare a man flirt with you without evidence of your guilt?" It was meant as a joke, to point out that he was probably flirting with her because he wanted to get to know her better, but she was oblivious.

"Precisely. I'm glad you see it my way, Sylv."

* * *

ON MONDAY MORNING I found myself sneaking glances at the newspaper article about Mr. Glass instead of working. The day before, I'd wanted to discuss his visit with Daisy again, but she was busy painting. When the muse caught her, it held on fast and didn't let go. Her responses to my questions were mere grunts or simply made no sense. When I asked whether she thought Mr. Glass was a magician, she said, "Hmmm." Given no further response, I decided that was an agreement. After all, his mother was supposed to be very powerful, and she'd probably wanted her children to be magicians too so had married one to make sure.

I leaned a hip against the desk and scoured the article once more for mention of him being a magician.

"Reading about me again, Miss Ashe?"

"Mr. Glass!" I dropped the newspaper on the desk, but it was too late. He'd seen me. He must think me an obsessive admirer. *Ugh.* Yet another humiliation to add to the list. "I was just, ah, reading the advertisement beside it."

He picked up the newspaper and read. "'La-Mar Reducing Soap. No dieting or exercise. Acts like magic in reducing double chin...'" He glanced at my chin. His mouth didn't move but those green eyes danced with humor. "'... abdomen, ungainly ankles, unbecoming wrists, arms and shoulders, large—" He cleared his throat and returned the newspaper to the desk. "If you really were reading the ad, may I point out that you don't need this soap."

My face flamed. There was nothing for it but to brazen it

out. I snatched up the newspaper and threw it in the rubbish bin. "No, you may not."

He laughed softly. "You may have been reading the article, not the ad, but you'd have no reason to deny that, would you? I mean, there's nothing wrong with reading it a second time. Or is it the third?"

It was more than that, but I wasn't going to admit it. The man was more self-absorbed than I'd realized. Daisy's first impression of him was perhaps the most accurate, after all. The abundance of good fortune had turned him into an egotist.

"Are you a member of the Society, Mr. Glass?" I asked.

"No. Should I join?" He glanced around, taking in the desk with the pile of old books, the shelving stacks that rose on either side of us, and the comfortable leather armchair. "I'm not much of a philosopher but perhaps I can reflect on life while you work. It's very quiet."

He made it sound like a curiosity, or even a criticism. "It's a library. It's supposed to be quiet. And there's nothing wrong with being left in peace with only one's thoughts for company."

"Depends on the thoughts," he said darkly. Before I could respond, he added, "I wanted to apologize for the way Alex and I spoke to you and Miss Carmichael on Saturday. We made you feel like suspects, and that wasn't fair." It wasn't confirmation that he'd removed us from his list of suspects. We were still on it. We were probably at the top.

I arched my brows, waiting for him to say more, perhaps even confirm or deny it.

He studied the cover of one of the books on the desk, fingering the frayed cloth edge somewhat absently. Why the hesitation? "I came to tell you something that occurred to me just this morning."

"Go on."

"I think you may be from a family of silver magicians, after all."

"Why do you think that?" I asked on a rush of breath.

"Your name is Sylvia."

My hopes had lifted, but now sank again. I nodded but did not tell him I'd already considered the connection. Indeed, it was so obvious that it was hardly worth mentioning at all. He couldn't possibly have come here just to tell me that. I waited for more, but none came.

"Is something the matter, Miss Ashe?"

"No," I said heavily. "You should go."

"Should I not have come to your place of work? There was no one downstairs so I decided to try my luck up here. Should I have signed in?"

"You didn't see Mr. Parmiter?"

He shook his head and shrugged, as if it didn't matter. But it mattered to Mr. Parmiter.

"Thank you for coming all this way to tell me my name, Mr. Glass." I winced. I hadn't meant to be sarcastic. Not out loud, anyway. "I appreciate it. But please don't trouble yourself with my little problem anymore. You must be terribly busy and—" I cut myself off and silently groaned as Mr. Parmiter emerged from behind the nearest stack. I hated that it hid anyone coming up the stairs from view. If I was preoccupied, like now, I didn't hear footsteps.

"Sir?" Mr. Parmiter barked. "Are you a member here?"

Mr. Glass extended his hand. "Gabriel Glass, at your service. I was just here to—"

"Are you a member?"

Mr. Glass lowered his hand. "No. I'm here to speak to Miss Ashe about—"

"Then kindly leave." Mr. Parmiter indicated the way to the staircase. "The library is for the use of members only."

Mr. Glass's jaw firmed. "You misunderstand. I work for

Scotland Yard." He produced a card and handed it to Mr. Parmiter.

Mr. Parmiter held it at arm's length and peered down his nose as he read. "Is Miss Ashe in trouble?"

"She witnessed a crime, and I came to ask her some follow-up questions."

"You should have spoken to me first and asked permission. Non-members are not allowed."

"Surely you can make an exception for the police."

"Your card says you are a consultant for Scotland Yard, not an actual policeman."

I wanted to crawl into the cavity under the desk and hide there. Mr. Parmiter had always been nice to the society's members, so I thought he just disliked women in general, or Daisy and me in particular. But his rudeness to Mr. Glass proved he loathed anyone associated with me, no matter how loose that association.

Mr. Glass held up his hands in surrender. "I hope I haven't caused Miss Ashe any trouble. It was unwittingly done. If someone had been on the desk downstairs, I would have checked first before going in search of her."

Since Mr. Parmiter was supposed to be on the desk, he took the comment as a slight on his work ethic. His lips quivered with indignation. "If you've quite finished," he bit off.

Mr. Glass touched the brim of his cap. "Good day, Miss Ashe, and thank you again for your assistance with my investigation." He apologized to Mr. Parmiter for keeping me from my work then left.

Mr. Parmiter swung around to face me. "You can see out the rest of the day, but don't bother to come in tomorrow."

My jaw dropped. I stared at him. "You're dismissing me because of a visit that I had no control over? That's not fair!"

"It's not just him. There's that silly girl who regularly sneaks in, as well as the makeup."

"I don't wear makeup!"

He sniffed. "Your paramour was the last straw. A Scotland Yard consultant indeed."

"He is!" I snatched the card from him and waved it in front of his face.

"Anyone can get fake cards made up. That man does not work for the police. He's too young to be a consultant. Either you've been duped or you're trying to fool me."

It took me a moment to gather my wits and find the words to express myself. But when I did find them, I grabbed my bag and rounded the desk. I might be shorter than Mr. Parmiter, but I liked to think he reeled back because of the fierce look on my face, not the fact that I stepped so close to him that we were almost toe to toe. "You should be ashamed of yourself for the way you treat people, but I doubt you have the depth of character to feel shame for your behavior."

He thrust out his chin, making it a good target if I were inclined to punch him. "You won't be getting a reference from me, Miss Ashe."

"I don't care." I tucked my bag under my arm and walked off. I couldn't bear to look at him any longer.

"Where are you going? You have to finish the day!"

"Deduct it from my wages."

I resisted the urge to give him a rude gesture as Daisy would do, but I did utter a string of expletives under my breath as I stormed out of the building. The member waiting at the front desk with a book made sounds of disgust through his overgrown moustache.

I exited the society building, crossed the road, and did not look back.

CHAPTER 4

*S*torming out may have felt cathartic, and it got my point across perfectly, but now I had no reference from my most recent employer. I spent the rest of the week answering job advertisements, speaking to agencies, and attending interviews. I applied for any work that looked remotely suitable. There was only one advertised position for a junior journalist, and I didn't even get an interview for it. When I inquired at the newspaper office, I was told dozens of men had progressed to the interview stage.

Now that the war was over, and returned soldiers flooded the employment market, it would be almost impossible to find a job traditionally done by men, so I gave up and applied for jobs usually done by women. The result was the same. They didn't want me either.

"It's so disheartening," I said to Daisy and Horatio when I entered Daisy's flat on Friday evening.

Horatio took my coat and hung it on the stand near the door. He planted a kiss on my cheek. "You sound like you need a drink. Daisy's mixing cocktails."

"Martinis," Daisy said from the sideboard.

I sat on the sofa. "Sounds exotic."

Horatio sat beside me. "What work have you applied for?"

"Everything! Telephone operator, shop girl, secretary…"

"Charwoman?" Daisy asked.

"Not yet, but I may have to."

Horatio pulled a face. "You're too pretty and clever for manual work."

"I'll work in a factory if I have to. I need the money."

"That explains the old coat you've been wearing. Let me guess, it's your only one?"

I put a hand to my lips in mock horror. "You mean people have more than one coat in their wardrobe?"

"Shocking, I know." He nudged me with his shoulder. "How desperate are you?"

"If I don't find work next week, I won't be able to pay for my room at the lodging house."

Daisy handed me a cocktail in a coupe glass and another to Horatio. "Is that such a bad thing? That place is a prison for single women, and that Mrs. Witless is the warden."

"Mrs. *Whitten* is not that bad. She has a great responsibility, keeping all of us safe."

Daisy grunted as she sat on the brown leather armchair, tucking her legs under her. The chair did not match any of the other furniture. Indeed, none of the furniture matched. The sofa on which Horatio and I sat was an ancient Georgian thing covered in tattered silk that had probably once been lustrous gold but had faded to the color of bone. Daisy tried to hide the stains with throws and cushions that smelled faintly of turpentine. Or perhaps the smell came from Horatio. A thick-legged dining table was being used as a desk for her sketches, as was another smaller table beside the sofa. All the furniture had been pushed to one side of the open space to make way for her easels and canvases, as well as the sideboard. The entire flat was devoid of knickknacks, except for a small bronze sculpture of a basset hound taking pride of place on a side table. The lack of clutter allowed more room for paintings, sketches and her bicycle, the latter hidden by the door when it was open. The eclectic ensemble of décor and furniture worked. Rather like Daisy herself.

Her studio flat was much larger than the space allocated to me in the lodging house, and I admit to being envious. The old building had been renovated and turned into flats, and the attic removed altogether to increase the height of the ceilings in the top-floor rooms. The newly created flats benefited from vaulted ceilings and plenty of light, perfect for an artist. Daisy accessed the bedroom on the mezzanine level via a rickety ladder that looked as though it would be difficult to navigate after a few cocktails. The lower level of the flat was one large open area that combined art studio, sitting room, dining room and kitchenette into one. A door led to a bathroom. There was no queueing for the bath for her, no cold showers if she left it too late, and no being shouted at through the door to hurry up. She had it all to herself. The rent must be quickly eating through her grandparents' inheritance, however. If she didn't sell some paintings soon, she might find herself joining me in the lodging house.

"You should see the signs posted up all over the lodging house walls, Horatio," Daisy said. "'Keep innocence,' 'Protect Your Virtue.'"

"Do the signs work?" he asked.

"No," both Daisy and I said at the same time.

He smiled into his cocktail glass. "Thank you for the hint."

I laughed softly. From what I'd learned of Horatio, he was an incorrigible flirt with a love of life, women, and probably men, too. Since losing my position at the library, I'd spent every afternoon with Daisy, and sometimes Horatio, lamenting my dreadful luck in finding new employment.

They were good listeners, supportive, but not practically helpful. I started to wonder if either of them had needed to look for work in their lives. Horatio was a successful artist, and managed to earn enough from his paintings to make a living, while Daisy survived on her inheritance.

She tilted her head to the side. "You don't need another lover, Horatio. You have Lucy."

"Lacy." Horatio shrugged. "She's all right, but she's just not *inspiring* me anymore."

"You're bored of her already? Honestly. You're as fickle as a butterfly in a spring garden."

"And just as lovely, too."

I laughed, and Daisy rolled her eyes.

Horatio snapped his fingers. "Sylvia! *You* can do it!"

I'd been about to sip my cocktail, but his sudden outburst made me spill a little down my blouse. "I may be desperate, but I won't be your lover."

"Not my lover, my muse."

Daisy leaned over and offered me a handkerchief. "Isn't it the same thing with you?"

"Sometimes."

Daisy and I arched our brows at him.

"Very well, *all* the time. But you can be different, Sylvia. All you have to do is sit for me and look ethereal. I promise not to touch you. Unless you want me to, of course."

"Would I be fully clothed?"

He chuckled but it quickly faded. "Oh, you were serious. The position of my muse requires you to be naked. But I promise I won't see your body as a man does. I'll view you through an artist's lens."

"Thank you for the offer, but I think I'll continue looking for other work." I sipped my cocktail. "This is fresh. What is it?"

"A martini," Daisy said. "Gin, vermouth and orange

bitters. It's popular in America. Well, it was before Prohibition."

"Poor sods." Horatio downed his cocktail in one gulp and held his glass out for Daisy to refill. "I need another. I don't take rejection well."

Daisy uncurled herself from the armchair and took the glass.

Horatio turned to me, a hand to his heart. "Despite the blow you've dealt me, I'm going to help you. I know where you might find temporary work."

I sat up straighter. "Where?"

"The Royal Academy."

My heart sank. "This would be for the same exhibition where I made a fool of myself, the butler dismissed me, and the patroness admonished me for daring to speak to a guest?"

"Lady Stanhope isn't a patron; her husband is an honorary member. She's just a rude cow who likes to feel important. Anyway, she won't be there, and nor will the butler. The private viewing is over, and now that it's the public's turn, Lady Stanhope makes herself scarce. She prefers not to associate with the common rabble. Ludlow is also superfluous. He's semi-retired and only worked during the private viewing at Lady Stanhope's request. Most of the extra staff who were employed for last week have already left. Those who are still there will probably want to pat you on the back. Your exit is legendary."

Daisy perked up. "It was rather fun, wasn't it, Sylvia?"

"Not really," I said with a shake of my head and a smile. It was better to laugh off humiliation than stew in it. Besides, I'd had enough of stewing. I wanted to forge ahead and forget. What did it matter what Mr. Glass thought of me? I'd never see him again.

"The job won't be in the kitchen or serving this time," Horatio went on. "Starting on Monday evening, they're rotating some of the paintings. Some will be removed alto-gether and returned to the owners or the artists, while others will be moved to different rooms based on feedback from the private viewing. The work all happens after hours. I heard the exhibition manager's assistant is unwell. I'm sure you could fill in until he gets back, Sylvia. Why not try your luck on Monday afternoon, when the manager is there?"

It was the best offer I'd had all week. It was the only offer. "I will. Thank you, Horatio. You're a gem."

Daisy handed Horatio a glass and he saluted me with it. "And if you change your mind, I'm still willing to take you on as my model."

"Thank you."

He looked pleased, despite my sarcastic tone.

"You bounce back from rejection quickly," I said.

"There is just too much to be happy about to be down for long."

Daisy leaned forward and clinked her glass with his. "Here's to new opportunities, new friends, and a new decade. I have a feeling it will be a thousand times better than the last one."

Horatio sighed theatrically. "Dear God, I hope so."

As did I.

"Speaking of new friends, have you seen that handsome Glass fellow since Monday?" he asked.

I shook my head. "I don't expect to see him again."

"Are you quite sure about that?" He winked at Daisy.

She blinked back. "Why would Sylvia see him? She lost her job because of him!"

I pressed my lips together to stop myself telling her his visit was merely the icing on the cake for Mr. Parmiter. The flour, eggs and butter were mostly her.

Horatio turned to me and pulled a face that Daisy

C.J. ARCHER

couldn't see. "Let me know if you do see him again. I'll give you some hints on how to flirt with men like him."

"She won't be flirting with him. Stop encouraging her, Horatio."

"Flirting can be a great way to obtain information."

Daisy sank in the chair. "I know," she muttered. "His friend knows it too, blast him."

"All I'm suggesting is that if Sylvia wants to find out if he still suspects you two of being involved in the kidnapping, she ought to be...friendly." He pushed himself up from the sofa and put out his hand to Daisy. "Now show me your latest masterpiece, Darling."

She drew in a breath. "Really? You want to see it? Marvelous!" She sprang off the chair and, grinning, asked us both to follow her.

I could throttle Horatio, but he seemed genuinely enthusiastic about looking at her pieces. It only proved even further that I knew nothing about art. Daisy's paintings were not to my taste at all. Even so, I managed to nod and smile at the appropriate times, and I was rewarded with her genuine happiness in return. Perhaps Horatio was only humoring her, but I was glad he did if this was the result.

* * *

NEXT TIME I SAW HORATIO, I would kiss him. When I arrived at Burlington House, late on Monday afternoon, I found the exhibition manager's office in turmoil. His assistant was still sick, and the work was piling up. It was easy to convince Mr. Bolton that I was capable of performing the necessary duties. I informed him that I'd been a journalist for a number of years and then a librarian, here in London, most recently.

"Your references?" he said without looking up from his paperwork.

I placed the ones I had in front of him. He quickly scanned them. Indeed, he did it so fast that he mustn't have noticed the one from the library was missing altogether and that none of them were recent.

He pulled a wooden box out of his top desk drawer and selected a rubber stamp from among several neatly arranged inside, as well as an ink pad. He stamped my references with the word ACCEPTED then stood and buttoned up his jacket. "You'll do." He indicated I should walk out of the office ahead of him. "Hang up your coat and take this clipboard."

Mr. Bolton was like a military commander with his barked orders and brisk assessment. After he asked me to wait in the corridor, and nipped back into his office to retrieve a short stick, the resemblance to a general was even more pronounced. He thrust it under his arm and marched on.

We spent the next two hours going from one gallery to the next, checking off the artwork against his list. He used the stick as a pointer, both at the art on the wall and at me when he wanted me to note something down. At the end of two hours, the six-man packing team arrived.

Mr. Bolton clicked his fingers at me. "The list, Miss Ashe."

I handed him the clipboard, but he handed it straight back. "Remove the main copy and keep it. You'll be needing it shortly."

I unclipped the top copy and returned the clipboard to him.

He passed it to one of the packers. "The paintings on the front page require removal. There are thirteen."

"Unlucky number," one of the packers muttered.

Mr. Bolton pointed his stick at the fellow. "You! You're new. What's your name?"

The packer rested an arm on the upright trolley's handles. "Tommy Allan, sir."

"There's no place for silly superstitions in this institution, Mr. Allan."

Mr. Allen ran his tongue around his top teeth and made a sucking sound. The heavy-lidded stare he gave Mr. Bolton was made more sinister thanks to the scar stretching from the corner of his mouth to his ear. Both of his ears were covered by his hair. I wouldn't be surprised if the ear near the scar had been damaged or was missing altogether. Scars like his were not unusual on former servicemen.

The head packer split his men into two groups, one of four and the other with two.

Mr. Bolton assigned me to oversee the moving crew. "Make sure they put the right pieces in the right places according to your list. I will oversee the packing team."

The group of four turned out to be the moving team. One of them was Mr. Allan. He was the first to move off, only to be called back by Mr. Bolton.

The exhibition manager ran through a list of dos and don'ts for both teams, most of it boiling down to not touching the paint. Going by the bored expressions of all the men, I suspected the lecture was unnecessary. Most had done this before.

When he finally finished, Mr. Bolton clicked the heels of his shoes together and pointed to the adjoining gallery with his stick. "Onward packing team!"

Two of the men followed him. Since my team was starting in the main gallery, we stayed put.

Mr. Allan spat on the tiled floor. "Thought I was done with toffs like him giving me instructions for a job I can do better than them."

One of the other packers glanced at me. "Better clean that up, Tommy."

Tommy Allan sneered at me before walking off. "Cleaning's a woman's job."

I bit down on my retort and walked off too, leaving the gob of spit untouched. Mr. Allan was not the sort of man I wanted to have a confrontation with, particularly on my first day. I would give him the opportunity to clean it up in his own time.

It was going to be a long evening.

We worked for four hours, by which time my crew were growing restless. It was late and we'd not stopped. Well, most of us hadn't; Mr. Allan had taken a ten-minute break to smoke a cigarette. I watched with growing irritation as the ash dropped onto the floor as he made his way around the room, perusing the paintings. When he finished, he dropped the butt near his foot and ground it with his heel.

When he stopped work again after four hours, I decided it was time for them all to have a break. I went in search of Mr. Bolton and found him with the packing crew in one of the smaller galleries. His two-man team held a painting between them as they carried it to a crate. Mr. Bolton stood to one side, reading a scrap of paper.

I approached. "Do you mind if we stop for a short while? The men are thirsty and tired."

He tucked the paper into his jacket pocket and checked the watch hanging from the gold chain at his waistcoat. "Very well. It is late. You two!" He pointed his stick at his men. "Finish up with that one for tonight. We'll resume again tomorrow evening."

I caught up to the two packers but had to wait as they maneuvered the large painting through the door. It gave me an opportunity to admire it. It depicted a country village street scene with horse-drawn carts, carriages and two pedestrians. It was pretty but otherwise unremarkable. Even so, I couldn't stop staring at it. It intrigued me.

The men turned it around to place it into the upright crate. Something in the corner at the back caught my eye. The canvas was torn. No, not torn. It had simply come away and folded over.

But how could that be? The canvas had looked undamaged from the front. It was stretched taut, just as a painter's canvas ought to be. There were no gaps, tears or folds. Was there a second canvas behind the village scene painting? I edged closer and reached out a hand to touch it.

"Miss Ashe?" Mr. Bolton barked. "What are you doing?"

I snatched my hand back to my chest and looked up upon hearing a snicker. Mr. Allan leaned against the doorframe between the two galleries, smoking.

Mr. Bolton marched up to me. "Go and see to your men, Miss Ashe. You! Mr. Allan! Don't just stand there!"

Mr. Allan blew out a puff of smoke from the corner of his mouth then dropped the cigarette butt on the floor. His lips twisted into a sly smile directed at me.

I steeled myself. "Please pick that up, Mr. Allan, and the other one, too."

"Didn't you hear me before? Cleaning's woman's work."

"The cleaners aren't here."

He merely shrugged and turned away. "Then do it yourself."

"But—"

He rounded on me, his eyes flashing. "But what? It ain't your job to clean up? That's only because you took a man's job." He stabbed a finger at the floor. "You should be on your knees scrubbing, and a man who fought for his country should be walking around here with a list and pencil. Instead, good men have to beg on street corners, their faces covered so as not to frighten the harpies who took their work." He'd lowered his voice so that only I could hear. It loaned a menacing edge to his words.

"Is something the matter?" Mr. Bolton called out.

Mr. Allan sucked air through his teeth, shot a glare at the exhibition manager, and walked off.

Mr. Bolton swallowed hard. "Please pick up the cigarette butts before you go, Miss Ashe." He marched into the next gallery, stick wedged under his arm.

The two men from the packing team asked me to step aside. They carried the narrow crate between them, the painting of the village safely stored inside. They settled it on the trolley and one man wheeled it off.

"Where is that going?" I asked the other.

"To the storeroom until the artist comes to collect it. It wasn't sold, so it will be returned to him. Apparently, it ain't good enough to stay up. Not when there are others that need a turn. Not like that beauty." He nodded at the wall at the end of the large gallery where the painting of the steamship powering through the ocean now hung. My crew had moved the seascape to pride of place as instructed by Mr. Bolton. Based on feedback from the private viewing, it was deemed worthy to be one of the first paintings to be seen as people entered the main gallery.

I agreed with the packer. It was a beauty and deserved prime spot.

I didn't mention the extra canvas behind the village painting to Mr. Bolton. He might be one of Mr. Glass's suspects, and I didn't want to ruin the investigation. Indeed, Mr. Glass might even be aware of the hidden canvas. Leaving it in place might be part of his plan to catch the thieves.

Even so, I decided to telephone him first thing in the morning. He wasn't at home, however. With only one telephone in the lodging house, I couldn't be sure I'd be notified if he returned my call, so I asked when he would be back. There was a muffled sound on the other end then a different voice came on the line.

"Who're you and what do you want?" the woman barked in a thick American accent.

"I, er—"

"It's a simple question!"

I held the receiver away from my ear so as not to be deafened next time she spoke. "My name is Sylvia Ashe and I have some information for Mr. Glass about the investigation he's working on."

"Gabe mentioned you. You can come over. The address is sixteen Park Street, Mayfair. Come now."

"Will he be home by—"

The line went dead. I stared at the receiver and eventually hung it up. It would seem I was going to see where Mr. Glass lived—in Mayfair, no less.

It was a pleasant morning, so I dispensed with my coat and wore my best outfit of black pleated skirt and matching jacket with a white blouse. A black cloche hat adorned with ribbon, the only new purchase I'd made since arriving in London, completed the outfit. All that black meant that by the time I walked to Mayfair, I was hot. It might be time to invest in some new, more modern clothes in more cheerful colors, but I needed to find work to pay for them, first.

Park Street was one of those London streets that only the wealthy could afford to live on. Number sixteen was located in a row of handsome red and cream brick townhouses with a set of steps parallel to the pavement leading down to the service area basement. I bypassed those steps and headed up the ones that led to the front door.

My knock was answered by an ancient butler who led me through to the drawing room. He instructed me to wait and disappeared before I could ask if Mr. Glass had returned. I took a turn around the large room. It was everything I expected of a Mayfair drawing room, complete with a lovely clock encased in a glass dome on the mantelpiece, gilt-framed paintings, and expensive looking furniture. The décor was somewhat dated, but it suited the grand old townhouse, and it wasn't cluttered like many houses decorated by women of Lady Rycroft's age. The only other drawing room of a large townhouse I'd seen had been packed with occasional tables, their surfaces covered with knickknacks, photographs, and a stuffed bird or two.

This drawing room was perfect, not a cushion out of place. I didn't dare sit down. If it wasn't for the cluster of framed family photographs on one of the tables, the room would have suffered from being too formal, but the photos made it homely.

I bent to study them and smiled at a picture of Gabe, aged about ten. He stood between two adults who must be his parents. I could see where he got his good looks from.

I straightened as a man sauntered into the room. He stopped and studied me so I studied him back, albeit with a tentative smile. He was an odd looking fellow, his age difficult to determine. He could be in his early thirties or all the way up to fifty or so. He was short and wiry, with sharp cheekbones and light brown hair that was arranged rather messily.

"Well, it's about time." The voice belonged to the person I'd spoken to on the telephone, and a woman at that, not a man. It was an easy mistake to make, dressed as she was in trousers, white shirt, and waistcoat. The sleeves on the shirt were rolled to her elbows and she wore no tie. When she came closer, I could see that her long brown hair was streaked with slivers of gray. She wore it tied up at the back of her head.

"About time?" I echoed.

"I thought you'd get here ages ago. You live in Bloomsbury, don't you? It doesn't take thirty minutes to get here from Bloomsbury."

"It does if you walk."

"Walk? Why'd you want to do that?"

"It's a nice day, and you said Mr. Glass wasn't back when we spoke earlier on the telephone. I thought I'd give him time to get here."

She grunted. "Sit down. You can tell me what you want to tell him. I'll pass it on."

I sat on the sofa. She sat on the chair opposite with her legs apart and her elbows out. Although her habits and manner were masculine, she was small and fine-boned. The odd combination was intriguing.

"Quit staring. A woman dressed in trousers ain't a strange sight, these days. The war saw to that."

I looked down at my hands in my lap. "Sorry."

"Go on, then."

"Pardon?"

"Tell me what you wanted to tell Gabe."

I glanced at the door, but no one was there. We were quite alone. I wished the butler hadn't left. This woman unnerved me. "I have some information about the case he's working on."

"So you said over the telephone." She signaled for me to continue with a flick of her wrist. "You can tell it to me, and I'll tell Gabe."

"I'd rather tell him in person. Is he expected home soon?"

She crossed one leg over the other and jiggled her foot up and down. "You can trust me, Miss Ashe. I live here."

Was she a servant, playing at being hostess while the master was out? Aside from family, who else would live in Lord and Lady Rycroft's townhouse?

Whoever she was, I wasn't going to tell her anything without Mr. Glass's approval. She didn't look like she was going to back down, either. We sat in a silence that grew weightier by the moment, she glaring daggers at me from

68

across the room as I tried not to be further irritated by that jiggling foot.

I only hoped I wouldn't regret my silence and that she wasn't someone close to Mr. Glass who I'd offended with my refusal to talk.

CHAPTER 5

*T*hank goodness the butler entered carrying a tray with teacups and teapot. He was as welcome as a cool breeze at the end of a hot summer's day.

"I never asked for tea, Bristow," the woman snapped.

"Miss Ashe might like it," he said. "She looks flushed."

"She won't be staying."

"Even so, providing tea is what a hostess does."

The woman bristled. "I ain't an idiot, and I've been in this country long enough to know the rules. I also know that when someone ain't staying long, there's no need to offer tea."

The butler picked up the teapot. "I'll pour, shall I?"

Mr. Glass walked in and stopped suddenly upon seeing me. Mr. Bailey, following behind, almost bumped into him. "Miss Ashe! This is a surprise."

I rose and shook his hand before sitting again. "I telephoned earlier and was told to come here. I have some information that you might find useful for your case."

"You were told to come here?" He turned to the woman, brows arched. She had not risen upon his entry, whereas the butler had straightened. She wasn't a servant then. "I see you've met Willie."

"Actually, we haven't been properly introduced."

He released an exasperated breath.

Mr. Bailey chuckled as he sat. "You're not in the Wild West anymore, Willie."

She gave him a withering look. "I was just about to do it." She jutted her chin out at me. "I'm Willie Johnson. Call me Willie."

"A pleasure to meet you."

"Don't speak too soon," Mr. Bailey muttered. He looked as though he was enjoying himself.

"Thank you, Bristow, that will be all." Mr. Glass poured the tea and handed a cup to me. "Willie is my father's cousin."

I stared at him and then her.

"I know. None of us can believe it either." He passed a cup and saucer to Willie. The withering look deepened as she took it.

"I want to apologize for her," he went on.

"It's quite all right," I said.

"She's got the manners of an alley cat and is even worse at the moment. She's trying to give up smoking. It's made her irritable."

"Alley cat!" Willie grunted. "More like a tiger."

"I would have said insect," Mr. Bailey chimed in. He was still smiling as he saluted Willie with his teacup.

She scowled back. "I quit smoking to support *you*, Gabe."

"I'm also trying to give up," he told me. "It was my mother's request just before she left for America. She doesn't mind the occasional cigar smoked in the evening, but she disliked my cigarette habit."

Most of the men had returned from the war as cigarette smokers. I'd heard someone say the government issued them to the soldiers to suppress their appetites because there was a food shortage at the Front. Whatever the reason, there were more people, not just men, smoking now than there used to be before the war.

"It's a big sacrifice on my part," Willie went on. "You only started during the war, Gabe. I've been smoking since I was six. That's a few years more."

"Quite a few," Mr. Bailey said.

"Quit it, Alex, or I swear I'll cut off your little toe when you're asleep."

Mr. Bailey grinned but wisely remained silent.

Mr. Glass looked to the ceiling and muttered something under his breath. "I'm very sorry, Miss Ashe. They're not usually like this."

Both Mr. Bailey and Willie looked unconvinced by this statement.

I sipped my tea to bide my time and gather my wits. This meeting wasn't going as I expected, and I wasn't yet sure what to make of it. I knew the upper classes could be eccentric, but that eccentricity didn't quite explain the dynamic between these three. Even Mr. Glass was confounding all the opinions I'd formed since reading the article about him. Perhaps I should have been warned that he wasn't going to conform to those opinions when I learned he worked for the police. It was hardly the sort of occupation the wealthy heir to a barony would take on.

Willie placed her cup on the saucer with a loud clatter that I suspected was to draw our attention. "You going to tell us this valuable information or just sit there?"

I looked to Mr. Glass and he nodded. "You can speak in front of her. She won't say a word to anyone."

She puffed out her chest. "I've worked many cases with Gabe's parents, back when they helped the police, and I was married to a Scotland Yard detective until he up and died on me." Her words may have sounded as though she felt betrayed by his death, but her eyes turned sad. She tried to hide her sorrow by lowering her gaze.

"I've been employed temporarily at the Royal Academy of Arts in the evenings, to assist with the moving and packing of some of the paintings." At the surprised looks of both Mr. Glass and Mr. Bailey, I couldn't help smiling. "Yes, they re-employed me after that debacle, but only because my new manager isn't aware what happened last time I worked there. It's an entirely different team. I started last night. As one of the paintings was being carried off, I noticed something behind the canvas. It appeared to be a second canvas. It was stretched across the frame like the one in front, but a corner had come loose."

Mr. Glass had lowered his teacup as I spoke, and he now sat forward. "Did you tell anyone?"

"No. I thought it best to inform only you in case one of the employees is a suspect."

"Thank you."

"So...?"

He frowned. "So...what?"

"Is one of the staff a suspect?"

"He can't tell you that," Mr. Bailey cut in.

"Do you think it has something to do with your art theft?" I asked.

Willie's gaze narrowed. "You ask a lot of questions for a librarian."

I bit the inside of my cheek to stop myself telling her I used to be a journalist. I got the feeling from the way Mr. Glass had described his experience with the reporter who wrote about his rescue of the drowning lad that he didn't like them. I didn't want him to think poorly of me.

"Librarians can't be inquisitive?" Mr. Glass shot back. To me, he said, "I do think it's linked. We hadn't been able to locate the stolen painting. Can you describe the painting it was behind?"

"It was a street scene of a country village." I described the buildings, colors and what the people in the painting wore. "It was pretty but didn't particularly stand out, which I suspect is why it was being taken down."

"Did anyone else notice the hidden canvas?"

"I don't think so, but I can't be certain."

"Who else was there?"

"The exhibition manager, Mr. Bolton, and six packers." I rattled off their names and Mr. Bailey wrote them down in a small notebook. I watched Mr. Glass closely. Either the names meant nothing to him or he was good at hiding his thoughts. "None look like the thug who tried to kidnap you," I added.

"Kidnap!" Willie exploded. "Gabe? What's she talking about?"

Oh no. I'd put my foot in it.

"Calm down, Willie," Mr. Glass said. "There was a small scuffle outside Burlington House. Nothing I couldn't handle."

"I knew I should have gone with you that day. Why didn't you tell me about it?"

"Because I knew you'd overreact."

"I ain't overreacting!"

Mr. Glass arched his brows at her.

She pointed a finger at him. "Your parents asked me to take care of you while they were gone. How can I do that if you don't let me come with you when you investigate?"

"Ordinarily I would," he said calmly, with more patience than most would employ under the circumstances. "But you weren't invited to the exhibition opening, and you would have looked out of place amongst the wait staff."

She crossed her arms. "I would not."

Mr. Bailey rolled his eyes. "You would have attracted more attention to yourself than Miss Ashe's friend did."

I ought to be offended on Daisy's behalf, but I found I couldn't be. She *had* made a spectacle of herself—and of me.

"Besides," Mr. Glass went on, "I'm perfectly capable of looking after myself, which you well know."

"Tell me what happened," Willie went on. "What did the kidnappers look like? How'd it play out?"

"Can we discuss this later?"

She glanced at me. "Fine. But I'm going to stick to you like a fly on a hog's ass from now on."

Mr. Bailey groaned, but Mr. Glass simply seemed resigned to the idea.

Despite his request to leave the discussion until later, Willie wasn't giving up yet. "I don't reckon the kidnapping's related to the art theft. If the thief got wind of your investigation, there's a dozen other ways to stop you or distract you. By trying to kidnap you, they're only drawing attention to themselves."

I agreed, and it was the point I'd been going to make when I brought it up. "Why not just kill Mr. Glass? Why kidnap him?"

All three turned to me.

I cleared my throat and gently put my teacup in the saucer and returned them to the table. "I've taken up enough of your time."

Mr. Glass glanced at the glass domed clock as he rose. "Shouldn't you be at the library now?"

"I no longer work there."

"Did you leave of your own accord or were you dismissed?"

"Dismissed."

"Why?"

"Various reasons, all of which boil down to Mr. Parmiter not liking me."

"Did he dismiss you because of my visit?"

I led the way out of the drawing room so that he couldn't see my face as I lied. But I didn't get the chance to speak. The butler's booming voice echoed around the tiled entrance hall.

"No, you cannot!" He slammed the door in someone's face. For an elderly man who looked like a sneeze would see him lose his balance, he was rather fierce.

"I just want a quick word!" shouted the person on the other side.

"Bristow?" Mr. Glass strode up to the butler. "Who is it?"

"It's that journalist again, sir."

Mr. Glass clapped him on the shoulder. "Thank you. I'll handle it."

Willie pushed past them both. "Let me." She jerked the door open and squared up to the man standing on the porch. "Get going or I'll shoot!"

The man stumbled backward, turned, and raced down the stairs.

She closed the door and dusted her hands. "He won't be back in a hurry."

Mr. Bailey opened the door again and stood on the porch, hands on hips. He frowned into the distance.

"You can't threaten to shoot people, Willie," Mr. Glass said.

"I wasn't pointing my gun at him, was I? It ain't a real threat unless you're holding a weapon in your hand. India doesn't let me carry it in the house." She puckered her lips in thought then smiled slyly. "But she ain't here no more."

"I'm also forbidding you from carrying it in the house. It should be locked away in the gun cabinet."

"It is," she said with a glare for Bristow as he opened his mouth to speak. He shut it again and melted into the shadows at the back of the entrance hall near the stairs.

Mr. Bailey re-entered the house and closed the door. "He's not going to give up that easily. Journalists never do."

I clutched my handbag to my chest.

Mr. Glass gave me a flat smile. "Apologies, Miss Ashe. We're used to it, but confrontations like that must be unsettling for you."

"It's fine."

Willie shook her head. "That one's persistent. Don't know why. It wasn't even that big a story."

Mr. Bailey agreed. "What else can he possibly want to know? You saved the lad and his father drowned. That's it." His dark gaze drilled into Mr. Glass. "Isn't it?"

Mr. Glass drew in a deep breath and smiled at me. "You shouldn't walk home alone. That journalist might be lurking around the corner and could accost you if he realizes you were just here."

"Why would he do that?" I asked.

"He'll think you have answers."

"Answers about what?"

Willie clicked her tongue. "That pig ain't the only one who's nosy."

I clutched my bag tighter. "Sorry. I don't mean to pry."

"You're not prying," Mr. Glass said quickly. "After witnessing that, it's only natural you have questions. You must be rattled. Let me drive you home."

"No!" Willie cried. "Dodson can take her."

"No one needs to take me," I said. "I can walk. I won't speak to that journalist, or any others."

"Even so, I'd feel better if I knew you'd avoided him altogether," Mr. Glass said. "They can be very persistent. Bristow, have Dodson bring around the Prince Henry."

"No!" Willie said again. "You shouldn't take her."

Mr. Glass shrugged. "Why not?"

"Because of the attempted kidnapping," Mr. Bailey said.

Mr. Glass nodded at Bristow, and the butler disappeared through a door that must lead to the service stairs. "I'm not worried about another kidnapping and nor should anyone else be. There have been no attempts since that time outside Burlington House over a week ago."

Willie still looked annoyed, and I was beginning to feel somewhat guilty. If something happened to Mr. Glass because of me, would his cousin come to the lodging house brandishing her gun? Would his friend, Mr. Bailey, blame me?

"I'll walk." I edged past them to the door. "It's a pleasant day, and I have errands to run. Goodbye and thank you for the tea." I let myself out and hurried down the steps, eager to get far away from the madhouse as quickly as possible.

* * *

I WENT to Daisy's flat, intending to spend the afternoon with her, but she'd been struck by her muse and conversation was out of the question. I blamed Horatio. Ever since he'd complimented her pieces on Friday evening, her efforts had become frenzied. There were sketches and half-finished canvases strewn all around the flat, as well as splashes of paint on the floor and on Daisy herself. I washed the dishes, which mainly consisted of cocktail glasses, and made her a sandwich. I made sure she'd taken a few bites and drunk a cup of tea before I let myself out.

I mixed with some of the other lodgers in the sitting room at home, intending to while away the rest of the afternoon playing Bridge before getting ready for my second evening of work at the Academy. But the arrival of Mr. Glass scuttled those plans.

"They let you out," I said, only half-joking.

"I had to use all of my persuasive efforts, but they did."

"They're worried about you."

He sighed. "Especially Willie. She has taken her promise to my parents to look after me very seriously. What she doesn't know is, they told me to look after her, and they told Cyclops to look after us all."

"Cyclops? As in the one-eyed giant of Greek mythology?"

"The one and only. He's Alex's father and a good friend to my parents."

Mrs. Whitten strode into the entrance hall where we were talking and stood with her hands clasped in front of her, all her double chins squashed into her neck in disapproval.

Mr. Glass smiled and doffed his cap. "I was about to leave." He waited for her to move off before he leaned toward me. "I've just come from Burlington House and want to give you an update on the investigation."

"Oh! That would be marvelous, but are you allowed?"

"I still can't divulge much, but I want you to know what came of your efforts last night."

Mrs. Whitten cleared her throat. She hadn't left, after all.

"May I take you for a brief drive, Miss Ashe?" Mr. Glass asked. "We can talk in the car."

It seemed like the best way to have a private discussion. I fetched my coat and hat and joined Mr. Glass outside. He stood beside a different car than the one his driver had picked him up in the day of the kidnapping. This one was a Vauxhall Prince Henry in clotted cream with a burgundy leather interior. The brass knobs and dials shone in the sunlight. With the top down, it looked very flash.

"You have two motors?" I asked as I climbed into the passenger seat.

"The other is my parents' car. It's usually kept at our country home with them. This one's mine, although it's getting old now. I had Dodson drive me in theirs to Burlington House because I knew parking would be difficult. I prefer to drive myself, so I usually take this one." He cranked the engine and climbed into the driver's seat. "Do you want to wear goggles? I usually don't bother in London. We won't be able to go fast in the traffic."

I declined the goggles too. Gabe pulled a lever on the steering wheel, and another attached to the outside of the vehicle near the windscreen, and we set off into traffic. With the grumbling engine and wind whipping past my ears, we couldn't hold a conversation. Perhaps we should have walked instead. The ride was rather thrilling, however. I'd been in motorized buses and cabs but being driven in a luxurious private vehicle was a different experience. I felt like a child being shown a new toy.

Mr. Glass must think me terribly unsophisticated. I didn't dare glance at him, and hid my smile behind my arm, raised in order to clamp a hand on my hat to stop it blowing away. I could see why he wore a driving cap and not a hat; it would have blown off.

We only drove for about ten minutes, heading south past the museum then through the West End theater district. Just past Leicester Square, Gabe pulled to the curb and turned off the engine. We were in an unremarkable retail area with many pedestrians walking past. Some stopped to admire the motorcar.

Gabe took no notice of them. He settled an arm on the back of the seat between us. "Next time you'll need different headwear. Something tighter or with a scarf that ties under your chin."

Next time?

"Miss Ashe, I wanted to thank you properly for the information about the hidden painting."

"Did you find it? Has it led to an arrest?"

"Sadly, no on both counts. I found the painting, the one with the village scene you described, but there was nothing behind it. It did look as though it had been tampered with, so that confirms your theory. At least now, thanks to you, I know for certain that someone from the exhibition is involved. It narrows the list of suspects considerably."

"What will you do next?"

"Keep investigating."

I waited for more, but none came. "I'm returning to work there tonight. Do you want me to look around? I can probably access some records or keep an eye on your suspects."

"I can manage." He tapped his thumb on the leather upholstery and frowned. "Perhaps you shouldn't return. Someone might suspect that you saw the stolen painting. I don't want to put you in danger."

"No one saw. Besides, I have to show up. I need that job."

"Ah yes, the library fiasco. That leads me to my reason for bringing you here." He indicated a covered entry between two identical shops, both painted in black and fronted with bay windows. The gap between them was no larger than a doorway, and if he hadn't pointed it out, I would have taken no notice of it. Carved into the lintel, above the entry, was the name of the street beyond. Crooked Lane.

I squinted but couldn't see beyond the entry. "I don't understand."

"I felt terrible for costing you the job at the Philosophical Society's library."

"That wasn't your fault."

"It was partially my fault, so I got you an interview at another library."

I stared at him.

His smile widened. "It's down there, in Crooked Lane. The librarian is expecting you. His name is Professor Nash, although he's no longer a professor. He retired some years ago."

"You know him well?"

"The library is…special to my family. It houses a collection of books about magic. Professor Nash spent years traveling all over the world to source books, manuscripts, letters, and all manner of documents that mention magic. There's nothing like his collection in the world. He's retired from travel now and just works in there, alone. It's time he had some help." He indicated me.

"*If* he employs me," I added. "Wouldn't he rather employ a magician?"

"He's not a magician himself, so he wouldn't have any qualms hiring an artless. Besides, at least one of the main financial backers is artless."

He was holding something back, and I could take a guess at what. "Does Professor Nash want an assistant, Mr. Glass, or are you foisting me upon him?"

He gave me a wry look. "Am I that easy to read?"

"I think you ought to drive me home. I don't want to upset the apple cart."

"You won't be. Nash is a good fellow, although somewhat eccentric. He has worked alone in that library for too long and is getting on in years. He needs an assistant, and I happen to think you'd be perfect for the job."

"Why?"

"Because you have experience, you're sharp-eyed and clever. You're also not currently working. Not to mention that Nash is rather hopeless and wouldn't get around to placing an advertisement. I'd have to do it. So, you're saving me time if you accept."

"I haven't been offered the position yet."

He got out and came around to my side. He opened the door and held out his hand to me. "Please, Miss Ashe, will you just speak to him? I feel awful for costing you the position at the society."

I hesitated but took his hand. "Very well. It sounds intriguing, and I'm not one to turn down a golden opportunity."

"Do you mind if you make your own way home? I have a suspect I need to follow."

I eyed the dark entryway again but still couldn't see through to the other side. Very little daylight must be getting through. "You're not sending me into a magical cave, are you?"

He grinned. "Do you want me to come with you?"

"I'll be fine. I'll just buy a loaf of bread and leave crumbs so I can find my way out again."

"It won't work. There are too many birds in the city. What if I promise to send in a search party if you haven't returned to the lodging house by nightfall?"

"That makes me feel much better."

I waved him off from the pavement before turning and heading through the entrance to Crooked Lane beyond. It was like stepping into another time. The buildings looked late seventeenth century to me, painted black with bay windows bulging into the cobblestoned lane. There was no pavement or vehicles—there was simply no room. If I stretched my arms wide, I could almost touch the bay windows on either side.

There was no one about. I expected to see pedestrians passing through, but I soon realized the short lane was a dead end. It should have been named a court or yard. It also wasn't crooked. Perhaps once, centuries ago, it had been open at both ends and acted as a throughway between the busier streets that bookended it. Progress and development had seen it shortened and the kink that gave it its name lost.

My footsteps echoed, bouncing off the brick walls that rose three levels high on either side. It was difficult to tell if the buildings were occupied or empty. Some on the ground level had a business name painted on the window, while others were unmarked, their curtains closed. Those that could be clearly identified were the sort that didn't rely on passing foot traffic for custom. The library was wedged between a solicitor's office and theater manager's office in a narrow building only one window wide. The sign above the window said THE GLASS LIBRARY.

This library wasn't simply meaningful to Gabe's family. It had been named after them. That was quite a connection indeed.

I pushed open the door, only to pause on the threshold and draw the familiar smell of old books into my lungs. It took me back to another library in another city, one I hadn't thought of in years. My days studying in that library had been some of my happiest. That too had been a private library, the collection owned by an elderly couple who delighted in having a girl reading their books after school.

The small front office contained a leather-inlaid desk that was mostly bare except for some writing implements, a black and brass candlestick telephone, and an open ledger. The light from a brass lamp angled onto the neatly ruled blank page. A coat and hat hung from the stand between the desk and a winding staircase. I gave these things only a cursory glance. My attention was almost wholly occupied by the room beyond.

The small office opened up to the library proper. At the far end, directly ahead, was a large fireplace, above which hung an enormous clock with brass numbers and hands. It must have been custom made to take pride of place above the stone mantelpiece.

As with the office, I gave the clock only a fleeting glance. The bookshelves interested me more. They were stuffed with books of all sizes, stretching to the high ceiling. I took a step toward the room, then another and another, and before I knew it, I was passing through the two black marble columns guarding the entryway. I'd joked with Gabe about disappearing into a magical cave, but it was no longer a joke.

Whether it was the clock, which I assumed contained Lady Rycroft's magic, or whether it was the nature of the collection, I was in awe.

I stood beneath the central chandelier, its dozens of lights blazing, showing off the shine on the polished wooden shelves and ladders, and the delicate floral motif in the ceiling plasterwork. I ought to feel small in this room, dwarfed as I was by the shelves, but I didn't. I felt comforted. Books were so familiar to me and reminded me of happy times. Before I learned to read, my mother or brother would read me to sleep. As I grew older, I devoured stories like other children devoured sweets. I loved to explore and have adventures from the safety of my bed. When I felt anxious, I curled up with a book and read. When I felt overwhelmed by grief, I read to stave off the loneliness. I was not alone when I had a book. Despite our numerous moves, I made sure that some cherished volumes came with me. It was only natural that this room made me feel a sense of belonging, of being home.

I only hoped the librarian would employ me because the longer I stood there, the more I knew I wanted to work in the Glass Library.

"You must be Miss Ashe," said a reedy voice behind me.

I turned and was surprised to see a familiar face.

CHAPTER 6

*P*rofessor Nash resembled an old book. A little bit crumpled and worn out, with a bent spine, but I was intrigued enough by the cover to find out more. He welcomed me with a smile and a sweep of his fine-boned hand, inviting me to sit in a reading nook I hadn't noticed before.

Tucked away at the back, the only light came from a low-hanging chandelier and a floor lamp beside the chocolate-colored leather sofa. A freestanding bookcase housed a small gilt clock, an urn that looked as though it hadn't yet been cleaned after its discovery at an archaeology dig, a bronze statue of a horse and other knickknacks, as well as books, naturally. Three more books were stacked on a sofa table beside a portable writing desk and silver candlesticks, and a disused copper coal scuttle had been re-purposed as a magazine holder. It was the perfect space for quiet reading, even more so than the reading nook at the Philosophical Society library. There was even a lap blanket for chilly days folded neatly over the arm of the sofa.

I took a seat at one end of the sofa, and Professor Nash

occupied the other. He seemed unconcerned that no one manned the front desk.

After introductions, I couldn't hold it back any further. The curiosity was eating at me. "Have we met before? You look familiar."

He adjusted his spectacles to peer at me closely. "You're not familiar to me, but Gabe said you used to work at the London Philosophical Society library. I'm a member there and have been to the library a few times."

"That must be it. I was probably tucked away behind one of the bookshelves on your visits."

"Mr. Parmiter didn't mention he had an assistant."

It was better to get it over with now. It would be less painful to broach the topic of my dismissal before I let my hopes rise. "Did Mr. Glass explain why I left my previous employment?"

"Not really. He told me he is to blame because he called on you there and Mr. Parmiter is a curmudgeon. His word, not mine." He smiled, making his eyes twinkle behind the spectacles. "I think he feels guilty."

"He does, and I'm concerned he's using his influence here to force you to interview me for the role of assistant. I do hope that's not the case. I don't want to be a bother."

"You're no bother at all. The truth is, I'm looking to slow down a little. It's time I employed an assistant." He clasped his hands together in his lap. With his stooped back, he looked as though he'd folded over like an envelope. "I might as well employ a friend of Mr. Glass's."

"Oh, we're not friends. I hardly know him."

"He clearly thinks you'd be good for the role, and I trust his judgment."

"You know him well?"

"Well enough. When he was a child, his parents would bring him to the railway station to meet me after I returned from one of my travels. He couldn't wait to find out what treasures we'd brought back. He liked the artefacts best and was always a little disappointed when our hoard was merely a few old books." He chuckled. "He was an inquisitive lad but an active one. He preferred being out of doors to reading."

"I was the opposite."

His smile widened. "Me too. Tell me a little about yourself, Miss Ashe. Gabe says you're new to London. Where are you from?"

"I lived in Birmingham before coming to London."

"You don't have an accent."

"I was only there for a year and a half. My mother and I moved there after the war. We moved a lot over the years."

He was polite enough not to ask why, but I could see he was curious. If he'd asked me to explain the frequent relocations, I would have told him the truth—I didn't know why my mother insisted we never stay in one place very long.

"Aside from the Philosophical Society library, what experience do you have?"

"That's the only librarian position I've held."

"What work did you do in Birmingham?" He might look like the quintessential mild mannered professorial type, but there was a shrewdness behind those spectacles. He'd sensed I was avoiding telling him more.

I suspected he would sense a lie too, so I didn't attempt one. "Please don't tell Mr. Glass this, but I was a journalist during the war."

"Ah. I see. I heard about his run-ins with reporters after he returned home after Armistice. They all wanted to interview the hero, the baron's son who'd survived four years of brutal fighting against all odds. I understood their curiosity, but it must have been annoying for him to be hounded like that. Anyway, I believe they gave up after a few months."

"Until recently. The story of him saving a boy from drowning has sparked interest again."

He leaned forward conspiratorially. "I see no reason to tell him about your prior profession. It will be our secret."

"If you employ me, that is."

He frowned. "Why wouldn't I employ you?"

"I, uh… I don't know."

"Well then, that's settled."

"It is?"

He put out his hand. "Welcome to the Glass Library, Miss Ashe. Can you begin tomorrow?"

"Yes!" I shook his hand enthusiastically. Perhaps a little too enthusiastically. He wiggled his fingers when I let go.

As we walked to the front door, I admired some of the books on the shelves as we passed. Some were quite old, going by the wooden covers and visible spine stitching. Professor Nash noticed my lingering gaze and my slowing pace.

"You like them?" he asked.

I brushed my hand along the spines. "You have a remarkable collection. Mr. Glass said you found these all yourself."

"Yes, along with a friend." He sighed. "We traveled together for a number of years, buying up everything we could find in all corners of the world. Some books we saved from being destroyed, and others are now available to all when before they were kept hidden. There are some cultures where magic is forbidden, you see. Magicians can't practice their craft for fear of punishment. Possessing just one of these books could lead to execution. When war loomed on the horizon, I chose to return home. Oscar continued on alone and met his end in the Arabian Desert. We had some grand adventures, he and I." His gaze lost focus for a moment, before sharpening again. "We have books about magic, alchemy and witchcraft, as well as an entire section on superstition. Ours is the largest collection of Asian works outside that continent. We even have some very old books printed on bamboo sheets."

"Remarkable. Can you read them?"

"Many, but by no means all. Some are written in ancient languages, long forgotten or difficult to translate. Some are written in code that I've yet to crack."

"It's wonderful that you named the library after Lord and Lady Rycroft. They must be honored."

He blinked at me. "Oh no. I mean, yes, she's honored, but the library isn't named after both of them. It's just for Mrs. Glass. India. She's the library's inspiration as well as a patron. Lord Rycroft has provided much of our funding, of course, but he'd be the first to tell you the library isn't named after him. He's artless," he added, as if that explained it.

It was my turn to blink owlishly at him. "Oh? I thought he must be a powerful magician too, like his wife."

"Goodness, no." He chuckled.

"And their son, Mr. Glass? Is he a magician?"

"Artless, like his father." He sighed heavily, as if this were a great disappointment to him. I wondered who else was disappointed by Mr. Glass's artlessness. I wondered if he was.

We shook hands at the door and I left, my step lighter than when I entered. As I exited Crooked Lane, I glanced over my shoulder, but the murky afternoon light made it difficult to discern the individual buildings, and I couldn't quite work out from here which one was the library. What a charming little street. Perhaps *charmed* was a better word. The sun had dipped low. Time had slipped by without me realizing it. I needed to hurry home and change for work. I had to finish the job I started at the Royal Academy of Arts.

It wasn't until I was halfway home that I realized I hadn't asked Professor Nash about my wage or working conditions.

Not that it mattered. Anything was better than what I had now.

* * *

To my surprise, Horatio was waiting for me in the lodging house sitting room. Two lodgers crowded close to him on the sofa, giggling at his story, only to spring apart when I entered. I suspected it wasn't my arrival that made them nervous, but Mrs. Whitten's, hot on my heels.

"You have far too many male guests, Miss Ashe," she said snippily. "A policeman is one thing, but an artist is quite another! Will he be here long?"

I assured her he wouldn't be then turned to Horatio. He leapt up and embraced me, kissing both my cheeks. It wasn't a wise thing to do in Mrs. Whitten's presence. She looked as though she'd explode with indignation. All of her chins shook violently.

Horatio took her hand between both of his. "Dear lady, don't fret."

She eyed him with suspicion. She wasn't going to succumb to a man's charms.

"Believe me, Sylvia is of no interest to me. She's far too insipid."

I ought to be offended, but at that moment, I didn't care. I had to get ready for work. "Is something the matter, Horatio?"

"Yes! Well, no, not really." He frowned. "You seem agitated. Is it because I said I have no interest in you? Dear sweet little thing. Don't be upset. You're somebody's type, just not mine."

"Miss Ashe!" Mrs. Whitten barked.

I sighed and rubbed my forehead. "Horatio, please. I have to go to work soon."

"Ah, yes! The Academy! The manager took you on?"

"I'm helping the packing team. Tonight is the last night."

"Oh? The assistant is well enough to return?"

"No, I'm giving notice. I'm starting a new job tomorrow, and working days *and* nights is too much. Hopefully Mr. Bolton's regular assistant can return, but if not, I'm sure he can find someone else. The work is easy."

"A new job! How wonderful. If one likes that sort of thing, of course." He pulled a face and, despite the situation, I laughed.

He eyed Mrs. Whitten over my shoulder then hooked his arm through mine. "Come with me into the corridor."

The two lodgers didn't follow us, but Mrs. Whitten did. Thankfully she kept going. She mustn't think Horatio a threat to my virtue out here where lodgers came and went at regular intervals.

Horatio and I stopped beside a small painting leaning against the wall. "This is for you." Instead of showing me, he picked it up and led the way up the stairs. "Quickly," he hissed. "Before she sees."

I unlocked the door to my room, and he bundled me inside.

"That was close," he said.

"I wouldn't count your chickens, Horatio. She knows everything that goes on in this building. She probably knows you're in here." I pointed to the canvas. "Is it one of yours?"

He turned it around. The unframed canvas was of Tower Bridge in the evening, partially shrouded by mist and rain. It was gloomy and I half expected to see a sinister figure lurking in the shadows if I looked closer. "It is. I see you like it. I painted it when I was gripped by melancholy."

"It's very...moody."

"It's yours." He set it down on the floor and leaned it against the bed.

Horatio had a piece in this year's Royal Academy of Arts summer exhibition. Thanks to that exposure, he could expect his work to sell for quite a lot of money. I wasn't an expert, but I suspected even a small, gloomy piece like this one would do well. "Thank you, that's very generous of you. But why are you giving it to me?"

"Because I like you."

"Even though I'm not your type?"

He flashed me a grin. "As a friend, you're everybody's type. You're as sweet and warm as a pot of hot chocolate."

I laughed. "Please don't give up painting to try your hand at writing. Now, if you don't mind, I really do need to get ready for work."

He turned around. "I won't look."

In case he did, I turned around too. I changed my blouse and threw on a different jacket but kept the same skirt. I tied the jacket's sash at my waist and checked my hair in the mirror. It was a little messy but would have to do. There was no time to rearrange it.

I opened the door and peered out, looking for Mrs. Whitten. "All clear."

Horatio handed me my coat and hat. "If I see her, I propose we make a run for it."

"That's easy for you to say. I live here."

"Then move. This place is awful anyway." He wrinkled his nose. "The light is dreadful and there are too many old books."

"Those are my books."

He mouthed an apology before ushering me out the door.

* * *

BURLINGTON HOUSE WAS peaceful at night. With the crowds gone and the doors locked, only the movements of the packing crew could be heard. The men kept their voices hushed, as if in deference to the cathedral-like galleries. My team knew what they were doing, which gave me the opportunity to wander around and admire the paintings.

A set of heavy footsteps approached from behind. I didn't look around. It wasn't necessary. I'd come to know each man's gait and the weight of his tread.

"It's all right for some," sneered Mr. Allan, the packer with the scarred face. "The rest of us are slaving away while you swan about doing nothing."

I finally turned around. "I'm happy to help. Tell me what you'd like me to do."

He struck a match and lit the cigarette dangling from his lips. "You'd only get in the way." He tossed the match on the floor near my feet and sucked on the cigarette.

I bit my tongue to stop myself pointing out that he couldn't have it both ways. Letting him rile me would only inflame the situation. Arguing was precisely what he wanted, and I wouldn't let him win.

I picked up the matchstick and tucked it into the pocket of his dust jacket before walking away in search of Mr. Bolton and his crew. I wanted to tell him this would be my last night.

He was not in the adjoining gallery, however. Whispered voices came from the next gallery over. They sounded harsh, spoken in anger, and as I drew closer, I realized one was a woman's.

"Mr. Bolton?" I entered the gallery but stopped short.

Lady Stanhope and Mr. Ludlow, the butler who'd dismissed me from the waitressing job, looked just as surprised to see me as I was to see them.

I turned and fled.

They recovered from their shock and pursued me. Mr. Ludlow caught my arm just as I was about to re-enter the gallery where my team was rehanging a painting. "What are you doing here?" he growled.

"I—I'm working for Mr. Bolton. He employed me to—"

"I fired you! Get out!"

I wrenched free. "If you'll just speak to Mr. Bolton—"

"I'll speak to him, all right. He clearly isn't aware of the sort of person he employed."

Lady Stanhope trotted up on her heeled shoes and looked me up and down. From her confused frown, I suspected she couldn't recollect our first meeting where she'd tried to stop me speaking to Gabe. I wasn't important enough to remember. "Ludlow? Who is this girl?"

"A waitress I dismissed for confronting the guests during the private viewing."

I bristled. "We were having a conversation, not a confrontation."

Lady Stanhope's face pinched as if my words tasted bitter. "You were not employed to have conversations. The guests don't want to be bothered by the staff." She shot Ludlow a frosty glare. "I knew having waiters this year would be a mistake. We should have left the food in the refreshment room like previous years."

The butler's nostrils flared in and out with every snorting breath. I wasn't sure if his anger was still directed at me or had been transferred to Lady Stanhope. He'd certainly sounded annoyed with her earlier, if his harshly whispered tone was anything to go by. That she'd let him speak to her like that at all was something I needed to think about another time.

Right now, I was worried about being dismissed on the spot. Mr. Bolton strode into the gallery. He pointed his stick at Mr. Allan and the other men who'd stopped to watch the exchange. "This isn't a theater show! Get back to work."

Mr. Allan's top lip curled up into his scar. The effect was a sinister sneer that sent a chill through me. He was enjoying my plight.

"Lady Stanhope?" Mr. Bolton gentled his tone. "What a pleasant surprise this is. I wasn't expecting you."

"I had some last-minute arrangements to discuss with Mr. Ludlow."

Mr. Bolton frowned. "Arrangements for what?"

She circled her hands around Mr. Bolton's arm and sidled closer. She bent her head to his and blinked up at him through her lashes. "We were just reconciling some costs. It's all finished now, and we both wanted to have another look at the paintings before we left for the evening." She steered him away. "Which is your favorite?"

I watched them go with a sinking heart. It sank further when Mr. Ludlow stepped into my view. He looked as though he couldn't wait to throw me out again.

"Collect your things and leave this instant," he snapped.

I gathered all my confidence and willed my voice to sound steady. "I work for Mr. Bolton now. I take my orders from him."

To my utter relief, Mr. Bolton returned. He'd overheard me. Granted, I'd spoken loudly enough that he would have heard me from the next room. "What *is* going on here?"

The butler drew himself up to his full height then proceeded to look down his nose at both of us. The exhibition manager's lips pursed. "This girl was employed as a waitress. I had to dismiss her for rudeness."

"She has been nothing but polite to me and the men."

Mr. Ludlow's nostrils expanded like a bellows. "Nevertheless, she cannot be re-employed."

"Nevertheless, if anyone is being rude to me, it's you, Ludlow. If I wish to re-employ her, that is my prerogative." His vehement defense surprised me. I hardly knew him and I'd not expected it. He must not like Mr. Ludlow.

Mr. Ludlow's jaw firmed. "But—"

"Ludlow!" Lady Stanhope snapped. "There's no point him hiring anyone else now. She'll have to do."

It wasn't much of a defense, but it worked. With a click of his tongue, Mr. Ludlow strode off, heading for the exit. Lady Stanhope shook her head at his back. "Carry on, Mr. Bolton." She left too, her strides less purposeful and her back stiff.

"'Carry on,'" Mr. Bolton echoed. "She has a nerve ordering anyone but Ludlow the Lug about. She has no authority over me."

"Ludlow the Lug has a good ring to it."

He didn't seem to be listening to me, however, as he watched Lady Stanhope retreat.

"I wonder what they were doing here. I don't believe the story about reconciling expenses, do you, Miss Ashe? The private viewing ended days ago, and expenses for the event should have been tallied before it began." He thrust his stick under his arm and marched off without waiting for my response.

I checked in with my men to see what progress they'd made, only to find Mr. Allan had gone missing. When he didn't return after ten minutes, I went looking for him. He wasn't in any of the galleries. The stairs were roped off, but Mr. Allan wasn't the sort to abide by rules.

I was about to slip under the rope when I heard a sneeze in the distance. It hadn't come from upstairs. I followed the sound to another set of stairs that led down.

I descended into the basement. It wasn't the part where the kitchen was located; it was the wrong end of Burlington House. I peered into one of the rooms off the corridor. Aside from broken crates, brooms, and other maintenance equipment, some dust covers protected large objects. Underneath could be furniture or artwork.

I was about to leave when I noticed one of the covers had

slipped off, revealing a life-sized classical statue of a naked man, missing its head. I entered the room and picked up the cloth to throw it back over.

With the cloth obscuring my view, the only warning I had was the sound of two footsteps before someone slammed into me, knocking me off my feet.

I fell onto my rear end, hitting a stack of crates on my way down, causing them to topple over. The cover and a cloud of dust enveloped me.

Then the door slammed shut.

CHAPTER 7

$\mathcal{B}$y the time I untangled myself from the cover, the
man was long gone. The smell of cigarette smoke
lingered, however. I threw the cover over the statue, turning
away as dust billowed from the cloth. I managed to suppress
my cough but not my sneeze.

A moment's panic quickened my heart as I tried the door
handle and it wouldn't turn. It was simply stuck, however,
and a little bit of elbow grease was all that was required.

I was about to leave when I noticed another dust cover in
the corner of the room had slipped off the flat crates stacked
vertically against the far wall. It had fallen onto a pile of more
dust covers that were carelessly discarded along with dozens
of cigarette butts. The entire room needed a good clean.

I grabbed a corner of the cover to haul it back over when I
noticed one of the crates was labeled Village High Street. It
must contain the painting of the village scene, behind which
the thief had most likely hidden the stolen painting. Mr. Glass
would have lifted this cover a few hours ago to look for the
canvas.

I closed the door behind me and headed back up the

stairs. My team had almost finished for the evening. Mr. Allan had returned and avoided eye contact with me for the remainder of the shift. I would have confronted him over his visit to the storeroom but I decided I preferred the peace and quiet. Confrontations set my nerves on edge.

I checked my list and marked several items as completed before going in search of Mr. Bolton. His team was also packing up. Mr. Bolton dismissed them all for the night and escorted me back to his office.

"I want to thank you again for hiring me, sir," I said as he handed me an envelope containing my pay. "But I'm afraid I have to give my notice, effective immediately. I've found permanent employment elsewhere, and I can't cope with a job during the day and this one in the evenings."

He extended his hand to me. "Congratulations on the new position." He didn't seem terribly concerned at being left in the lurch, although that could simply be me misinterpreting his no-nonsense manner.

"I'm sorry if my sudden departure leaves you in a bind. I do hope your regular assistant will get well soon."

"I'm sure he will. Goodbye, Miss Ashe."

I shook his hand. "Goodbye, Mr. Bolton." I gathered my bag and coat and left.

Outside, I cursed my ill luck. It was raining, and I hadn't brought an umbrella.

I was about to brave the wet weather and hurry down the steps to the courtyard when I heard a noise like shuffling feet to my left. I squinted into the shadows of Burlington House's wide portico, but it was too dark to see anything.

I continued on my way, not daring to investigate who—or what—made the noise. The courtyard was empty. The packers had left, and Mr. Bolton was still inside. I walked as quickly as I could to Piccadilly, where the streetlights provided some security. I found a cab and headed home. It wasn't until the cab door closed and we were on our way that I finally felt as though I was no longer being watched.

* * *

THE MORE I thought about it, the more the exchange with Lady Stanhope and Mr. Ludlow bothered me. Their explanation for their presence at Burlington House didn't ring true. Like Mr. Bolton, I was suspicious of their story about reconciling expenses. My suspicions only grew as I recalled their conversation in the adjoining gallery. While I'd not overheard any actual words, there was no doubting the heated tone, nor the fact that most of the anger came from Mr. Ludlow, and it was directed at Lady Stanhope. A butler shouldn't speak that way to his employer.

I telephoned Mr. Glass in the morning and told him my suspicions. He thanked me and asked if I could meet him to discuss it further.

"I can't. I'm starting work at the Glass Library today."

"Nash will give you a lunch break."

I was about to protest that I might work through lunch to make a good impression on my first day, but he hung up after saying a hasty goodbye.

I walked to Crooked Lane, drawing in a deep breath as I passed through the entrance. The air smelled fresh after the overnight rain, thanks to the lack of motorized traffic. The buildings and narrow entrance kept the fumes and noise out.

Professor Nash looked up upon my arrival and smiled. "Welcome to your first day, Miss Ashe. Come in, come in." He stood and buttoned up his jacket. "You may hang your coat there and leave your bag..." He looked around the floor and, unable to find a suitable nook, opened the large bottom drawer of the desk. He pushed aside its contents to make space. "In here will do. There is a key if you'd like to lock it for safekeeping. It's here somewhere..." He eyed the surface of the desk then rummaged through the top drawer.

"Don't worry," I said. "There's nothing valuable in it." I deposited my bag in the bottom drawer and hung up my coat on the stand near the stairs.

"We'll begin with a tour. There's not much to see in the front office, and you're already familiar with the layout of the ground floor. That's where I keep the most popular books, the general primers on magic, histories, that sort of thing. The least valuable, shall we say, although some are still quite rare and all have a scholarly value, if not a high monetary one. Onward and upward!"

He led the way up the winding staircase to the first floor. At the top of the stairs, I stopped and gasped. The room was even more spectacular than the ground floor. The ceiling was higher and even more ornate with the same leaf motif as downstairs repeated but painted in vibrant springtime colors with golden accents. A narrow mezzanine clung to the walls above our heads. Accessed by a spiral staircase, it was only wide enough for one person to browse the bookshelves, or two to squeeze awkwardly past one another. An arched window spanning the full height of the room was cut in half by the mezzanine. The window overlooked Crooked Lane, allowing plenty of light to pour through. The good lighting made it the perfect spot for reading, both at floor level and on the mezzanine, which jutted out just enough at the window to fit an armchair. The reading nook on the floor level was larger than the one downstairs. Aside from another chocolate brown leather sofa, there were two matching armchairs and side tables. A desk faced the window, its surface bare except for a globe at one edge and some writing implements in a brass stand.

Professor Nash drew my attention to the bookshelves, some of which had glass doors. "On this floor, we keep the more valuable books and papers." I failed to see how a few panes of glass would stop a determined thief, even when they were locked. "Some of these items are very old, others are newer but rare. And as you can see, we have some magical objects up here, too."

"Oh? Which ones have magic in them?"

"The glass doors. The magic in them should stop them breaking easily. Same with the mirror." He nodded at the large mirror hanging above the fireplace. "That bronze statue, the globe over there on the desk, the plaster ceiling, and most of the furniture."

"Remarkable," I said on a breath. "Does the clock above the fireplace downstairs contain magic?"

"It does. India—Lady Rycroft—put her magic into it. She made it especially for the library."

I felt foolish for asking my next question, considering I'd just accepted a position in a library dedicated to magic, but I had to. Besides, Professor Nash would find out sooner or later that I knew very little about the topic. "Forgive me, but I'm not quite sure what Lady Rycroft's magic does. I assume it makes timepieces run perfectly, but is that all?"

His face lit up. My naïve question had the opposite effect than I'd expected. Instead of thinking me a fool, he was enthusiastic about sharing his knowledge. "It's not all, no. She can also extend the magic of another magician." At my blank look, he went on. "Most magicians only know one spell; a spell based on what is desired most from that object. So, for glass, you would want it not to break. For wood, you don't want it to burn. For iron, you want strength. For a map, you want to find a location, and for a precious metal or gem, you want more."

"More?"

"Yes. More of the same. That's why those are very rare. Gold magic has died out, for instance."

"And silver?"

He frowned. "I believe that has died out too."

"What about art, like paintings? What does their spell do?"

"That's a good question. I'm not sure." He pushed his spectacles up his nose. "The problem with the spells is that their magic doesn't last forever. It fades. The length of time the magic lasts is dependent on the strength of the magician. It can last mere hours if made by a weak magician, or as long as decades. I've come across some magical objects where the magic is still in it centuries later. Many classical buildings from antiquity have survived for this very reason—they used stonemason magicians." He put up a finger to emphasize his next point, although it required little emphasis. His bright-eyed expression was compelling enough. "India knows a spell that can *extend* magic. Not just her magic, mind, but magic put into an object by other magicians."

I could see how that would be related to her watchmaking magic. Both spells were related to time. "Is that why she's considered so important to the modern history of magic?"

"Not really, no. She rarely uses that spell. She's remarkable for a number of reasons, all of which stem back to her lineage. In her family tree, several magical lineages converge and through the wonder of genetics, she has inherited great power. For one thing, she doesn't need to *speak* a spell. She can just *think* it. But most rare of all, she can create new spells."

"That does sound useful."

He gave me a grim smile, and I suspected there was a story behind her spell creation. "She doesn't use her magic much, anymore. She decided some time ago that the possibilities are too dangerous if new spells fell into the wrong hands. Her greatest achievement is her advocacy for magicians, both in this country and around the world."

I knew they were persecuted as witches in the Middle Ages and then more recently the craft guilds wouldn't give magicians licenses to trade, but I hadn't been aware of Lady Rycroft's role in ending that persecution.

"India championed magicians," Professor Nash added. "The guilds finally agreed to allow them to live openly and to trade freely, as long their goods were sold as luxury items which incur a luxury goods tax. It was the only way to create harmony between the artless and magicians. It was quite nasty there, for some time. Quite nasty indeed."

"Mr. Glass says you're not a magician."

"That's correct. I'm descended from iron magicians, but I didn't inherit it."

I studied the objects he'd pointed out as being magician-made. The glass and mirror were just plain panes, but the turned wooden legs of the desk and table were intricate, as was the plaster ceiling. "I've learned something today. I thought a magician's power lay only in making objects they manufacture more beautiful."

"It's part of their power, but a spell isn't required to make a beautiful thing. A magician's products are naturally more appealing than those made by an artless craftsman. It's why a magician who doesn't know they are a magician is capable of making something of great beauty and wonder. It's an innate talent all magicians possess. Spells do something else, something more."

"A magician can have a talent for their craft without realizing it?"

"Oh yes. It's not until the carpenter magician whittles his first stick that he finds he has an affinity for woodwork. You asked about an artist's spell before, and I answered that I wasn't sure what their spell would do. The mere fact a piece of art has been painted by a magician already makes it more appealing than one painted by a regular artist, so I can't think how adding a spell would enhance its beauty. Make the colors more vibrant, perhaps? Make it more lifelike?" He shrugged.

I touched the silver ring on my finger. It was plain, with no engraving. I didn't want to put a sharp tool to it to try my hand at silversmithing in case I destroyed the ring. I felt no particular affinity for it, either. But perhaps my brother had. Perhaps that was why he suspected he was a silver magician.

"There's one final part to my tour." Professor Nash indicated I should follow him with a crook of his finger. We headed down the aisle between two shelving stacks to the end. The wall was occupied by more shelves neatly packed with books.

Professor Nash pointed to one covered in red leather on the middle shelf. It didn't look old, but the top of the spine was a little worn. What an odd place for wear and tear to appear first. I tilted my head to read the black lettering on the spine but didn't get the opportunity. Professor Nash pulled the book off the shelf, but only halfway. Something behind the book clicked. With a secret little smile, he pushed on the bookshelves.

A section gave way and swung open.

I drew in a sharp breath. "Now you're just teasing me. A hidden passage inside a library? Have you been reading my childhood diary and discovered all my favorite things?"

He chuckled. "I can tell that you and I will get along famously." He reached in and switched on a light.

Beyond was an empty room the size of a cupboard with another door at the back. "This is the vestibule. That door there leads to my rooms."

"You mean you live in here?"

He nodded. "Go in. Take a look."

"Are you sure?"

He smiled. "Quite sure."

I passed through the vestibule and pushed open the other door, revealing a small flat beyond. In some ways, it reminded me of Daisy's flat, with a mezzanine level for the bedroom, although Professor Nash accessed it via a spiral staircase rather than a ladder. It wasn't as light as hers, but it wasn't dark either. High windows let in enough light for us to see. It was smaller than her flat, but it looked comfortable, if somewhat masculine, furnished much the same as the reading nooks in the library.

"You may use the kitchen or bathroom facilities up here whenever you need to," Professor Nash said.

"But this is your home."

"Never mind that. I'm a neat person." He pointed to a trap door in the ceiling of the mezzanine bedroom. "There's an attic full of books and other documents that require cataloguing in there. Once you've settled in, you can get started on them."

We returned downstairs and he went through some policies and procedures. The library was open to anyone. It didn't operate on a membership basis like most libraries. None of the books could be checked out, however. Anyone was welcome to stay and read in one of the nooks, but everything belonging to the library had to stay in the library.

"As much as we want to keep the collection free for anyone, it does present a problem when it comes to borrowing," he told me. "We can't rely on borrowers to be honest about their address, and not everyone carries identification with them. We found that out the hard way, many years ago, when some people simply never returned the books. I spent a lot of time finding them, so I don't want them to go missing. We changed our policy after that."

"I look forward to hearing about your adventures," I said.

"I'm afraid I'm not the greatest storyteller. My traveling companion was better."

"Oscar, was it?"

"He could tell a fine tale. He was a journalist, like you. He gave it up to travel with me almost thirty years ago. Speaking of Oscar." He scanned the bookshelves behind the desk and plucked out a book with a bright orange cover. "This is a copy of his first book." He handed it to me. "It'll give you a good introduction to magic."

The title read THE BOOK OF MAGIC: The facts, myths, histories and rites of sorcery in England and around the world as written by a modern magician. The author's name was Oscar Barratt.

"What type of magician was he?"

"Ink. A rather pointless magic, as he put it, but he could make it float prettily in the air."

"Thank you. I'll start tonight."

We continued to work throughout the morning as Professor Nash showed me what jobs he would require me to do. There weren't many. The library was set up to run efficiently, and without members or borrowers, an entire component of librarianship was eliminated.

I was in the middle of re-shelving some books on the first floor when I turned around and got the fright of my life. Mr. Glass stood at the end of the aisle, one broad shoulder leaning against the bookshelf, his arms and ankles crossed. The pose was relaxed but his gaze was sharp and filled with amusement. The man had a habit of finding my embarrassing moments funny.

"Sorry," he said. "I thought you would hear my footsteps."

"I was lost in thought." I shelved the final book and walked towards him.

He stepped aside but didn't move away altogether. "Ready for lunch?"

I had to turn side-on and edge past him. Even so, I still

brushed up against him. He didn't seem fazed, but my face heated. That only made him smile again.

I quickly put some distance between us and turned away, tucking a strand of hair behind my ear. "I'll check with Professor Nash first."

Professor Nash was quite all right with me taking lunch. I suggested an hour, but he said to take as long as I needed. I got the impression Mr. Glass had already checked with him before coming upstairs to find me. I wasn't sure what to make of that. I supposed it depended on whether he'd used his influence to coerce the professor or not. From their friendly exchange, it was difficult to tell.

"Busy morning?" Mr. Glass asked as we walked side by side along Crooked Lane.

"Not really. There were no patrons."

"I hope you won't find it too dull."

"If there's nothing to do, I can always read. Not that I'll do that, of course. I'm sure there'll be plenty of work to keep me occupied." I bit my lip. I needed to remember he was the son of the library's patron. Admitting to him that I would read while I should be working was a poor career move.

"Don't worry. I won't tell Nash. I'm quite sure that's how he spends most of his day, anyway."

"Why did he hire me if there's not enough work for two?"

He simply shrugged. "What do you make of the library?"

"It's wonderful," I said on a breath. "So many books, and the reading nooks look so cozy. Professor Nash seems nice. He's very enthusiastic about magic."

"More enthusiastic than most magicians."

We walked westward, and I had a horrible feeling he was going to take me somewhere flash like the Ritz. Not even my best outfit was suitable for lunch somewhere so exclusive. We changed direction, however, and found ourselves in the streets behind Leicester Square. He stopped at a restaurant named Le Café De Paris on the corner with chairs and tables arranged out the front.

He pushed open the door, and I breathed a sigh of relief. I would fit in here. The patrons were dressed casually, and the tables were covered with plain white tablecloths. Large mirrors made the interior look bigger than it was, and the modern paintings gave it an artistic flair. Several diners sat alone, hunched over books or sketching on pads, coffee cups and ashtrays at hand. Others sat in small groups engaged in intense conversation. A friendly waiter led us to a spare table by the window.

Mr. Glass ordered a bottle of red wine and asked for the menus. Thankfully the dishes were ones I recognized and not in French. We both ordered roast beef.

"It's not quite the same as a genuine French café, but I give the owners points for trying," Mr. Glass said.

"It's probably not a wise business decision to offer frogs legs and snails to English diners."

"Neither dish tastes as awful as they sound, by the way."

"You've tried them?"

"During the war. I was in Paris for a few weeks in '18."

"I thought you spent all of the war on the front lines."

His eyes narrowed ever so slightly. "You've done your research." He glanced at the man seated at the next table as he ground a cigarette butt into the ashtray. Mr. Glass's thumb began to tap on the table surface. "As the war came to an end, I was needed in Paris."

"You were an officer, weren't you?"

"Captain." The tapping increased its rhythm. "Do you mind if we talk about something else?"

"Of course. Sorry." I could kick myself. What former soldier wanted to discuss the war with a woman he hardly knew? I searched for another topic. "The art in here is…interesting."

He studied the painting on the wall opposite. "Is that one body with two heads or two people?"

"Those are people? I thought it was just a collection of geometric shapes."

He flashed a grin. It was utterly disarming. "It's fortunate neither of us wants a career as an art critic."

"My brief stint at the Royal Academy proved that point to me," I said. "Although none of the paintings in the exhibition looked anything like these."

"The Academy isn't known for being at the forefront of the artistic movement. Speaking of the exhibition, tell me more about the meeting between Lady Stanhope and Ludlow."

I repeated what I'd told him over the phone that morning. "It may mean nothing," I finished. "But I thought it worth mentioning."

"It's definitely suspicious." He raised his glass to me. "Thank you for bringing it to my attention, Sylvia. May I call you Sylvia?"

"Yes."

"Call me Gabe."

"Are you sure?" I blurted out.

"Quite sure."

My face heated again, but I had nothing to hide behind. He didn't smile or seem to find amusement in my embarrassment this time, but I still felt like a fool. Fortunately, the waiter brought our food, drawing Gabe's attention away from me.

"Which gallery were they in when you overheard their heated conversation?" Gabe asked as he cut into his beef.

"The main one."

"Were they near a particular piece of art?"

I finished chewing as I thought back to when I'd stumbled upon them. "Do you recall the seascape with the steamship?"

He'd been about to eat a morsel of beef but lowered his fork. "I do."

"They were near that. We moved it the night before, to a more prominent position, since it was so popular. Is that a clue?"

He didn't answer immediately but continued to eat. I suspected he wouldn't answer me, citing the excuse that he wasn't allowed to talk about the case with a civilian.

But he proved me wrong. "It may be important, but I'm not yet sure. There's still so much we don't know about this case."

Since he was in a talkative mood, I might as well try my luck and ask more questions. "What *do* you know?"

This time he didn't hesitate. "That it's likely someone at the gallery is involved in the theft." He picked up his wine glass and sipped, watching me over the rim. "I should probably start at the beginning."

I stayed silent, not wanting to shatter his trust in me.

"Scotland Yard employ me only on cases that involve magic or magicians. I was called in for this case when the owner of the stolen painting claimed it was done by a magician artist. At least, that's what the owner claimed."

"You don't think it's magical?"

"I have no opinion one way or another. The painter is long dead, so he can't be questioned. He lived a century ago, in a less enlightened time, when magicians were persecuted. Paint magicians never revealed their talent out of fear they'd be ostracized by the Royal Academy. That's the closest thing to a guild artists have. The stolen work was done by a little-known artist named Jean-Baptiste Delaroche. He wasn't very prolific. This painting is one of only three in England."

"If no one knows whether the painter was a magician, why did the owner buy it?"

"She bought it for a low price from a dealer she claims

had no idea about fine art. She suspected it was magician-made, so when she took it home, she invited a sculptor magician to verify it for her. She never got a second opinion."

"Why a sculptor magician, not a painter?"

"She said he was an acquaintance and she trusted him. He sensed the magic in the Delaroche and gave his professional assurance to her."

"Is he under suspicion for the theft?"

"He is on my suspect list, but I'm yet to connect him to the black market for art, which is where the painting most likely is destined."

"When was it stolen?"

"Two days before the exhibition opened for private viewings. It was on loan from the owner for the duration of the exhibition and had just arrived at Burlington House. Some time that afternoon or night, it disappeared. Only the frame remained."

"It must have been placed behind the village painting until such time it could be squirreled out of Burlington House."

"Precisely. You'd make a good detective, Sylvia."

"Unfortunately, my nose will have to remain buried in books rather than other people's business since the police don't employ women."

"Their loss."

We ate in silence for a few minutes as I tried to make sense of the case. "The thief has to be someone with access to Burlington House after hours."

"Not necessarily. People came and went all afternoon. Deliverymen, the exhibition manager and his assistant, even some artists who delivered their work personally."

"The packing team?"

"And them. In theory, any of the staff employed that day, including Ludlow."

"And Lady Stanhope? I assume she was there going over last-minute details with Ludlow."

He nodded. "As a friend of the painting's owner, she also knew it was magical."

"You think the seascape is also magical, don't you?"

He finished his meal then sat back. "It seems likely. According to the experts, it's technically perfect. To me, it's simply a beautiful piece. Other Philistines seem to agree."

I smiled. "Including this Philistine. Can you have an independent magician verify it?"

"I didn't want to draw attention to it, but now I'm worried it's too late. The exhibition manager has moved it to a new, more prominent location, and two of my suspects were seen having a heated discussion near it." He dipped his head in a bow. "Without you, I wouldn't have known."

"Perhaps a guard can be employed to watch it."

He refilled our wine glasses and picked his up. "You were there during the first private viewing. Did you notice anyone paying it particular attention?"

"I wasn't employed to notice anything except the hors d'oeuvres on my tray, as Mr. Ludlow delighted in reminding me before he fired me."

One side of his mouth kicked up in a small smile. "I doubt that stopped an inquisitive person such as yourself."

"I did see a few painters nearby who seemed to be discussing it. Then Lady Stanhope joined them. She was friendly towards them and they seemed to like her."

"They can't afford not to like her, at least to her face. Their livelihoods depend on her patronage. She's a great art lover."

And artist lover, I suspected, going by the way she flirted with Horatio that day. "What do you make of her?"

"I'd never met her before that day."

"I thought she moved in the same circles as your parents."

He chuckled. "Do you think everyone with a title are friends?"

"No, of course not."

He looked at me as though he knew I was lying.

I cleared my throat. "I think I know where we can find out more about her." At his arched brows, I added, "From the way she was touching Horatio, I think they're more than mere acquaintances."

"Let's ask him, shall we?"

"Now?"

"The sooner the better, before the thief tries to steal the seascape." He paid what we owed and headed for the door.

I grabbed my bag and hurried after him. "But I have to return to work."

"I'll have a word with Nash. I'm sure he won't mind." He smiled as he opened the door for me.

I warred with myself on the walk back to Crooked Lane. It was my first day at the library. Should I take time off, even for something as important as the case? I decided to ask Professor Nash if it was all right and change my plan if he seemed reluctant.

"Wait out here," I said to Gabe when we arrived at the library. "I don't want you influencing his decision."

Professor Nash didn't flicker an eyelash when I told him Gabe wanted me to help with his investigation. Indeed, he seemed unsurprised by the request.

"The work will still be here when you return," he said cheerfully.

"I'll make up any time lost by staying back late the rest of the week."

"That won't be necessary. Gabe is paying your wage so if he finds another purpose for you, then so be it. The work here will get done eventually."

I blinked slowly at him. "I assumed I was being paid by

the library. I know Lord and Lady Rycroft are patrons, but aren't there others? And isn't there a board or committee that oversees things like employment and wages?"

"No, you don't understand. *Gabe* is paying your wage. Not his parents or the other patrons. And the committee are hopeless. They wouldn't have made the decision to employ an assistant in one day. Good lord, no. It would have taken them weeks. Gabe informed me that your predicament was urgent and you needed to be employed immediately. He's paying your wage until such time as the committee gets around to meeting and discussing the role of assistant."

I must have had a stupid look on my face because Professor Nash leaned forward and squinted at me.

"Is everything all right, Miss Ashe? Did you eat an eel pie from the street seller on the corner? They're notoriously awful. No, of course you didn't. Gabe would have taken you somewhere nice."

I stared back at him, still trying to digest what he'd told me and what it meant. Gabe was paying the wage of a woman he hardly knew out of his own pocket, for an assistant's position that hadn't existed before today and, to be quite honest, wasn't needed. Why?

And what did he expect in return?

CHAPTER 8

"*Y*ou should have told me," I said to Gabe.

He sheepishly dug his hands into his trouser pockets. "Ah. I see Nash spilled the beans. I hoped you wouldn't find out for a while yet. At least until you'd settled in."

"Why didn't you tell me you were personally paying my wage?"

"Because I didn't want you to find out."

I shot him a withering glare. I probably should be more careful than ever about what I said around him. Being from a wealthy and titled family was one thing, but he also had the power to have me dismissed or to dock my wages. I ought to find it unnerving, but I was too angry to worry. My temper, which was slow to ignite, had just had a load of fuel dumped on it.

"I didn't want you to find out because I was worried one of two things would happen. You'd either start treating me like an employer or you'd be angry. At least one mystery is solved today."

"I'm glad you find my predicament amusing. Add it to the tally of all the other things." I stormed off along the lane.

He easily caught up to me with his long strides and fell into step beside me. "I do not find you amusing. In fact, right now I find you to be the exact opposite." He blocked the exit, forcing me to stop too. "I didn't say anything because it's only a temporary arrangement. As soon as the committee get around to ratifying your employment, your wages will be paid by the library's fund."

"Which your parents pay into."

"Among other people." He stepped aside. "I felt guilty for costing you the other job, Sylvia. When I realized you needed the money, I thought you'd be perfect for the Glass Library. But I also know the committee are hopeless, so I took the matter into my own hands. I should have been honest with you. I'm sorry."

I pressed my lips together tightly in the hope it would keep my emotions in check. The flush in my cheeks was from anger this time, not embarrassment. But that anger was rapidly fading with every blink of his velvety green eyes.

"You pitied me," I said.

"No." I arched my brows and he sighed. "I did it out of guilt, not pity."

"What do you want from me, Gabe?"

"Right now, I want you to speak to Horatio." Somehow, he managed to look like an innocent schoolboy. I blamed those eyes and the way the long dark lashes fanned them with every blink. Eyelashes like that were wasted on a man.

I marched out of the lane and turned left.

"My motor is this way." He pointed right.

The top was up on the Vauxhall, which was just as well since clouds were gathering. He cranked the car while I climbed into the passenger side. Once the engine began to rumble, he sat beside me. We drove without speaking until we reached Horatio's building.

As soon as he turned the car off, he turned to me. "Can we go back to being friends, Sylvia?"

"We weren't friends to begin with."

"Then let's start now."

"You're my employer, Gabe." I got out and closed the car door with an emphatic slam to get my point across. "In fact, I think I should call you Mr. Glass again."

"Please don't." He strode alongside me toward the building. "Sylvia, there's no need for this. I assure you I have no ulterior motives. It's a business arrangement, nothing more."

"I know that." I heard my snippy tone and loathed it. I tried hard to school my features, but it wasn't easy. Not when emotions whirled within me, tangling together until I could no longer identify each individually.

I tried to shove aside the little voice in my head that told me I was overreacting. But it wouldn't be silenced. It spoke the truth. I *was* overreacting to the situation. Gabe admitted he did it because he felt guilty, and that the arrangement would change once the committee were on board. He'd given me an assurance ours was purely a working relationship.

So why was I bothered by it? Why didn't I want to be friends with this man?

My reaction made no sense to me, so I couldn't blame him for his deep sigh as he headed into the building. I couldn't expect it to make sense to him either.

* * *

I'D EXPECTED Horatio's flat to be large, as befitting an artist who exhibited at the Royal Academy's summer exhibition. It was only about the same size as Daisy's, without the mezzanine level. A wooden screen separated the bedroom from the rest of the flat, which acted as a studio. At first glance, the painted screen looked bright and summery with birds flying across a blue sky. But on closer inspection, the landscape they flew over was littered with blackened stumps mired in mud.

Horatio's hands were clean; we hadn't interrupted him painting. He invited us to sit and looked around for uncluttered chairs. "Apologies for the mess, but I've hardly had time to blow my nose, let alone tidy up."

"May we see your latest work?" I asked.

"Certainly not. It's not finished. You may look at those." He flapped a hand at the paintings leaning against the wall. They were avant-garde, like the ones we saw in the café, not at all like the realistic painting he'd given me or the one he exhibited at the exhibition. I wondered which sold better.

Gabe told him we needed to know about Lady Stanhope for an investigation. "Sylvia says she saw you two conversing at the exhibition, and we hoped you could tell us what she's like."

Horatio's eyes lit up. "Is she a suspect in a crime?"

"I can't answer that."

He gasped. "She is, isn't she? Why else would you be here? What has she done?"

"As I said, I can't answer that."

"Has she finally tried to poison that dull old goat she married?"

"Horatio," I chided. "You know Gabe can't tell you. Anyway, you ought to be careful or you'll become a suspect too. I saw the look she gave you at the exhibition. If she poisons her husband, it would be because of you."

His face paled. "Me? But I didn't encourage her! Oh, you're joking. It's not very amusing, Sylvia."

"It is to me."

Horatio crossed his arms and gave me an arched look. "We're not lovers."

I raised my brows.

He sighed. "Very well, we were, but just the once. It was a few weeks ago, and it won't happen again."

"Does she know that?" From the way Lady Stanhope touched him at the exhibition, I suspected she wanted their arrangement to resume.

"She does now."

"What's she like?" Gabe asked.

"She doesn't like being refused. She told me she'd have me blacklisted by the Academy if I didn't go back to her. She doesn't realize that I don't care. The artwork shown by the Academy is as boring as the people who run it. They only want to show the same thing they've shown for decades. They haven't noticed that the world has changed. People want to be inspired and moved by art. They're tired of cows and cottages."

"Why did you want to exhibit there if you're not interested in the Academy's opinion?" I asked.

"Exhibiting at the summer exhibition fulfilled a lifelong dream. But it's a dream I had years ago. That sort of art doesn't interest me like it used to. After the war, I moved on to more modern, experimental styles. I don't want to dwell in the past. Nobody our age does," he added heavily.

Gabe nodded at the wooden partition with the birds flying over the war-ravaged landscape. "The Somme?"

"Passchendaele."

Gabe gave a grim nod. "I was there."

Horatio shook his head as if shaking off the memories. "I'm not the only artist whose work Lady Stanhope put forward to the selection committee, if you understand my meaning."

Oh. Right. Horatio had agreed to the affair to get his work exhibited. Once he'd secured his place in the exhibition, he'd ended it. Other artists had, too.

C.J. ARCHER

"She wasn't very discriminate," he went on. "Freddie Duckworth would never have got a place if it weren't for Lady Stanhope. Brilliant sculptor but, like me, his usual style isn't the sort the Academy likes. He made a piece specifically for the exhibition on the off chance it would be accepted. Surprise, surprise, it was—*after* his liaison with Lady Stanhope."

At the mention of the sculptor, Gabe shifted his weight. It may have meant nothing, but I wondered if it was the sculptor magician who'd verified the stolen artwork was done by a magician.

"I'm not sure what she got out of their liaison, to be honest," Horatio went on. "Freddie's more of a gargoyle than an Adonis."

"Perhaps she enjoyed his company," I said.

"Your naivety does you credit, but if you saw him, you'd agree." He clicked his fingers. "You did see him, as it happens. He was standing with us that day at the private viewing when Lady Stanhope came up to me."

"When you were studying the seascape?"

"Which seascape?"

"The one everyone loved, with the steamship powering through the water."

"I remember that one. A fine piece."

"Lady Stanhope was seen having an argument with Ludlow the butler," Gabe said. "He seemed to be angry with her. Would you say she's the sort to allow a servant to speak sternly to her?"

Horatio snorted. "Is any lady that sort?" When neither of us spoke, he added, "I imagine Ludlow is looking for other work now. She would see that he was dismissed." He leaned forward, conspiratorially. "So, tell me, what is Lady Stanhope supposed to have done?"

I glanced at Gabe, but he simply stood and buttoned his

jacket. "Thank you for your time."

Horatio shot to his feet. "Come now, you can tell me. I've been an immense help answering all your questions. I deserve to know what you think she has done."

"You weren't that much help," I said.

Horatio wagged a finger at me. "I expected more from you, Sylvia. We're friends. You know I'd keep anything you told me to myself."

"You tell Daisy everything."

"She doesn't count." When he could see neither of us would give in, he clicked his tongue and followed us to the door. "I thought your new job was in another library, Sylvia, not working with the police."

"I'm working at the Glass Library, but Gabe wanted me to accompany him here since you and I are friends."

He smiled slyly. "I understand."

I managed to keep my features schooled but was betrayed by my flushed face. As much as I wanted to retort that he was quite wrong, I didn't want to draw attention to myself.

"No," Gabe said levelly, "I don't think you do."

* * *

I EXPECTED Gabe to take me back to Crooked Lane, but instead he drove down a narrow mews in Bloomsbury and stopped at the front of a building that looked like a coach house or motoring garage. Going by the potted flowers beside the door, I suspected it was now a private residence. After many of the larger townhouses in the area were converted into flats, the accompanying mews behind them were also converted.

I joined Gabe on the pavement. "Does Freddie Duckworth live here?"

"Yes. I met him when I wanted confirmation that the

stolen Delaroche was indeed the one he verified as being magical."

"Did you ask him where he was on the day it was stolen?"

"Thinking like a detective again, I see. I did ask. And no, he didn't have an alibi. He was at Burlington House delivering his sculpture. He had access to the painting, but so did a lot of people."

"If he's guilty, how does Lady Stanhope fit in?"

"I don't know."

"Are you going to ask him about her?"

He shook his head. "Not yet. Not until I know if it's relevant. I don't want him deducing that he's one of my suspects." He knocked on the blue door. "Today I just want to ask him about the seascape."

While calling someone ugly was not something I would ever do, Horatio was right when he said Freddie Duckworth was no Adonis. He did himself no favors by combing his thin hair over his bald patch in an attempt to hide it and wearing what could best be described as a large potato sack with holes cut out for his head and arms. He used the smock to wipe gray dust off his hands, but he didn't seem to be aware it was also on his face.

"Come in, come in." He ushered us inside to the sitting room with jerky movements of his bone-thin hand. There was no sign of any half-finished sculptures, so I assumed his studio was upstairs. There were several finished ones, however. None were what I'd describe as classical, like those in the exhibition. They were all of faceless bodies in twisted, unnatural poses. "Tea?"

"We can't stay long," Gabe said. "We wanted to ask your professional opinion about one of the paintings in the Academy's exhibition."

Freddie's gaze slid to me. He didn't seem to recognize me from that day at the private viewing, but I remembered him as one of Horatio's friends. He wasn't as flamboyant as Horatio but seemed no less self-assured as he offered us seats with an expansive sweep of his hand. He was small in stature with busy fingers that tapped and drummed throughout the conversation. His face was thin too, his cheeks sunken beneath the shadow of a beard.

Usually when I saw a starving artist, I assumed they were poor. But the furniture was new and well-made, the carpet plush, and the grate clean. It smelled like it had been recently blackened. Like most bachelors, I doubted he kept his own house. He probably had a charwoman come in. The sitting room was also filled with statues, mostly of nude women. I kept my gaze on Freddie.

"You can trust Miss Ashe," Gabe assured him. "She's working with me on the case."

I arched a brow, but he didn't notice.

"The painting in question is a seascape with a steamship plowing through the water. Do you remember it?"

"Of course. And if you want to know if it was done by a magician, then I can confirm that it was."

"How do you know?" I asked.

"I'm a magician. I can sense magic in objects."

"What does 'sensing' magic feel like?" Ever since Gabe had mentioned it, I'd wanted to know.

"The magic leaves behind some residual warmth which a magician can feel. But it's not like the usual heat from a fire or hot water. It's different. I can't explain it. It's something only another magician can understand." He gave me a look which was more sympathetic than apologetic. He felt sorry for us artless, as if we were somehow lesser.

Gabe thanked him and led the way to the door. "One more thing. Are you absolutely sure the stolen painting was done by a painter magician?"

Freddie started to laugh but cut it short. His jaw worked

and his lips moved, but it took three spluttered attempts before he ground out, "Am I certain? Am I certain! Mr. Glass, you come from a family of magicians. Of all the artless, you should be aware that a magician simply *knows*."

Gabe put up his hands. "Forgive me. I wasn't questioning your expertise."

"You were." Freddie strode past us and jerked open the front door. "If this is the thanks I receive for assisting the police, then kindly leave." He might not be as flamboyant as Horatio, but he was far more dramatic.

The slammed door almost hit Gabe in the back as he exited behind me. "I suppose I should expect nothing less after questioning a man's professional integrity."

"Do you genuinely believe he was lying about Delaroche being a magician painter?"

He opened the motor's passenger door for me. "We only have his say-so that the painting contains magic."

"Can't another magician check the other paintings done by Delaroche?"

"There are very few in existence. Scotland Yard is chasing up professional opinions on all of them. Even if magicians can't sense magic in them, that doesn't mean the stolen one wasn't magical. Perhaps Delaroche put a spell on it but not the others. Some persecuted magicians used their spells only rarely, some never did and have gone to their graves leaving no magical items behind. The fear of being discovered was very real. In the nineteenth century, when Delaroche was alive, they might no longer be burned at the stake for witch-craft, but they could lose their livelihoods, their friends, and their reputations."

Gabe's mother must have faced that kind of ostracism. To have overcome that and pushed for reform was bravery indeed.

"Professor Nash explained to me that a magician who

126

doesn't use a spell still produces better products than an artless craftsperson," I said.

"There's usually something more compelling about them, it's true."

"But when a spell is added, the product becomes superior in some way. For clocks, it's to run on time, and so forth. But he wasn't sure what a spell could do for a painting."

"Keep the colors vibrant for longer?" He shrugged in the same way as Professor Nash had when posing the same question.

I climbed into the motor and glanced at the sky. It was growing late. I asked Gabe for the time when he slid into the driver's seat.

He flipped open the lid on his silver pocket watch. Unlike most men nowadays, he didn't wear a wristwatch. "It's four-thirty. I'll return you to the library."

We drove to the entrance of Crooked Lane in a silence that was less tense than earlier. My temper had cooled and, while I didn't like his subterfuge, I decided I had no choice but to accept it. I wanted to keep the job at the library and that meant accepting that Gabe was personally paying my wage until a different arrangement could be made.

It also meant I had to maintain a professional distance from him. It was for the best.

I was about to tell him that when we pulled to the curb, and he switched off the engine. But before I could speak, he got in first.

"So, are we friends again?" He looked directly ahead as he asked it, almost as if he didn't care about the answer. Or was worried what my answer might be. When I didn't speak immediately, he finally turned to look at me. He frowned. "Sylvia?"

I ought to lecture him about professionalism and remind him again that we were not friends and never could be. But something stopped me. He'd gone very still, except for the drumming of his thumb on the steering wheel. And his green eyes drilled into me with an intensity that warmed my skin but also stretched my already taut nerves. I'd seen that same look in men who'd returned from the war before, but it was always fleeting and never directed at me.

It both chilled me and thrilled me. Made me want to reach out and stroke away the grim set of his lips. Every part of me became aware of him, of his stare, the tapping thumb and, most of all, his close proximity.

Someone pounded on the door with their fist, breaking the spell. My already rapidly beating heart felt as though it burst out of my chest.

"Gabe!" It was Willie, his brash American cousin. "Gabe, get out right now or I'll wrench this door open and pull you out myself!"

CHAPTER 9

$\mathcal{W}$illie might be a similar size to me, but I doubted anyone took her lightly. I wasn't about to. I certainly couldn't ignore her, standing outside the motor with hands on hips and a frown on her face.

Gabe swore under his breath. "Sorry about her."

"I don't think she likes me," I said.

"She's angry with me, not you."

"For ignoring the directive to stay home?"

"I left the house without her." He opened the door and got out. "Willie, what are you doing here?" Something to his right caught his attention. His shoulders stooped. "You too?"

Alex strode up, looking as annoyed as Willie although somewhat less murderous. "We've been looking everywhere for you!"

"I've been following up a lead with Sylvia."

Alex and Willie turned to me. Alex greeted me cordially if a little stiffly.

Willie crossed her arms over her chest. "Did you really *need* to take her with you?"

Gabe's jaw firmed. "Yes."

"You shouldn't leave the house without one of us," Alex snapped.

"Both of us," Willie added.

"If the kidnapping attempt is linked to the investigation, then continuing to investigate is the worst thing you can do. You should be taken off the case." As Alex said it, he lifted his gaze and nodded at a man approaching. "I'll speak to my father."

Alex's father was as much of a giant as his son. Both were solid, tall men, but the elder Mr. Bailey was more thickset compared to Alex. It wasn't his size that had me gulping as he drew closer, however. It was the black leather eyepatch over one eye and the scar that leaked from the patch's lower edge to his cheek. Storybook pirate villains were less menacing.

Then he ruined the effect by smiling at me. It was a smile as large as the man himself. "You must be Miss Ashe, the professor's new assistant." His American accent was as thick as Willie's, his voice as deep as his son's.

"How did you know?" Alex sounded indignant.

"I'm a detective."

I shook Cyclops's hand. "It's a pleasure to meet you, Detective Bailey."

"Just call me Cyclops. Everyone does."

"Be honest, how did you find out about her?" Alex asked again.

"Bristow told me about Miss Ashe's visit to the house yesterday and that Gabe offered her a job here at the library."

"The old gossip," Willie muttered with a shake of her head.

"You guessed Gabe would be here just from that?" Alex asked.

"You don't get to be a detective inspector without having

sharply honed instincts, Son." He smiled and clapped Alex on the shoulder.

Alex looked skeptical about his father's explanation but didn't press him again. "I was just telling Gabe that you should take him off the case. It's not safe."

"Do not take me off the case, Cyclops," Gabe said. "I'm making progress."

"Ain't you listening, Gabe?" Willie all but shouted. "The closer you get to finding the thief, the bigger the danger. Alex is right. You've got to stop. Let someone else take over now."

Gabe removed his driving cap and dragged his hand through his hair to ruffle it. "If the kidnapping is linked to the case then the next person is going to have the same problem. But I don't think it is. It doesn't make sense to kidnap me. It won't change anything. It won't stop Scotland Yard investigating."

Willie exploded with a string of expletives until Cyclops ordered her to pipe down. She fell into a stroppy silence.

I cleared my throat. "If you'll all excuse me, I have to get back to work."

"Thank you for your help, Sylvia," Gabe said. "I appreciate it."

I didn't think I'd been of much assistance. He could have called on Horatio without me. But I didn't think mentioning that in front of the others would help his argument with them.

He turned to Cyclops. "Are you returning to Scotland Yard? Sylvia and I think another painting could be the next target for the thief. Security should be tightened at Burlington House for the remainder of the exhibition."

Cyclops shook his head. "I'm heading home. You go. My sergeant will arrange it."

"I'm also going to arrange for the sculptor magician to

inspect the painting and confirm whether it is or isn't magician-made. I'd wager it is, but I want to be sure."

Alex opened the motor's passenger door. "I'm coming with you." He slipped inside while Gabe cranked the car. It grumbled to life.

Before he climbed into the driver's side, Cyclops stopped him with a hand to his shoulder. "There's a journalist watching your house. Bristow says he's been there all day."

Gabe nodded his thanks.

I headed through the covered entrance to Crooked Lane beyond, leaving behind the hubbub of the city. Or so I thought.

Willie and Cyclops followed me. The problem with a dead-end street is that there's no escape. I couldn't get rid of them. So I rounded on them.

"Is there something else?" I said in the friendliest voice I could muster.

Willie stabbed a finger at my face, stopping only inches from my nose. It wasn't easy, but I remained where I stood, willing my feet not to take a step back, no matter how much I wanted to. "Stay away from Gabe. He's almost back to the person he was before the war. I don't want anything—or anyone—to jeopardize his progress."

"Willie!" Cyclops barked. "Don't be rude. And if you think Gabe's ever going to be the same as he was before the war, think again. Besides, he was reckless and a bit of a prick in those days."

"He was more fun. I liked him better."

"That's because recklessness is your meat and potatoes." He turned to me. "She's as mad as a feral cat."

The insult seemed to slide off her. I suspected these two had flung worse at one another for years and no longer took offence.

"You have the wrong end of the stick." I was about to tell

them that Gabe and I were just friends, but in truth, we weren't even that. "He came to me," was all I said.

Willie opened her mouth to speak but Cyclops grabbed her by the shoulders and steered her in the direction of the lane's exit. "Go home, Willie."

She gave him a rude hand gesture and marched off, out of the lane.

Cyclops released a long breath. "Sorry about her. I'd like to say you get used to her, but you don't. Hard to believe she's been married twice."

"You've known her a long time?"

He smiled wistfully. "Decades. I was in my twenties when I met Willie, Matt and Duke."

"Duke?"

"Another friend. He moved back to America years ago, got married, and now has a horse ranch with his wife and two sons." He spoke softly, his voice thickening with emotion. He must miss Duke.

"If you'll excuse me, I should return to work," I said. "I've been absent for hours."

"Don't worry about Professor Nash. He's a good man. He won't fire you without good reason."

"He can't anyway. Gabe employed me. He's paying my wage."

Cyclops's eye widened then narrowed as he glanced over his shoulder in the direction of the lane exit.

"It was nice meeting you," I said and walked off toward the library.

"Just a moment, Miss Ashe." Cyclops fell into step beside me. "I came to ask you about the kidnapping."

I stopped and blinked up at him. He hadn't come here in search of Gabe. He hadn't used his detecting skills to find him. He'd come to see me, and Gabe just happened to be here.

He winked. He must have followed my train of thought. "Don't tell them. It keeps them on their toes if they think I know everything."

I couldn't help smiling. He was the most surprising man. "What do you want to know?"

"Gabe and Alex made it sound like a minor incident, but I got the impression they weren't telling me everything. You were there. Tell me what really happened."

"A man tried to force Gabe into the car. There was also a driver and another man in the back seat who aimed a gun at Gabe when Gabe got the attacker in a headlock."

Cyclops rubbed the back of his neck. "Dammit," he muttered.

"None of us saw the face of the man with the gun. As Alex ran up, the attacker got back into the car and it drove off."

"Was anything said? Any threat to give up the investigation?"

I shook my head. "Just the man with the gun ordering Gabe to let the thug go or he'd shoot. Did they not mention him?"

"They did not," he said darkly.

"They didn't want you to worry."

"That's probably it. Gabe's tired of folk fussing."

"Why do they fuss?"

He leveled his gaze with mine. "He's an only child and spent four years at war. His parents tried not to cosset him, but they have a lot of friends who've looked out for him over the years."

"Like you and Willie."

He put up his hands in surrender. "Don't put me in the same category as her. I have four of my own to worry about, three of them daughters. Willie doesn't have children. Gabe's like a son to her. She worries about him, especially now that India and Matt have gone overseas."

"They mustn't be too worried about him if they left."

"He's come a long way since leaving the army. They also knew he needed his own space and time."

It seemed odd to add time, but perhaps Lady Rycroft was somewhat obsessed with it, considering she was a watch-maker magician. "Cyclops, was Gabe really on the front lines for the entire four years?"

"He was." His gaze narrowed. "Why?"

I shrugged. "It just seems…incredible that he wasn't seri-ously injured."

His eye narrowed even further. "That's what the journalist who keeps pestering him says."

"I should go." I turned and hurried to the library.

It was clear Gabe wasn't the only one who disliked jour-nalists. First Willie and Alex, now Cyclops too. All voiced a negative opinion about my former profession. If I was going to see them again, I'd be worried about accidentally revealing it.

But my association with Gabe and his friends was finished. I had no reason to see them again. He might pay my wages, but he had no need to call on me anymore.

I pushed open the door and breathed in the scent of leather covers and paper. It was a relief to be away from those people and immerse myself in my work after a trying afternoon.

But a small voice inside me admitted that it had not been an awful afternoon. Not in the least.

* * *

DAISY SAT on the edge of the desk in the reading nook on the first floor of the library, one long leg crossed over the other. She placed her hands on the desk surface behind her and leaned back, closing her eyes. She looked like an artist's model, perfectly positioned where the sunlight could capture the colors of her hair, from blonde to strawberry and every shade in between.

"This library is much better than the Philosophical Society one," she said.

"You're only saying that because Professor Nash let you stay when he found you."

Daisy had hidden under the desk when the professor returned after his lunch break. He must have heard her voice because it was the first place he looked when he joined me. She and I had both held our breaths as she crawled out, but he'd only smiled, pushed up his glasses, and welcomed her to the Glass Library. He'd left us to talk, even saying that he didn't want to intrude.

"It reminds me of my grandfather's library," she went on.

"Really? How large was his house?"

She hopped off the desk and threw herself onto the sofa. She lounged into the corner and picked up the book on magic by Oscar Barratt that the professor had loaned me. I'd stayed up well into the night reading it and continued over my lunch break. She flipped through the pages then put the book down again. "Horatio told me you called on him yesterday with Gabriel Glass."

"We asked him about Lady Stanhope. He knows her rather well."

"There's no need to wiggle your eyebrows like that, Sylv. I know what you're implying without the facial theatrics."

I lowered the book on tribal witchcraft I'd been studying. "Are you jealous? Do you like Horatio in that way?"

"Lord, no. I'm not jealous of him and that old crow. I'm just a little disappointed you didn't include me in all the fun."

"It wasn't fun. Gabe and I were working."

She twisted her mouth to one side then the other. "Why did he need you when he has Alex?"

"I think he was avoiding Alex."

She snorted. "I can't blame him for that. I'd do everything in my power to avoid him too. The man is rude and arrogant." She suddenly sat up. "I've been thinking about your predicament."

"What predicament? I have a job now—"

"Not that. About your brother's notion that you're descended from silver magicians. You've given up too easily."

"I wouldn't say that. I was pre-occupied with finding work. Besides, we came to a dead end when the Silversmiths' Guild couldn't find any Ashes in their archives."

She stood and strode to the nearest bookshelf. "There must be some books about silver magicians in here."

"Not specifically."

"One of them must mention silver magic in *some* capacity. Even just a paragraph or two."

"It's possible, but it would take a lifetime to go through them all. I can't even read many of them."

"Ask the professor to translate."

"He told me he doesn't know any silver magicians." But that wasn't quite what he'd said. He claimed silver magic had died out. It wasn't the same thing as *never* having known a silver magician.

Daisy grasped my hand and dragged me away from the nook. "Come on. Let's confront him."

"It's my second day," I whined. "I don't want to be difficult."

"You're not being difficult. We'll call it research. Librarians love research."

We found Professor Nash at the front desk with a cup of tea in one hand and a book in the other. He put down the tea upon seeing us, but not the book. "Are you leaving, Miss Carmichael?"

Daisy rounded the desk and perched on the edge near him, forcing the professor to scoot his chair back to avoid being bumped by her knees. "Not yet. Sylvia has a question for you." She nodded at me to continue.

"I don't want to bother you if you're busy," I said.

The professor gave me an encouraging smile. "You're no bother. How can I help?"

"It's a research question about magic."

He put down the book and gave me his full attention. Daisy gave me a smug look.

"Do any of your books mention silversmith magicians?"

"Several mention silver magic. Do you want a general primer or something more in-depth?"

"I'm specifically after the names of silver magician families."

He frowned in thought. "None mention names that I can immediately recall, although there are some texts written in Medieval times that I haven't looked through in a while. They might reference specific magicians."

"Nothing recent?"

"No." His frown deepened. "Miss Ashe, this is the second time you've asked me about silver magic. I'm thrilled you have an interest in magic, but why that discipline in particular?"

"My brother thought he—we—are descended from silver magicians. I didn't have the opportunity to discuss it with him before he died, but now I'm curious to know more too. Not that I agree with him. I have no affinity for silver objects. Daisy and I asked at the Silversmiths' Guild, and Ashe is not a name that appears in their archives."

"And your mother's maiden name? Grandmothers' maiden names?"

I lifted a shoulder. "I'm afraid I don't know them."

His lips formed a tight O. Clearly he thought it curious

that my mother had never told me her own maiden name. I suspected he wanted to ask why but was too polite to ask.

I wished I'd never brought it up. "I'm sure James was mistaken. His notes were probably just the ramblings of an exhausted soldier. Let's forget I mentioned it."

"Everyone has a right to know where they came from, Sylvia," Daisy said gently.

My mother thought differently. She hadn't told us her maiden name, never mentioned my father or grandparents, and wouldn't even tell us where she was originally from or where my brother and I had been born. It had crossed my mind more than once that we were adopted, but James looked too much like her not to be her natural child. While I was a little like her with my small stature and gray eyes, those traits were common enough that I didn't feel absolutely certain she was my mother. I didn't have her coloring, for one thing. My hair was lighter, almost blonde in bright light, and freckles dusted my nose and cheeks in the summertime. My mother's hair was brown before it went gray, and freckles wouldn't dare appear on her skin or she'd have tried to lighten them with lemon juice as she'd once tried with mine.

Professor Nash pushed his glasses up his nose. "Miss Carmichael is right. Besides, I'm intrigued now so you must pursue it, Miss Ashe."

I sighed. "I suppose it can't hurt to see how far we get with our research."

"Excellent. However, books may not be of assistance in this case. The last time you asked me about silver magic, I told you there are no living silver magicians. As far as I am aware, that's true." He poked the air with his finger to punctuate his next point. "However, I do recall India telling me about a silver magician she'd met. It was around the time of the riots in the spring of ninety-one."

At least I knew Gabe wasn't lying to me about not

knowing a silver magician. I didn't know his precise age, but if he was born before 1891, he would have been very young.

"Her name was Mary something," the professor went on. "No, that's not quite right. Merry, Marion... Marianne!" He thumped the desk with his fist in triumph. "That's it. Marianne. I can't recall her surname, though. I am sorry."

"Ring any bells?" Daisy asked me.

I shook my head.

"She may have been a relative, an aunt or cousin, something like that." Daisy sounded as enthusiastic as Professor Nash. "What else can you tell us about her, Prof?"

"Nothing. I never met her. India did. India and Matt. Pity you can't ask them. Try Cyclops or Willie. They were all joined at the hip back then. If India and Matt met her, it's likely their friends did too."

The idea of speaking to either Cyclops or Willie again didn't appeal to me at all. Willie clearly didn't like me, and Cyclops had given me a somewhat threatening look when I'd brought up Gabe's incredible wartime feat. He seemed to place me in the same category as the journalist who was pestering Gabe.

"You should call on one of them this evening," Professor Nash said. "I'm sure they'd both be happy to answer your questions. Willie in particular likes to tell stories of their adventures."

I smiled and nodded and let him think I would do just that.

Daisy gave me a skeptical look, however. She knew me well, despite our relatively short acquaintance. Fortunately, she had errands to run before the end of the day and had to leave.

Nor was she waiting for me when I arrived back at the lodging house. Someone else was, however.

When I opened the door to my room, my heart leapt into

my throat and pounded out an erratic rhythm. I should have taken that as a warning.

But I did not.

I closed the door behind me and stumbled innocently into the wasp's nest.

CHAPTER 10

*L*ady Stanhope stood in the middle of my room, a look of disgust on her face. I wasn't sure if it was directed at me or her surroundings. My room may have been small, the furnishings simple, but it was clean and tidy. I could only guess that she was disgusted with me.

She would have been an attractive woman if she smiled more. It would seem she only reserved her smiles for young artists. I wished Horatio were here to diffuse the tension.

He might not be here, but I could use his name. "Did Horatio tell you where to find me? We're good friends, you see, and—"

"I don't care who your friends are."

So much for that idea. She didn't even flicker an eyelash. I expect nothing about this woman moved involuntarily, not even a flap of her skirts in the breeze. The stiff fabric would see to that. Her movements were controlled, contained, and designed to convey superiority and authority. On anyone else, they would feel practiced, but I suspected they were innate to her now. Perhaps she'd rehearsed them in front of a mirror many years ago until they became second nature.

The only time I'd seen that visage slip was when Ludlow had spoken angrily to her. She'd probably been in shock. It wouldn't be often that a servant raised his voice to her.

Lady Stanhope stepped toward me, her chin lifted at an arrogant angle. She eyed me coolly. "Who *are* you?"

"I'm Sylvia Ashe."

"I mean, who are you? Who do you work for?"

I leveled my gaze with hers, determined not to show how anxious this meeting made me. "I'm just an assistant librarian. I was briefly employed as a temporary assistant to the exhibition manager at the Royal Academy."

"Do you work for the police?"

"No."

"They spoke to me about a...situation that you witnessed at the gallery. You were the only witness, Miss Ashe. Tell me how the police knew about it if you didn't inform them?"

"I don't work for the police," I said again.

She walked slowly around the room, picking up things and studying them before putting them down. Again, I was reminded of someone who was aware of every move she made and chose them for maximum impact. Every slide of her finger across a book cover was done on purpose, every pinch of her lips and every glance.

She picked up a framed photograph of my mother, James, and me, taken when we were small. "No father?"

"What do you want, Lady Stanhope?"

"I want you to know that you can no longer work for the Academy. You've been blacklisted across all departments. You can't even be employed to take out the rubbish."

"That doesn't affect me. I've found other employment."

"Ah yes, the Glass Library."

"How do you know where I work?"

"I asked." She glanced at the door as she said it. Some of the other lodgers knew where I worked now. It was not a secret, and they had no reason not to tell her. "Don't cross my path again, Miss Ashe. Am I clear?"

"Abundantly."

She studied the photograph again. "They're dead now, aren't they? You're alone in the world." She must have learned that from the loose-lipped lodgers too. "What a sad thing it is for a young woman to be alone in London."

"I have friends."

She smiled, her lips stretching into a thin gash amid her pale face. "We both know it's not the same. Friends won't miss you like family would if something terrible were to happen to you."

I swallowed heavily.

She strode past me and left.

I rushed to close the door and locked it. I leaned back against it and released a pent-up breath. That woman had no power over me. She couldn't affect me. I no longer worked for the Royal Academy and was gainfully employed out of her sphere of influence.

So why did I feel the prickle of unease creeping across my skin?

* * *

I WAS BEING FOLLOWED.

The sensation wasn't new to me. I'd been aware of someone watching me on the night I left Burlington House for the final time. But I was quite sure that person hadn't followed me across the courtyard, mostly because there was nowhere to hide in the courtyard. I would have noticed them in the vast open space. This time, there were many places for someone to hide every time I turned around in an attempt to catch them. Recessed doorways, parked vehicles, and mailboxes all provided excellent coverage, but it would be just as easy to blend into the crowd of pedestrians also making their way to work. Men's clothing didn't differentiate much.

I quickly ruled out Lady Stanhope. There weren't many ladies about. Mr. Ludlow, however, was a likely suspect. He might have the same idea as his co-conspirator and want to threaten me too.

When I reached the entrance to Crooked Lane, I decided to confront him. I waited but couldn't see him, however. I couldn't see anyone suspicious. Pedestrians continued past me, their faces unfamiliar.

I entered the lane and hurried to the library. I was about to open the door when a hand clamped over my mouth and my arms were pinned to my sides. I was pulled back against a muscular body.

"What did I ever do to you?" The snarling voice belonged to Tommy Allan, the packer with the scar.

I tried to wriggle out of his grip, but it was too firm. He was much stronger than me. Panic fluttered in my chest. I cried out, but my voice was muffled by his hand. Professor Nash wouldn't hear me.

"Girls like you make me sick. You're all the same. You judge me without knowing a thing about me." He spat the words, spraying spittle on my neck. "Was I the first person you thought of when the pigs questioned you? Huh? They want to find a thief, and the first person you thought of was the ugly man with the scar. Does my face frighten you? Do I scare you?"

I managed to utter a muffled "Yes." It was true. He did scare me. But the more he spoke, the more my mind cleared. My fear was still raw and ice-cold, but it was no longer over-whelming. With the clarity of mind came the memory of combat lessons taught by my mother. She'd also been afraid, but of what, I still didn't know.

What I did know was that to extricate myself from

Tommy's grip, I had to stomp on his toes, elbow him in the gut, turn and kick him in his masculine parts. Once I recalled my training, the four moves came back to me effortlessly.

When he was bending over, clutching his nether region and expelling a hiss like a leaking gas pipe through clenched teeth, I opened the library door. "Professor Nash! Telephone the police, please!"

"Miss Ashe?" came his voice from deep inside. "What's the matter?"

Tommy grunted in frustration, and perhaps pain too, and limped away.

"It's your character I find ugly, Mr. Allan," I called after him. "Not your face."

Professor Nash appeared at the library door. "Miss Ashe? Who is that fellow?"

"A suspect in Gabe's case."

He gasped. "I'll telephone him immediately."

"No!" I followed him inside and closed the door. "It's not necessary. Mr. Allan made his point and I made mine."

The professor bade me sit on the chair at the front desk. "You look a little shaken. I'll make you a cup of tea."

It was true. I couldn't stop shaking. Now that the initial rush of energy had dissipated, my confidence had faded with it. I couldn't believe I'd fought off Tommy Allan and managed to toss a quip out too.

"Thank you, Mother," I muttered once the professor was out of earshot. Her many lessons in self-defense had finally been useful.

To be quite honest, I hadn't known I had it in me. I'd never had cause to put her training into practice and never thought myself capable, particularly against a man. It felt extremely satisfying, to say the least.

But that didn't stop me shaking.

I was still shaking when Professor Nash returned with a cup of tea. He hovered nearby while I sipped, perhaps concerned I'd be suddenly overcome with an attack of the vapors.

By the time I finished the tea, I was feeling calmer.

Or so I thought. When the door suddenly opened, I jumped, knocking the empty teacup onto the floor.

"Miss Ashe!" Gabe rushed in and clasped me by the shoulders. His concerned gaze swept over my face. "Are you all right?"

I nodded, despite my nerves twitching all over again. This time it was from my reaction to his touch and the way he studied me intently, looking for signs that I was about to crumple into a tearful heap. I didn't want to like that troubled look in his green eyes, or the way his strong hands felt as he rubbed my shoulders, but I did.

I liked it very much.

"I'm sorry, Miss Ashe," Professor Nash said. "I know you didn't want me to, but I telephoned him when I made the tea. I thought it for the best."

Gabe released me and straightened. "You didn't want him to call me? Why?"

I sighed. Professor Nash was right. Gabe needed to know. Tommy Allan was a suspect, and the confrontation could be a sign of his guilt.

Gabe tilted his head to the side and crossed his arms. "Are you still upset about me paying your wages?"

I looked away before his deep-sea gaze saw more than I intended it to. "I didn't want to be a bother."

He dropped to his haunches in front of me. "If I've given you the impression that you're a bother, I'm sorry."

It wasn't fair to let him think that when he'd admitted he'd felt guilt, not pity. "That came out wrong. What I meant to say was, I handled the situation. I doubt Tommy Allan will confront me again. But you should have been informed. He claimed you questioned him."

"I did, yesterday. I didn't mention your name, but he must have realized the intelligence came from you." He stood and sat on the edge of the desk, arms once again crossed over his chest. "How did he find out where you worked?"

"He followed me from home. He probably got the address from my employee file at the Academy."

"It was fortunate he waited until you reached the library to attack so Nash could help."

"Oh, I had nothing to do with it." The professor had stepped away to give us some privacy, but not far enough if he still overheard. "He was gone by the time I realized something was amiss."

They both looked at me, expectant.

The door opened, saving me from responding. Alex strode in and took in the situation. "Are you unharmed, Miss Ashe?" At my nod, he added, "I was there when Gabe received your telephone call. I drove him here and have been parking the motor."

"I'm fine, thank you. I was just about to tell Gabe that Tommy Allan hasn't been the only thorn in my side. I had a visit from Lady Stanhope last night."

Gabe swore under his breath.

"Who is Lady Stanhope?" the professor asked.

"Another suspect," Gabe said. "I spoke to her yesterday, too. Did she threaten you, Sylvia?"

I nodded. "Her threat wasn't accompanied by violence, but it felt more sinister, if that makes sense."

"Sinister? I didn't get that impression from her. She was very helpful and answered all my questions."

Alex grunted. "Of course she's helpful to *you*."

"What does that mean?"

"It means she'll be polite to you because you're the

Rycroft heir. She sees you as her equal. She wouldn't be as helpful if I were asking the questions."

Gabe looked offended by the suggestion. If he knew my thoughts, he'd be even more offended, so I kept them to myself. I suspected Lady Stanhope was polite to him for reasons other than his class. He was young and handsome, her favorite type of man.

I, on the other hand, was someone she thought she could easily intimidate and manipulate. While I liked to think neither was true, I was still rattled by her visit.

Gabe scrubbed a hand over his jaw. "Her visit is telling. Clearly, she didn't like you informing me of her altercation with Ludlow. Because she's guilty of the theft? Embarrassed I know how a servant treated her? Or something else?"

"I reckon she's embarrassed," Alex said. "People like her unleash their claws when they feel humiliated."

"Have you considered that Tommy Allan might be working for Lady Stanhope and Ludlow?" I asked. "He can move around Burlington House easier than her. Packers are coming and going all the time during setup. No one would notice if he went into the storeroom where the Delaroche painting was kept, but Lady Stanhope and Mr. Ludlow would be more recognizable."

"I think you're right," Alex said. "Gabe?"

Gabe pushed off from the desk. "We'll call on Burlington House to find out where Tommy Allan lives and we'll pay him a visit. If he's merely the muscle, rather than the brains, he might point the finger at whoever hired him when we tell him how much trouble he's in. He also needs to know that if anything happens to Sylvia, he'll be held to account. Come on."

I half-rose from the chair only to sit back down again when I realized he was speaking to Alex, not me. I would dearly like to face the man who'd attacked me and let him see I wasn't afraid of him, but I didn't dare do it alone.

"Perhaps you'd like to go too, Miss Ashe," Professor Nash said loudly so that Gabe could hear. "It may be a healing experience for you to confront that fellow." I wasn't sure how he realized it was what I needed, but I was grateful to him.

"Only if you can release her for a few hours," Gabe said. "And if Sylvia wants to come too, of course. I wouldn't want to be seen to use my position—"

Alex smacked his fist into Gabe's shoulder. "Shut up. You can see she wants to join us."

I mouthed a "Thank you" to Professor Nash and slipped out of the library ahead of them. Gabe and Alex fell into step on either side of me in the lane.

"Maybe Tommy Allan is the one watching you, Gabe," Alex said.

"You're being watched?" I asked.

Gabe gave his friend a glare over the top of my head. "It's probably just that journalist."

"Or it could be the kidnapper," Alex said. "And the kidnapper could be the thief."

Gabe released a measured breath. "Don't, Alex."

I got the feeling they were exchanging glances over my head again, but I was too busy looking for the person or persons following Gabe to notice. I couldn't see anyone watching us as we climbed into the Vauxhall, nor following us in their own vehicle. We drove too fast for a horse-drawn carriage to keep up. Even a motorcar would have struggled. Gabe wove in and out of the traffic with abandon. With one hand keeping my hat in place and another clutching my bag, I slid from one side of the back seat to the other like a tennis ball.

I was grateful when we pulled to the curb outside Burlington House, at which point Alex declared we hadn't been followed. He'd been checking over his shoulder the entire journey.

We found Mr. Bolton in his office, but he was on the telephone. The assistant, Mr. Driscoll, invited us to sit and wait in the outer office, but his friendly smile slipped when I introduced myself. He returned to his task of stuffing flyers into envelopes.

"I hope you're feeling better," I said.

He looked quite well to me. He was mid-twenties, handsome, with a hairstyle that defied gravity at the front. It was only when he bent his head forward that I realized the upswept fringe was meant to detract from the balding patch near the back.

"I am. Thank you." His tone was clipped, not inviting more conversation.

I sat on one of the wooden chairs, my bag on my lap, and waited.

Gabe, however, had taken Mr. Driscoll's stiff response like a bull to a red rag. He charged right in. "You were sick? I hope it wasn't the flu."

"It wasn't."

"What ailed you?"

"A cough."

"You stayed away from work because of a cough?"

"One can never be too careful these days." Mr. Driscoll cleared his throat and made a show of stretching his neck out of his collar.

"Do you have access to the employee files?" Gabe went on.

Mr. Driscoll finally met his gaze, his eyes wide. "No!"

One side of Alex's mouth twitched with his smirk.

Gabe reached across the desk and picked up a file. "Isn't this one?" He read the front. "'Archibald Makepeace.'"

Mr. Driscoll snatched the file back. "Please sit down. Mr. Bolton will be with you in a moment."

"You're lying."

"No!" It came out as a high-pitched squeak. Mr. Driscoll cleared his throat again. "I assure you I haven't lied."

Gabe's jaw suddenly firmed and his demeanor changed. "Someone gave out the home address of Miss Ashe." He kept his voice low, menacing, a far cry from the friendly one I was used to. "Was it you?"

Mr. Driscoll closed his eyes and blew out a measured breath. "Yes. Yes, it was me. I gave Lady Stanhope her address."

Gabe pressed both hands on the desk and leaned in. "You should be fired for that."

Mr. Driscoll nodded quickly. "Yes, sir, you're right. I apologize. It was very unprofessional of me."

"Don't apologize to me."

Mr. Driscoll's rapid nods continued as he his gaze shifted to me. "I am very sorry, Miss Ashe. But Lady Stanhope was most insistent and I...I felt as though I couldn't say no."

Gabe glanced over his shoulder at me, his brows raised, asking if I was satisfied with the apology.

"Apology accepted," I said.

At least now we knew where the leak had occurred. But I wasn't entirely sure Lady Stanhope had passed on my address to Tommy Allan. It wasn't necessary for them both to warn me off, unless they didn't know about the other's visit. If they were working together, and if Lady Stanhope had given him my address, shouldn't they have known?

Mr. Bolton marched out of his office and regarded the three of us in turn, offering a nod to the men and a "Good morning, Miss Ashe," to me. "Come into my office." He spun on his heel and marched back inside.

I half expected Mr. Driscoll to beg us not to inform his

employer of his indiscretion, but he merely watched us go with a sigh of relief.

Mr. Bolton regarded us from the other side of his desk. "I didn't know you two knew each other. Now. Tell me what I can do for you." He barked it out like an order.

"I was accosted by Mr. Allan, the packer," I said. "It happened outside my new place of work, but he followed me from home. Do you know how he got my address?"

Mr. Bolton's no-nonsense demeanor slipped a little more with every passing moment. "My dear Miss Ashe, that's dreadful! Dreadful indeed. I assure you, neither I nor Driscoll have given out your address."

"You can't account for your assistant's actions," Gabe said.

"I suppose not, but I still can't imagine he would do such a thing. Man's as straight as an arrow." Mr. Bolton glanced at the closed door then his gaze slowly shifted back to Gabe. "Do you think this is related to your investigation into the theft, Glass? Is that why you've accompanied Miss Ashe?"

"It's a possibility."

Mr. Bolton huffed and huffed again, shaking his head. "It pains me to think of Tommy Allan being caught up in this mess, but I suppose I can't defend him merely because I feel sorry for him." He indicated the side of his face. "It must be difficult for him, what with the scar. Miss Ashe, I feel somewhat responsible and must apologize. Tommy met you here, and if I'd known what would happen, I would never have put you in harm's way by employing you."

It took all my self-control not to retort that Tommy was the one he should regret employing.

"Is Mr. Allan in today?" Gabe asked. "We need to re-question him."

"I'm afraid he left our employ. As with several on the packing team, he was hired on a temporary basis only."

"Do you have an address for him?"

"Driscoll!"

Mr. Driscoll opened the door and peered through the gap like a rabbit sniffing for predators before emerging from its burrow. "Sir?"

"Give them the address of Tommy Allan."

"Yes, Sir."

Mr. Bolton dismissed us with a curt nod, and we followed Mr. Driscoll back to his desk. He looked through his files then wrote an address on a piece of paper. He handed it to Alex, all the while avoiding our gazes.

We didn't head outside straight away but went to check on the seascape on display in the main gallery. It was still there, attracting the most attention. A policeman stood beside it, gazing idly back at the art lovers as if he were a piece in the exhibition. He exchanged some words with Alex before Alex rejoined us.

"All's well," he reported.

Outside Burlington House, Gabe and Alex discussed the likelihood Mr. Driscoll had told Tommy Allan where I lived, and if he did, why he hadn't admitted it when he admitted passing on my details to Lady Stanhope.

I wasn't listening very closely, however. The last time I'd crossed the Burlington House courtyard, I'd felt as though I was being watched. There were several people about now and it was broad daylight, but I didn't experience that feeling this time.

We drove to Lambeth on the other side of the river, an area of London I'd not yet visited since arriving in the city. With good reason. I'd seen worse slums. Indeed, I'd lived in worse when my mother's meager wage was our family's sole income. Once James started to earn a living, our situation improved, and each subsequent move resulted in slightly better accommodation than the last.

The street on which Tommy Allan lived was crammed

with terraced houses squeezed together to fit in the maximum number. The only remarkable thing about them was their uniformity—three levels high, two windows wide, brown brick and black doors with the paint peeling off.

London's air was never very clean but in Lambeth, the smoke stung the eyes and clogged the throat the moment we stepped out of the motor. The nearby industry was the lifeblood of most residents, providing employment, but the thick air couldn't be good for the health of those who spent all day, every day, breathing it in.

Alex wanted to wait by the motor to protect it from the dirty fingers of children. He stood sentinel, arms crossed over his massive chest, doing his best impression of a villainous henchman.

Gabe had made a half-hearted suggestion that I remain in the motor, but I was still determined to confront Tommy Allan. I doubted he would be home, however. It was the middle of the day. He'd probably found new work by now.

I was right. He wasn't there, according to the woman who answered Gabe's knock. Indeed, he no longer lived there. He'd moved out. The woman was his former fiancée, and she was relieved to see the back of him.

"I made him pack his bags and sent him on his way. I put up with him long enough on account of him coming home from the war all broken and scarred. But they sent him back with a few cards missing from the deck." She tapped her temple. "His drinking got worse, and when he was drunk, he got angry. He took that anger out on me and my sister." She jerked her thumb over her shoulder which I took to mean her sister was inside. "A bit of shouting don't bother us, but when he hit her, well, that was it. She's my only family, and I got to protect her. I told Tommy to leave. Threw his things outside, right where you're standing. Best thing I ever did."

"Where can we find him now?" Gabe asked.

She settled a hand on her out-thrust hip. "He fell in with a bad lot after I kicked him out, but I don't reckon he moved in with any of 'em. They ain't got no room and they ain't the sort to help out their fellow man in his hour of need." She heaved broad shoulders in a shrug. "I reckon he's just living by his wits." She chuckled, revealing a missing tooth on the bottom row. "That's a joke, 'cause he ain't got none."

"Are you telling us he's homeless now?" Gabe asked.

"That'd be my guess. Try the poor houses for returned soldiers."

Gabe thanked her and she disappeared inside. We returned to the motor where Alex was in conversation with a group of local men, all smoking. Gabe sighed. "We could do as she says and try the poor houses, but he could very well be on the streets. Finding him will be impossible."

One of the men dropped his cigarette butt on the ground and smothered it with the heel of his boot. There were dozens of cigarette butts littering the pavement, many of them blown by the wind against the brick walls where they formed small piles.

I'd seen a pile of cigarette butts recently, but they'd not been blown around by the wind. If I was right, they'd all been discarded by one man. "I think I know where Tommy has been living," I said, unable to keep the triumph out of my voice. "Get in. I'll show you."

CHAPTER 11

$\mathcal{I}$t hadn't occurred to me at the time that the bundle of dust sheets on the storeroom floor at Burlington House was the bedding of someone living there. But now that I knew Tommy Allan was homeless, it made sense. The cigarette butts had been the clue. The pile beside the bedding had to have been made by a heavy smoker who spent a great deal of time there.

Every night, Tommy pretended to go home after his shift finished, but doubled back before the doors were locked and snuck into the basement storeroom. He'd probably been sneaking back in when I'd left on my last night. He'd slipped into the shadows and watched me until I was off the premises altogether.

I folded my arms to suppress my shiver.

"You're cold," Gabe said as we descended the stairs behind Mr. Bolton.

"I'm fine."

Mr. Bolton pushed open the door and I showed them where I'd seen the bedding and cigarette butts. But the dust covers had been placed over artwork and the pile of cigarette butts had been disturbed. Going by the rat droppings, it was obvious what had disturbed them.

"He hasn't been here for a few days, at least," Gabe said. "He must have found other accommodation."

I shivered again. The chill settled into my bones and remained there.

With a reassuring hand on my lower back, Gabe steered me out of the storeroom and up the stairs. Neither of us spoke until we were out of Mr. Bolton's hearing, but Gabe's pace slowed as we crossed the courtyard.

He glanced through the gate to Piccadilly, where Alex was waiting with the motor, then he stopped altogether. "I don't mean to frighten you, Sylvia, but you could be in danger."

The thought had already occurred to me. Indeed, it was all I could think about. While I'd told him earlier at the library that Tommy wouldn't dare attack me again, my bravado had since vanished, replaced by a strong dose of reality. It was unlikely Tommy had been frightened off altogether. All I'd really achieved was to anger him further and alert him that I was capable of some self-defense moves. He wouldn't be caught by surprise next time.

"He knows where you live and work," Gabe went on. "So I think you should move into my house."

I stared at him. Then I started laughing.

He did not join in. He simply looked back at me, his face grave.

I sobered. "You weren't joking."

"I think it's the best solution, at least until he's caught. You're too exposed at the lodging house."

"I could stay with Daisy or Horatio."

"And place them in danger too?"

He had a point. "But I hardly know you."

"Very well, let's see. I'm twenty-nine years old, an only child, and was brought up on the family estate in Dorset. My favorite food is anything that doesn't come out of a tin can and my favorite season is spring. I like animals and used to be scared of the dark until I was eight."

"What happened at eight to make you no longer scared?"

"Willie gave me a puppy. It slept on my bed with me."

Despite my anxiety, I couldn't help smiling. "You make her sound quite sweet."

"There are many words to describe Willie, but sweet isn't one of them."

"What will she think of me moving in?"

His smile widened. "That sounded like a yes to me."

"And Willie?" I prompted.

"Don't worry. I know how to handle her."

He might, but I didn't. I wasn't sure being under the same roof as someone who disliked me was better than living in the lodging house, despite the extra comforts a large Mayfair residence provided.

We set off again across the courtyard toward Piccadilly. "Alex also lives with us," he said.

"He doesn't live with his parents?"

"He did until my parents left for America. The arrangement suited us both. He wanted to get out of a crowded house—he has three sisters—and I wanted the company."

"Weren't Willie and the servants enough company for you?"

"Bristow and Mrs. Bristow are elderly, and the other servants don't live-in. And you've met Willie. Do I need to say more?"

I laughed. "Very well, I'll move in. But only on a temporary basis."

"Good. I'll return you to the library then go home and have the housekeeper make up a room for you."

"You should also warn Willie. I don't want to turn up on the doorstep unannounced."

* * *

UNFORTUNATELY, Willie wasn't at home, so Gabe informed me when he collected me from the lodging house at dusk. I'd returned there after work to pack and waited for him in the sitting room with my two suitcases and a hat box, the sum of all my belongings.

Mrs. Whitten had lectured me about ruining myself and then informed me I could never return there for fear of "infecting" the other girls with my immorality. I didn't bother trying to tell her the arrangement wasn't what she imagined. She wouldn't believe me. Nor did I inform Gabe that I was barred from returning. It changed nothing.

Willie still wasn't back when we arrived at number sixteen Park Street. The housekeeper, Mrs. Bristow, the ancient wife of the ancient butler, showed me to the guest bedroom. The window was open to let in fresh air, but the room still smelled a little stale. It was quite a feminine room with floral wallpaper on the wall behind the bed and a blue and white vase filled with pink roses on the dressing table. I supposed it was decorated in Lady Rycroft's style, not her son's, just like the rest of the house. From what I'd seen of it so far, it was tastefully done with comfort in mind rather than fashion. Daisy would probably find it out of date, but I found it warm.

Mrs. Bristow proceeded to tell me about the rest of the occupants and servants while I unpacked. The Bristows were the only live-in servants nowadays. Mrs. Ling the cook, Sally the maid, and Dodson the chauffeur, all lived in their own homes with their families. There was no footman, something which seemed to trouble the matter-of-fact housekeeper, probably because it meant her aging husband had no help. Nor was there a lady's maid, as Willie had no need of one, and Gabe didn't want a valet.

"You look capable of doing your own hair and mending," Mrs. Bristow said, giving me a thorough inspection.

"My mother was a seamstress."

"Is that so?" She gave me another going-over, this time squinting through her spectacles to get a better look. She gave a nod of approval. Indeed, I'd go so far as to say she seemed pleased.

I tucked the small suitcase containing my brother's and mother's things under the bed. "Tell me about Willie. Has she always lived here?"

"Off and on. She moved out each time she married and moved back in when the husbands died. A word of warning, Miss Ashe. Don't joke about her murdering them. She doesn't like it."

I gawped at her. "*Did* she kill them?"

Mrs. Bristow tapped the side of her nose and winked.

I watched her waddle out of the bedroom with a sense of doom. What had I got myself into?

"Dinner is at eight," she said.

"Do they dress for dinner?" I looked down at my outfit and sighed. I couldn't do much better. "Never mind."

I changed my blouse and redid my hair then headed downstairs in search of Gabe, intending to be as amiable a house guest as possible. I stopped on the second floor landing at the sound of Willie's angry voice.

"How's it going to look, Gabe?"

"Sylvia's safety is more important than what people think," he said.

I was surprised to hear that a woman who wore men's clothing was worried about convention and what people thought. She must care about him a great deal to worry about his reputation.

"This ain't about what *people* think, Gabe, and you know it," she went on. "How're you going to explain it?"

"I'll be honest."

"That's the dumbest idea you've had, excepting the one where you invited her to move in. Say she's a cousin."

"I'm not going to lie, Willie."

"Then you're going to have to suffer the consequences. And there will be consequences."

"Willie," Gabe chided, "stop worrying. It's not like you."

She muttered something inaudible then added, "Alex, why didn't you stop this?"

Someone sighed heavily, probably Alex at being dragged into the argument. "It's Gabe's fault that it's not safe for Sylvia in the lodging house so you have to understand he feels responsible. But I agree with you, she could have been put up elsewhere."

"I disagree," Gabe said at the same time Willie said, "See!"

"Do you both think so little of me?" Gabe went on, exasperated. "There's nothing to worry about because I don't think of Sylvia that way."

"It ain't about what *you* think, Gabe. It's about how it *looks*. You invited a pretty woman to move in—that looks like you've got feelings for her."

"The only feeling I have for her is guilt."

It was fortunate I hadn't got my hopes up or they'd be bursting like balloons now. Even so, my ego was somewhat deflated.

Willie growled in frustration. "If I'm being the sensible one in this conversation, you know trouble's brewing!"

The floorboards creaked and I ducked behind a large potted palm. Thankfully Willie stormed off down the stairs without looking in my direction. I waited for the front door to slam before I emerged from my hiding place.

But I did not enter the room. I didn't want to face Gabe. My presence was clearly a problem. Willie was right. My living here compromised Gabe. The twenty-nine-year-old son of a wealthy baron had excellent marriage prospects, but not if everyone thought he kept a mistress.

I turned to go.

"I have a telephone call to make," I heard Gabe say.

I picked up my skirts and raced up the stairs, but I wasn't fast enough.

"Sylvia! Wait."

I stopped and closed my eyes. Bloody hell.

"You heard that, didn't you?" he asked quietly.

I had to get this over with now. If I let this situation simmer below the surface, it could get much worse when it finally, inevitably, boiled over. I turned to face him. "I did."

"I'm sorry about Willie."

"Don't blame her. She's right. I'll pack my things and stay in a hotel tonight. Tomorrow I'll look for another lodging house."

"You won't go back to the same one?"

"Uhhh…"

"Mrs. Whitten won't let you back, will she?" He took the remaining steps two at a time until he was just one step below me. He still towered over me. "Ignore Willie. She's overreacting."

"You don't owe me anything, Gabe."

"We're friends, and friends help each other."

"We're not friends. You made it clear that you're doing this because you feel guilt, not out of friendship."

He caught my hand only to immediately let it go again. He cleared his throat. "Stay for dinner then see how you feel after that. I've invited Alex's entire family. If you're not convinced to stay after speaking to Cyclops and his wife, Catherine, then I'll drive you to a hotel myself."

"Won't they think as Willie does?"

"We'll soon find out."

"But I've got nothing suitable to wear for dinner."

"You're dressed perfectly for a casual affair with just a few close friends. Now, I have to make a telephone call. Alex will make you a cocktail in the drawing room, and I'll return shortly."

Alex led the way down the stairs to the drawing room, a room I'd already been in during my previous visit. While it wasn't as cozy as the sitting room upstairs, it was still inviting.

Alex made cocktails at a drinks trolley then handed one to me. "It's a martini."

"Daisy's new favorite drink. They were popular in America before prohibition, so she told me."

"She has friends there? Family?"

"I don't know. I think she has magazines sent over. She likes to keep up with the latest in everything."

"She does strike me as someone who'll change her hair-style as often as the wind changes direction."

"You say it with disapproval, but I think she'd be rather pleased that you noticed."

He was about to take a sip of his cocktail but suddenly looked up. "Why?"

Daisy would hate me hinting that she might be interested in him, considering she didn't yet realize she was interested. "Isn't any woman pleased when a man takes notice of her?"

"I didn't. Well, I did, but that's only because she's very obvious." He sipped his cocktail, a thoughtful frown on his face. "I'm surprised you two are friends. You're very different."

"She's outgoing and I'm quiet?"

"You're stable and she's impulsive." It wasn't the worst thing he could have called her.

"I think Daisy and I complement each other. Speaking of obvious people, I overheard the conversation Gabe had with Willie, earlier. She's very much against me staying here. As are you. I want to assure you, I'm leaving after dinner. I don't want to compromise Gabe's reputation in any way."

He lowered the glass. "You think we're worried about his reputation?"

"Well...yes. You both mentioned how it will look to other people. And I agree. It will look...inappropriate."

He scooted forward on the chair, cradling the glass in both hands. He fixed me with an earnest stare. "You're right. It will look that way. But we're not worried about what strangers think, and nor is he. We're worried—"

He closed his mouth and sat back in the chair when Gabe entered. His gaze tracked his friend as he made himself a martini at the drinks trolley then joined me on the sofa.

Gabe lifted his glass in salute to each of us in turn, "Cheers." It wasn't until he sipped that he noticed Alex watching him. "Everything's fine, just as I told you it would be. She's coming to dinner too."

Alex glanced at the clock on the mantel. "She must be keen to get here by eight."

"She'll be late."

"Naturally," Alex muttered.

Gabe smiled, but it was hesitant, perhaps even a little concerned. "There'll be another dining with us," he said to me. "Her name's Ivy. She's my fiancée."

CHAPTER 12

$\mathcal{T}$hank goodness I hadn't just taken a sip of my martini or I might have spat it out all over the lovely rug in surprise. Gabe had never mentioned Ivy. He'd never even given me an inkling that he was engaged.

I supposed it was an odd thing to insert into a conversation simply for the sake of mentioning it. The topic of women had never come up between us. The only time anyone had alluded to Gabe's popularity with the opposite sex was when Cyclops implied he'd been rather wild before the war. I wondered if Ivy was someone he knew then or a more recent addition to his life.

"I look forward to meeting her." It was true. I did look forward to seeing the woman who could attract such a paragon as Gabe. I couldn't decide whether she would be beautiful and elegant or down-to-earth and athletic. When I'd first met him, I would have guessed the former, but now that I knew him a little better and saw the type of friends he kept, I was leaning toward the latter.

"She says she looks forward to meeting you too," he said.

"Now I know why Willie and Alex were worried about

me staying. They're right, by the way. I can't stay. It's not fair to Ivy."

"She's a good sport."

"No woman is *that* good a sport. If you don't know that, you clearly don't know women very well."

Alex chuckled into his cocktail glass. Gabe grinned too. I had the feeling I was on the outside of an inside joke.

"Just wait until you meet before you make a hasty decision about staying or leaving," Gabe said.

Bristow entered and announced the arrival of Mr. and Mrs. Bailey, and their daughters Ella, Mae and Lulu. Alex kissed the cheeks of his mother and sisters and accepted a hearty clap on the shoulder from his father. Gabe followed in his footsteps and the Baileys greeted him warmly, as if he were another son who'd recently moved out of the family home. The two families must be close.

The three sisters tried, and failed, to hide their scrutiny of me before introductions were made. Their mother was more polite, warmly shaking my hand and not giving me the obvious once-over. She was a willowy woman, with blonde hair shot through with silver and fine lines fanning from the corners of her eyes that deepened upon her smile. I suspected she smiled a lot. There was just something sweet about her, yet a little bit cheeky too. I'd wager she appreciated a good joke.

Her eldest daughter, Ella, couldn't have been much younger than me. She seemed a little more reserved than her two sisters, who lost interest in me the moment the cocktail glasses were handed around. Not that their father let the youngest, Lulu, have one, which caused her to flounce off in a huff and throw herself into one of the armchairs. Mae accepted a glass with a triumphant smile directed at her little sister that only made Lulu's pout deepen. Mae sipped, gave

Lulu another smug smile then turned away and pulled a face at the taste.

Catherine joined me on the sofa and nodded at the three men, talking quietly near the door. "We've only been here two minutes and already they're discussing a case."

"There were some developments today," I said.

"So Gabe told me when he called and invited us to dinner. He said you were attacked. Are you all right, Miss Ashe?"

"Please call me Sylvia. And yes, thank you, I am. The attacker ran off when I hit him in the..." I cleared my throat. "When I fought back."

She smiled. "I'm glad to see you're not helpless. Nate wants to teach the girls some moves to defend themselves. Mae has no interest whatsoever. She thinks it'll make her too masculine. And Lulu does whatever Mae does. Ella has taken to his lessons with enthusiasm, though." She looked at her eldest who was hovering near the men. I'd thought she was there because she was infatuated with Gabe, but now I realized she was merely absorbing everything they said. Like her sisters, she was very pretty, but they were tall and slim like their mother where she was tall and more powerfully built like Cyclops.

"Are you staying here until this blows over?" Catherine made it sound like an innocent question, but I suspected she was very interested in the answer. As someone who probably saw herself as a mother figure to Gabe, now that his parents were out of the country, it made sense that she wanted to make sure I didn't intrude on his relationship with Ivy.

"There's been a misunderstanding. I'm leaving after dinner and will stay at a hotel."

She nodded sagely. "That's for the best."

"I'll explain as much to Ivy when she arrives."

"So she is coming." Catherine didn't pose it as a question or sound surprised. Indeed, she made it sound like it was a given. "Don't worry. I'm sure she'll say all the right things." She watched Gabe and leaned closer to me. "Did he tell you anything about her?"

"No."

"I see."

"Gabe and I hardly know one another," I clarified.

She took a sip of her cocktail, her gaze still on Gabe. Then she suddenly turned to me. "They hardly knew one another when they got engaged. It was very sudden. None of us had met her beforehand. It was 1917 and Gabe was on leave for two weeks. They met at the beginning of those two weeks then by the end, they announced they were getting married."

"Is he always so impulsive?"

She smiled sadly. "He used to be. By the time the war ended, that zest for living, that urgency to experience all life has to offer, vanished. It was as if the hardships of the past four years filed off the wilder parts of him. Willie says the war took away the best of him and left behind a shell, but I disagree. I think it took away the unnecessary parts and exposed the better man underneath. While everything about the war was dreadful, it did teach Gabe to slow down and savor his good fortune instead of take it for granted. Life probably would have done that eventually, but war sped up the process."

"Is that why they haven't married yet? They're savoring their engagement? I'm sure it's a very special time for them both."

"I think they just want to get to know one another better. There was very little chance for them to be together immediately after the announcement, of course, and Gabe didn't return home again until two months after Armistice. When he returned, he threw himself into his work with Scotland Yard. He needed something to do. He has been kept busy this last year." She glanced at the photograph I'd noticed on my last visit of a young Gabe standing alongside his parents. "With India and Matt away, the wedding will be pushed back further. Gabe would never marry without them present."

"When will they return?"

"They didn't say."

It seemed a little unfair not to give a firm date when their son's happiness hinged on them being home.

Gabe broke away from Cyclops and Alex and joined us. "Another martini?"

I declined and Catherine had barely touched her first one. He sat down next to her and opened his mouth to say something when a woman walked in. He rose again and smiled at her.

"Ivy. Come in." He kissed her cheek.

She linked her arm with his and smiled up at him. "I made it, and it's only a little after eight. Aren't you impressed?" She took his hand and stepped back so he could admire her before closing the gap again and placing his hand on her waist.

"I am. You look as beautiful as always, but I did say not to dress formally."

She laughed. "Darling, you know nothing about fashion." As she talked, her gaze scanned the room until it landed on me.

One of my guesses about her was right. She was a sleek beauty. Her statuesque figure suited the slim-fitting copper-colored sleeveless silk dress with the cluster of crystals at the cinched waist. Her dark hair was cut short like Daisy's but fell perfectly straight without a strand out of place. Daisy looked like she'd just got out of bed whereas Ivy looked as though she'd stepped out of a fashion magazine. The diamonds at her throat, ears and wrist left me in no doubt that she matched Gabe in wealth as well as height and good looks. They were a beautiful couple. Heads must turn when they walked into a party together, just as we all watched them now.

Gabe introduced me to Ivy as his "friend from the Glass Library."

She gave me a warm smile. "Gabe told me what a traumatic day you've had. You poor thing. It must have been awful being attacked like that."

"I was a little shaken afterward, but I'm all right now."

"I'm sure my Gabe took good care of you. Protecting those in need is something he does so well and so willingly."

"She fought the attacker off by herself," Gabe said. "She didn't need me."

Ivy's eyes widened. They were as lovely as the rest of her, all golden brown, framed by long lashes darkened by soot mixed with petroleum jelly. "How extraordinary. But she does need you now, doesn't she?"

"I'm only staying for dinner," I assured her.

She blinked those big eyes at Gabe. I wondered if she knew how innocent it made her look, how beautiful too. "You told me she was staying here until the attacker was caught and the investigation concluded."

"There was a misunderstanding," I said before Gabe could say otherwise. "I'm definitely leaving after dinner."

Ivy took my hand in both of hers. "Nonsense, Sylvia. It's much too dangerous for you to stay anywhere else. This is the safest place you can be with Gabe here to protect you."

"And Alex," Gabe added.

Ivy squeezed my hand and gave me a tentative smile. "Promise you'll stay?"

I glanced at Gabe. He merely lifted a shoulder in a shrug. "Perhaps just for tonight, but only if it's all right with you," I said to Ivy.

"It is. Now, you must tell me what it's like working in the library. It sounds fascinating."

One of the younger Bailey girls snorted, earning a glare from both her parents.

Everyone was saved from hearing about my work when Bristow announced dinner was ready. We filed through to the dining room and took our seats.

There was one place too many at the long table.

"Is Willie joining us?" Cyclops asked.

"That's anyone's guess," Gabe said. "She left in a huff because she was worried about Ivy's opinion of Sylvia staying here."

"She was worried about me?" Ivy asked. "I didn't think she liked me."

"Of course she likes you."

"Then why does she scowl at me all the time?"

"She scowls at everyone," Cyclops assured her.

"Especially Gabe's women," Alex added. When all heads turned to him, he cleared his throat. "I meant his women in the past. Now it's just one woman. That's you, Ivy. She scowls only at you." He snatched up his wine glass the moment it was filled by Bristow and drank somewhat gratefully.

Ivy laughed. "Then I'll consider myself fortunate every time she scowls at me from now on."

Bristow was in the middle of serving bowls of consommé when Willie sauntered in, a thumb hooked through her belt loop like a cowboy. She smirked upon seeing Ivy but didn't refer to the earlier argument she'd had with Gabe. He looked relieved.

"Consommé again?" she said as she sat. "I miss our former cook."

"It's not Mrs. Ling's fault," Gabe said. "There's been a war, in case you hadn't heard."

"Rationing's ended. She can get butter now."

Cyclops sighed. "I missed butter."

Willie grunted. "You wouldn't know it."

"Are you calling me fat?"

Willie slurped her consommé loudly.

"Ignore them," Catherine said to me. "When Willie is around my husband, he turns into a large child."

Cyclops tucked his head down and concentrated on his soup.

"Tell us about yourself, Sylvia," Catherine went on. "Gabe says you're new to London. Where are you from originally?"

It was a question I dreaded being asked, but one I'd learned to deflect. "Nowhere in particular and yet everywhere in England, or so it seems. Have you always lived in London, Catherine?"

She gave me a brief account of her life, including her years working for her watchmaker brother. Her family had been close to Gabe's grandparents, and she'd been a lifelong friend to Gabe's mother, India.

"Are your family watchmaker magicians too?" I asked.

"No. India is the only one left, as far as anyone knows. Gabe didn't inherit it."

"Inherited magic can skip a generation," Ivy pointed out with a small smile for Gabe.

He didn't seem to notice, however. He was concentrating on his consommé.

"Everyone in this room is artless," Willie said. "Except Ivy."

"Oh?" I blurted out. "How interesting. What's your magical craft?"

"I wish it was interesting, but it's only leather," she said.

Willie dismissed Ivy's self-deprecation with a wave of her spoon. "Don't sell yourself short, Ivy. Her family are bootmakers," she told me. "Their boots are real good. The pair they gave me have lasted two years and still look like new. But you don't have to take my word for it. The government reckons they're good too. So much so, they gave Hobson and

Son Bootmaker a contract to supply British soldiers with footwear in the war. Hobson's boots were worn in the trenches by our nation's finest."

"'*Our* nation?'" Cyclops teased. "So you agree you're more English now than American?"

"No. You twisted my words."

"He didn't," Alex said. "You admitted it. You're an Englishwoman through and through." He grinned at his father, who grinned back.

"I'm as American as Annie Oakley and Colt pistols." Willie pointed her spoon at Cyclops. "You're the traitor to your country with your English accent and your hoity toity ways."

We all stared at her. Then everyone burst out laughing. Cyclops's accent was as American as hers, and while I didn't know him well, he seemed the opposite of hoity toity.

As the dinner went on, I grew more and more comfortable. Gabe's friends were nice, although Willie didn't look at me, let alone strike up a conversation with me. I couldn't quite work out why, considering Ivy didn't seem to have a problem with me staying.

The Baileys and Ivy made up for Willie's rudeness, however, and by the time dessert was served, I felt quite relaxed in their company. The lull could also be because of Mrs. Ling's comforting food. She was an excellent cook. Her veal sweetbreads and filet mignon were heavenly, and the pudding drenched in a thick sauce was delicious. If I ate like this every night, I'd need to take out the waistline of my skirt.

We retired to the drawing room afterwards for port, which I declined. Ivy accepted a glass from Gabe then patted the seat next to her on the sofa, signaling for him to sit.

"Have you heard from your parents, Darling?"

"They sent a telegram yesterday."

"And?"

He blinked at her. "And what?"

"Did they give a date for their return?"

"No."

Her lips tightened ever so slightly, but the small sign of her displeasure quickly vanished, replaced with a smile.

Cyclops and Catherine exchanged glances. "I'm sure they won't be gone long," Catherine assured Ivy.

Ivy's smile wavered.

Willie picked up a deck of cards and began shuffling them, despite no one mentioning playing. She seemed to be doing it without thinking, as if it were something she did to keep her hands occupied. Perhaps it helped as she tried to give up smoking. "They won't be gone long. They won't want to miss your wedding."

Gabe's thumb tapped the sofa arm. It made no sound, but the military rhythm was unmistakable. I'd heard the drums in the brass bands keeping the same beat in the numerous parades held since Armistice. "There won't be a wedding until they return. Ivy understands."

She clasped his arm above the elbow. "Of course I do. My mother, however, is a little frustrated."

Gabe patted her hand and gave her the sort of smile one gives an elderly person who's repeated the same thing for the third or fourth time.

"They won't be gone long," Willie said again, her fingers flipping cards with the deftness of a conjurer.

Cyclops and Catherine exchanged another glance.

"I hate weddings," Willie suddenly declared.

"Then why'd you have two of them?" Alex asked.

"I didn't get married for me, I got married for others. Living in sin is all right by me, but some people get a real bee in their bonnet about it. Both of my husbands insisted."

"Don't listen to her," Cyclops said to me, his eye twinkling with humor. "She loves weddings. She always cries."

Willie sneered at him and returned to her shuffling. She made no mention of starting a game and soon afterward, Cyclops, Catherine and the girls gave their leave. I retired too so that Gabe and Ivy could have their privacy, although I needn't have bothered as Alex and Willie stayed behind.

I was climbing into bed a few minutes later when I heard soft masculine voices saying goodnight to one another. Ivy must have left almost straight after me.

I sank into the mattress with a sigh. The foot of the bed was warm thanks to the stoneware pot filled with hot water that Mrs. Bristow had placed there, and the sheets smelled faintly of lavender. It was a shame I was leaving tomorrow. The hotel rooms I could afford would be nothing like this.

* * *

"DID YOU SLEEP WELL?" Gabe asked me the following morning at breakfast. He sat opposite Alex at the dining table. Willie was nowhere in sight.

"Very well, thank you."

I must remember to thank Mrs. Bristow for the bed warmer before I left, and for the other small kindnesses. She'd left me a handwritten note on the pillow explaining how the morning routine worked in the household. To some, it would seem like a trifling thing, but to me, knowing the routine was more of a comfort than the soft mattress. It meant I didn't sit down and wait to be served, but served myself from the sideboard, as if taking breakfast in grand houses was something I did every day.

As I sat, I caught Gabe watching me over the newspaper he was reading, or pretending to read. He folded it up and placed it to one side. "We'll drive you to work this morning."

"Thank you, but please don't go out of your way."

"We're not."

Alex looked up from his newspaper, frowned at his friend, then continued to read.

"What happens with the investigation now?" I asked.

"We'll watch Ludlow and Lady Stanhope. Perhaps their movements will give us a clue. Cyclops assured me that Scotland Yard will commit as many men as they can to finding Tommy Allan."

"It'll be a near impossible task," Alex said from behind the paper.

Gabe flicked him a glare, but Alex didn't notice. "Don't worry," he assured me. "I'll have a word with Professor Nash when I take you to work and make sure he keeps the door locked."

"There's no need for that. Patrons should be allowed to come and go freely."

"They can knock."

Alex folded up the paper. "And the library has very few patrons anyway."

Gabe offered me a newspaper from the pile beside him. He had several, some of them dailies, at least two were weeklies. I sifted through them until I found one that looked interesting and opened it without reading the front page.

I gasped as an article caught my eye. No, not the article, but the photograph of the too-handsome man scowling at the camera.

"What is it?" Gabe asked.

I quickly turned the page. "Nothing."

Both Gabe and Alex were looking at me now. "Show me," Alex said.

I bit the inside of my cheek.

"You know we're going to read it eventually, so you might as well get it over with."

I sighed and turned the page back. "It's an article about Gabe. They used the same photograph as last time."

"The one taken after you rescued that boy," Alex added.

"After his father drowned," Gabe said heavily.

"That wasn't your fault."

Gabe accepted the newspaper from me and read the article. He passed it to Alex who set it down between us so I could read too. Gabe sighed. "That journalist isn't giving up."

According to the byline, the article had been written by Albert Scarrow, the same fellow who wrote the article that had initially led me to seek out Gabe at the exhibition. While that one was a news report on the boating accident, this article was more of an opinion piece. Indeed, it was wildly speculative and posed more questions about Gabe than factual information.

Questions such as why did the boy claim Gabe held his breath for several minutes under water, and how did he survive four years of war without injury? Both were seemingly impossible feats.

"This is bollocks." Alex pushed the newspaper away. "It's lazy journalism."

"He's just trying to find answers to a couple of curious events," Gabe said. "It's his job to speculate."

"It's his job to find facts to back up his claims."

"He hasn't made any claims, merely raised the questions. Nor can he find facts because there aren't any. I haven't given him a quote he can use."

"Then I will. I'll tell him where to shove his speculation."

"You'll leave him alone, Alex. He'll eventually give up."

Alex gestured in the general direction of the front door. "And in the meantime, we have to put up with him watching the house, waiting for you?"

Gabe's jaw firmed. "Leave it be, Alex. You're frightening Sylvia."

"Don't mind me." I reached for my coffee cup and resumed reading the newspaper as I sipped. I didn't take much of it in, however. Albert Scarrow had raised two very interesting points. While Gabe's time at war could be chalked up to luck, surviving several minutes under water was something else altogether.

"The boy made a mistake," he said, as if he could read my mind. "Children have no concept of time."

As the son of a horology magician, I suspected he had a very good understanding of it.

* * *

GABE STRAPPED my large suitcase to the rear of the motor with some reluctance. He'd tried to encourage me to stay longer at his house, but I refused. It was Saturday and I was only working a half day; I would go in search of new accommodation in the afternoon. He respected my wishes and gave in. I kept the hat box and smaller suitcase in the backseat with me as he drove the Vauxhall to Crooked Lane.

Alex remained in the vehicle while Gabe and I headed through the entrance into the lane itself. He carried both my suitcases while I held onto the hatbox.

A short man with a needle-thin mustache and oily hair parted down the middle stepped out of the shadows of the buildings. "Mr. Glass! Can you comment on the speculation surrounding your war record and the incident on the Isle of Wight?"

Gabe wedged the smaller suitcase under his arm and placed his free hand on my back, ushering me forward. "No comment."

The journalist whipped out a pencil and notebook from his pocket and trotted alongside us. "How long do you think you were under water for?"

"I can't recall. Not that long. I took a breath."

"Which is it? It wasn't long or you took a breath, or you can't remember?"

Gabe stopped and squared up to the journalist. "Are you Albert Scarrow?"

The man touched the brim of his Homburg. "The one and only."

"Mr. Scarrow, kindly respect my privacy and that of my friends. Stop following me."

"I'm not following you."

Gabe's eyes narrowed. "You didn't follow me from my house?"

"No. I've never been to your house. I don't know where you live."

Gabe's hand, still touching my back, pressed a little firmer. "Then how did you know to find me here?"

Mr. Scarrow pointed at the library door with his pencil. "It's common knowledge that the Glass Library is owned by your family."

"They don't own it. They're patrons. And?"

"And I thought if I waited long enough, someone who works there will arrive. No one answered my knock this morning." He scratched his cheek with the end of his pencil. "I wasn't expecting you to show up, but I consider it a sign that I'm on the right path with my hunch."

Gabe went quite still. He must have realized the same thing as me—if Albert Scarrow didn't know where he lived then he couldn't have been watching the house the other day. So who had? Another journalist? The kidnapper?

"Mr. Glass, what about your war record?"

Gabe and I strode away, but Mr. Scarrow trotted alongside us and repeated his question.

"I have no comment," Gabe growled. "You should leave."

"Excuse me, Miss, but can you tell me what you think of Mr. Glass's incredible feats?"

Gabe suddenly grabbed the journalist by the jacket lapels. His fist twisted the fabric, forcing Mr. Scarrow to rise onto his toes. He hadn't let go of my bags. "I warned you," he growled.

Mr. Scarrow's face flushed as blood rushed to his head. Gabe's grip may be tight but not so tight that the journalist couldn't emit a small squeak.

I clamped a hand over my mouth to smother my own squeak of surprise. I didn't know where to look or what to do. Gabe always seemed so calm, but now he was a tower of fury. I couldn't reconcile the man with the balled fist and clenched jaw with the gentleman I'd come to know.

Had this side of him been there all along?

I didn't get a chance to think about it further. A shot suddenly rang out, and I found myself on the ground, flat on my back, beneath Gabe's body.

CHAPTER 13

*G*abe had made sure that I didn't slam into the ground by circling his arm around me and shielding me from the worst of the impact. I wasn't winded, but I was certainly left breathless. I suspected that was more from the close proximity of the handsome man whose athletic body pressed against mine than any physical exertion.

Gabe's breath quickened too, warming my cheek. He stared at me, unblinking. Very few people hold one's gaze, let alone with such intensity, so when it happens, it can feel like the ground is shifting. Usually it's an unnerving experience, but with Gabe, it was intoxicating.

"Sylvia." His whisper brushed my lips.

"Gabe!" That was Willie's voice, shrill and demanding. "Gabe, get up!"

Gabe momentarily closed his eyes then pushed himself to his feet. He reached down and assisted me to stand too. That's when I saw Willie a few feet away, hands on hips. Alex was speaking to an older gentleman at the door to the solicitor's office, his gestures calming. Professor Nash had emerged from the library.

Mr. Scarrow was on his knees, arms over his head. He tentatively peeked out. Seeing no immediate threat, he got to his feet and scampered out of the lane, glancing over his shoulder at Willie as he did so.

"Have you gone mad?" Gabe snapped at her. "You can't shoot at people!"

She wasn't holding a gun, so I wasn't sure how he knew it had been her. "I didn't shoot *at* him. I aimed at the sky."

"There are former soldiers still shell shocked from the war!"

Willie nibbled on her lower lip, her shoulders slumping. "I forgot about that."

"Apologize to Sylvia."

Willie's spine stiffened. She crossed her arms again, flattening the jacket at her hips and revealing the outline of a gun tucked into the waistband of her trousers. "That man wasn't leaving you alone, Gabe."

"I had it under control."

"He was annoying you."

"You can't shoot every time someone annoys you."

"The world would be a better place if I could." She sighed and put up her hands in surrender. "I'm sorry I fired my Colt, but I ain't sorry for scaring him off."

Gabe scrubbed a hand over his face. His nerves looked more shattered than mine. His comment about former soldiers and shell shock may have been more personal than he made out.

"Why was he bothering you, anyway?" Willie asked. "Is he her man?" She nodded at me.

"I don't have a man," I said.

"Woman?"

I blinked at her. She blinked back. "No."

"He was a journalist," Gabe said.

Willie spat on the cobblestones.

"What are you doing here anyway?" he went on.

"You were gone by the time I got home this morning. I wanted to ask you if there's anything I can do for you today on the case. Bristow said you were taking Sylvia to work so I drove the Hudson to meet you here."

Alex joined us just as Daisy entered the lane wheeling her bicycle. She paused, taking in the scene, then approached.

"You all look a little stunned," she said. "Did I miss something exciting?"

"Only Willie shooting at a journalist," Alex said, regarding Daisy coolly.

"I didn't shoot *at* him!" Willie cried.

Daisy gasped. "You've got a gun? Where is it?"

Willie parted her jacket to reveal the firearm.

Daisy's eyes lit up. "I've never used one before."

Alex groaned. "This meeting is a bad idea."

"No one asked your opinion." Daisy turned her back on him. "Sylvia, why are your bags on the ground?"

Gabe picked them up, handing the hat box to me. Thankfully the suitcases had remained closed. Having my underthings strewn over Crooked Lane for everyone to see would be humiliating beyond words.

"I had to move out of the lodging house. I stayed at Gabe's last night. He was bringing me to work this morning when a journalist made a nuisance of himself. Gabe's cousin, Willie, scared him off by shooting into the sky."

"I hate journalists," Willie told her. "They're vultures."

"Not all of them," Daisy said. "I didn't know her when she was one, but I'm sure Sylvia was an excellent journalist."

Gabe, Willie and Alex all turned to me. Gabe looked disappointed. The other two looked as though they wanted to aim Willie's gun at me.

Daisy's gaze flicked between them. "What have I said?"

Willie stepped closer. We were a similar height and size,

but I suspected she could tear me to shreds if she wanted to, despite being twice my age. My mother's combat lessons would be useless against Gabe's fiery cousin. "I can't believe we let you into our home!"

"I'm not a journalist anymore. I'm a librarian." I gestured to the Glass Library. "I stopped being a journalist after the war. All the men came home and there was no longer any more work for me, so I changed careers." I was aware of my rambling but couldn't stop. Willie made me nervous.

She jutted her chin forward. "So how do we know you're not trying to be a journalist again by reporting on a big story?"

"I'm not!"

"What big story?" Daisy asked.

Willie took another step toward me. "If I find out this is all a ruse to get Gabe to trust you, I'll—"

"Willie!" Gabe grabbed her arm and jerked her back. "That's enough. Sylvia's not lying to us."

"You're too trusting."

He let her go and strode toward the library, one of my bags in each hand. Daisy and I followed, she still wheeling her bicycle.

"What story?" she whispered to me.

"I'll tell you later," I whispered back.

"She can carry her own bags, Gabe!" Willie called out.

He ignored her and I heard Alex scold her for being rude.

Daisy leaned her bicycle against the library wall and followed Gabe and me inside. Professor Nash greeted us at the front desk with a nervous little smile. I suspected he'd heard the entire exchange but was too polite to comment on it.

Gabe set down the bags behind the desk. He looked harried. I had a sudden urge to stroke his hair and massage the tension from his shoulders, but I couldn't even bring myself to meet his gaze.

"I'm sorry about Willie," he said on a sigh. "I feel like I'm always apologizing for her, lately. She's usually difficult but not always like this. Something's bothering her."

"Sylvia's former career," Daisy said.

"It's more than that."

"I'm not a journalist anymore," I blurted out. "Nor do I want to return to that profession. I like being a librarian. It suits me. I wasn't trying to ingratiate myself with you to spy on you for a story or anything like that."

He smiled sadly and touched my elbow to stop me talking, only to quickly let go again. The smile vanished. He rubbed his jaw. "You don't have to explain yourself."

"I do," I said earnestly. "I don't want you to think I deliberately kept the information to myself to trick you."

He clasped my shoulders and dipped his head. "I believe you, Sylvia."

A rush of relief made me feel giddy.

His grip tightened to steady me. "I'll have a word with Willie. I'll make sure she believes you too."

Nobody could make anyone believe something they didn't want to, no matter how compelling. I suspected Willie was determined to continue to dislike and distrust me.

"It doesn't matter," I said. "I won't be seeing her again." The unspoken implication being that I wouldn't be seeing him again, either.

He knew it, too. He let me go and stepped back. He looked away and, with a stiff nod, bade us goodbye and left.

I released a pent-up breath when the door closed behind him. "Well, I didn't think it possible but today has been even more nerve-wracking than yesterday."

"Why?" Daisy asked. "What happened yesterday?"

"I'll tell you after I finish work at midday." I glanced at the door.

She didn't take the hint. "Why can't you tell me now?"

"Because I have to work."

"Professor Nash won't mind. Will you, Professor?"

"Not at all," he said cheerfully. "Your company is most welcome, Miss Carmichael."

Daisy beamed. "See? Now, tell me everything. What's Gabe's house like? Is it enormous? Is the furniture made of gold?"

I laughed. It felt good to laugh. I needed it. Daisy knew just what to say to make me feel better. She giggled too.

"Go through to the reading nook," Professor Nash said, ushering us toward the main part of the library. "I'll make tea. I think we could all do with a cup."

"But I have work to do," I said.

"It'll still be here on Monday."

Daisy took my hand and dragged me toward the nook as Professor Nash headed up the stairs. "Your new manager is a vast improvement on your old one."

We drank tea as I filled Daisy in on the events from the previous day and told them both about the dinner party. The professor was not concerned with me socializing when I ought to be working. He was concerned for my wellbeing and insisted I go with Daisy to begin looking for somewhere to live.

I insisted on staying in the library until midday. I sent Daisy on her way after she finished her tea and said I'd come to her place later. Then I headed into the stacks to re-shelve some books.

They were on all manner of topics, from witchcraft in the Middle Ages to a cult based on metal magic in ancient Persia. I flipped through the pages of each one before slotting them into place on the shelves according to the code Professor

Nash had given me. Since the Dewey Decimal System wasn't granular enough, he'd invented his own cataloguing code. I'd planned to take the list home with me to memorize it but had not yet had the chance. Hopefully things would settle down once I found new lodgings.

I re-shelved the last book on a bottom shelf and, as I straightened, a collection of books caught my eye. They were all about art magic, from modern art to ancient and even cave paintings. My fingers skimmed across the spines as I read until I reached one focusing on modern painter magicians.

I took it to the reading nook on the first floor and settled on the sofa. The light streaming through the enormous window bathed the alcove in a soft glow. I scanned the contents page then skipped to the chapter on paintings. Indeed, there were two chapters. That in itself was revelatory and the reason for the division became more obvious as I read the Introduction.

According to the author, magical paintings could be separated into two categories. One type was for art painted by artists whose magical talent lay in the process of mixing the paint itself. Paint was made from mixing pigments with a resin that allowed the paint to adhere to a surface, and solvents to bind the resin and pigment together. The painter magician's magical talent lay in the combining of these ingredients. They could use a spell to create the perfect color and sheen. They could also apply it to the surface with perfect strokes to create the desired outcome, although no spell was needed for that. The magician's innate talent achieved a beautiful result with or without a spell. The book likened this type of art magician to a watchmaker magician. Time pieces are made up of different metal components, but the magician is not a copper or steel or other type of metal magician. They are a magician who puts it all together in a way that makes it run smoothly and efficiently. A paint magician mixes the ingredients and applies paint in a way that is eye-catching.

The second type of magical painting was quite different. In fact, the magicians that created this type of art were not considered *paint* magicians at all. Their talent was in the *surface* the paint was adhered to. Usually it was a canvas, but it could be any type of surface, such as plaster, metal, ceramic or enamel, to name just a few. The stolen Delaroche was painted on canvas, so it was possible Delaroche was a canvas magician and not a paint magician at all. We didn't know because he was long dead, and he'd kept his magical specialty a secret out of fear of persecution.

I flipped the pages until I reached the detailed section on canvas magicians. I knew a painter's canvas was made from cloth stretched over a frame, but that was the limit of my knowledge. According to the book, canvas is a woven fabric mostly comprised of cotton with a heavy thread weight. The magician who makes a magical canvas is actually a cotton magician. They could theoretically make magical objects of any kind where cotton is used, such as clothing, but they tended to specialize in canvas as a result of family tradition. Cotton was an old magic with many branches of specialty.

I didn't see how knowing about the two different types of magic would help solve the theft, but it may be relevant.

I tucked the book under my arm and went in search of Professor Nash. I found him at the front desk on the telephone. He signaled for me to approach then gave up the chair and handed me the receiver. "It's Gabe. He wants to speak to you."

I leaned closer to the mouthpiece. "This is Sylvia."

His greeting crackled down the line. "I wanted to see if you're all right after this morning's episode."

"I'm fine." I glanced at the desk clock. It was almost midday, time for me to finish work. It would be easier to show him the book rather than try to explain the different magics over the telephone. "Will you be home this afternoon?"

"I'm at Burlington House. There was an attempted theft of the seascape overnight. The attempt failed." I heard a voice in the background then Gabe came back on the line. "Sylvia, I have to go. Are you sure you're not injured from when you hit the ground?"

"I'm all right, thank you."

"Good. Well, goodbye."

"Wait!"

But he'd already hung up. I returned the receiver to its hook. "Professor, may I borrow this book until Monday?"

"Of course. Does it hold a clue?"

"I don't know, but it's worth showing it to Gabe for his opinion."

"You should leave now to catch him at Burlington House."

"It's still ten minutes to midday."

He waved off my concern. "Leave your suitcases here and collect them later. And be careful."

With the book still tucked under my arm, I grabbed my purse, hat and jacket and headed out the door.

* * *

DESPITE THE ATTEMPTED THEFT, visitors to the exhibition were still allowed in and out of Burlington House. Policemen stood at the entrances to each gallery, keeping a watchful eye on the artwork. I paid the entry fee then asked a constable where I could find Gabe. He directed me to Mr. Bolton's office.

The door to the exhibition manager's outer office was open, but the door to his office was closed. The assistant, Mr.

Driscoll, had taken that as an invitation to plant his ear to it to listen in.

I cleared my throat.

Mr. Driscoll jumped. He hurried toward me, his cheeks flushed at being caught eavesdropping. "Miss Ashe! What are you doing here?"

"I need to speak to Mr. Glass. Is he in there?"

"Yes. I mean I believe so. I'm not sure, that's why I was trying to hear. I couldn't make out their conversation, and if I could, I would have instantly backed away." The more he protested, the more I didn't believe him.

"I'll wait out here for him."

Mr. Driscoll seemed to make up his mind about something. He signaled for me to walk with him. "I'm sure they won't mind an interruption if it's very important."

I hadn't said anything of the sort, but I kept my mouth closed. I was as keen to hear what they were discussing as Mr. Driscoll was.

Mr. Driscoll didn't wait for his knock to be answered. He simply opened the door. The unexpected act allowed us to overhear Mr. Bolton mention a name. Tommy Allan.

Gabe and Alex both swiveled in their chairs to see who interrupted them. Gabe rose and offered me his chair. "Is everything all right? Did something happen at the library?"

I refused the chair. "Nothing happened. Everything's fine. I discovered something in this book that I wanted to show you. It might be relevant. I was willing to wait outside…"

The three men looked to Mr. Driscoll, lingering in the doorway. He stammered an apology and backed out of the room, closing the door.

Gabe patted the back of the vacant chair, but I refused again. "I don't want to intrude."

"You're not. Mr. Bolton was just telling us that he saw Tommy Allan running away from the crime scene. You might as well stay to hear what he has to say since you're heavily involved in the case now."

I sat, and Gabe remained standing beside me. He nodded at Mr. Bolton to proceed.

The exhibition manager sat forward, hands clasped firmly on the desk. "As I was telling Mr. Glass and Mr. Bailey, I was doing my rounds last night after the public left when I saw a figure near the seascape. Indeed, he had it off the wall."

"I thought the police were watching it," I said.

He separated his thumbs before tapping them together again. "The constable on duty was in the adjoining gallery, checking on another sound he thought he heard there. The figure was alone in the main gallery. As I said, he was holding the seascape in his hands. I assumed he was about to make off with it. I must have made a sound or gasped because at that moment he turned. It was Tommy Allan. He dropped the painting and ran out of the gallery. I was re-hanging the picture when the constable returned."

"You didn't try to stop Tommy Allan?" Alex asked.

"I would have if I'd had my stick with me." Mr. Bolton picked up his pointing stick and whipped it through the air, practicing the strike he never got to make. "I didn't want to risk trying to stop him without a weapon on me. I informed the constable, and he went in search of the culprit, but to no avail."

"The constable has already given us his account," Gabe told me.

A brisk knock on the door was followed by Mr. Driscoll re-entering. He'd probably been eavesdropping again. He opened his mouth to announce the arrival of the magician sculptor, but Freddie Duckworth pushed past him.

"Good afternoon, all." He went around the room, shaking our hands heartily. His trembled slightly. "I wasn't expecting so many people, but this is an excellent turnout.

It's good to see Scotland Yard taking this investigation seriously."

"Why wouldn't we?" Alex asked.

Freddie drew a flourish in the air with his fingers, answering with a non-answer. He seemed excitable today, like an active boy cooped up inside too long. The wisps of hair he'd so carefully combed over the bald patch on our last visit now stood up on end as if he'd repeatedly run his hand through them. He perched on the edge of the desk and smiled. Considering the reason for our presence at Burlington House, it was out of place.

"Can we see the painting now, Mr. Glass?" he asked. "I am so looking forward to it. I do hope it proves to be magician-made. I know the artist. Not very well, mind, but we have some friends in common." He shot to his feet. "Shall we, gentlemen? And lady, of course." He smiled at me as he extended his hand.

I took it as I rose. Freddie exited the office first, unable to wait for me. I quickened my strides to keep up with him, passing the watchful Mr. Driscoll.

Mr. Bolton accompanied us to the main gallery and instructed his staff to move the public away from the seascape. More people milled around it than any other painting.

Freddie stood in front of the painting and stroked his chin as he studied it carefully. "Take it down. I want a better look."

Mr. Bolton pointed his stick at two of his staff who carefully removed the painting from the wall and held it between them. It was the size of a card table surface.

Freddie slowly circled it. He got up close, crouching to inspect it from all angles. He reached out as if to touch it but stopped a few inches away. He was feeling for magic. "Interesting."

"What is?" Gabe asked.

Freddie circled the painting again, stopping behind it. He waved a hand at the back of the canvas. "It's only magical from the front."

"What do you mean?"

"It also *feels* different to the Delaroche."

"Go on," Gabe pressed.

"I can feel the magical warmth in this painting from the front. The other one, the stolen Delaroche, was magical all over, front and back."

"What does that mean?" Alex asked.

Freddie shrugged.

But I think I knew. "The Delaroche was done on a magical canvas, but this one is done with magical *paint*." I opened the book to the relevant chapter. "I found this in the library. It describes two types of painter magician. One has a talent for the paint itself, mixing it, creating it and applying it. The other type has a magical talent for the painting *surface*. In the case of the stolen Delaroche, perhaps the reason you could feel the magic all over is because the canvas itself held the magic, not the paint. In the case of this seascape, the *paint* is magical."

"That's why you could only feel it on the front, Duckworth," Gabe said. "Because the paint is only applied to the front."

We all turned to look at the seascape being carefully hung back up on the wall for all to admire.

Mr. Bolton asked for the book.

Alex scratched his head and frowned. "I don't understand. Was Delaroche a magician or not?"

"Unlikely," Gabe said. "Unless he was a canvas magician, and he made them as well as painted on them."

"It's probably cotton, not canvas," I pointed out. "Cotton is the primary component of canvas."

Gabe looked impressed. "You've learned a great deal about magic already."

"I think I've learned more about raw materials than anything."

Alex studied the painting, frowning in thought. "So the artless Delaroche painted on a magical canvas, raising his picture from ordinary to extraordinary."

"I wonder if he knew," Freddie said.

Alex wagged a finger at the seascape. "But this had to have been done by a paint magician. Is that right?"

Gabe, Freddie and I nodded.

Mr. Bolton handed the book to Alex. "The magic in the paint means Mr. Duckworth here could only feel the magic in the front, not all over as with the Delaroche."

Freddie wiggled his fingers and grinned. "I'm so glad I could help solve the case."

"It's not yet solved," Alex pointed out.

I joined Gabe, staring at the seascape. "You definitely felt magic in both paintings, Mr. Duckworth?" I asked.

Freddie nodded. "If I were a paint magician, the seascape would have felt stronger to me than the Delaroche, and if I were a canvas magician, the Delaroche would have been more compelling to me personally."

"Cotton magician," I corrected him.

"But I am neither so, although I was drawn to the magic in both, neither artwork felt very intense to me, merely mildly so."

The way magic worked was fascinating, although I still didn't quite understand what he meant by "felt."

Alex handed Gabe the book and he read as we walked away. At the exit to the main gallery, he mumbled an excuse and told us to go on ahead. Alex continued on with Mr. Bolton and Freddie, but I slowed my pace and lost them in the crowd. I doubled back and watched as Gabe stood in front of the seascape again.

He reached out but quickly withdrew his hand before touching the painting, his fingers curling into a fist.

I ducked out of sight and hurried for the exit before he saw me. I found Alex waiting by the main exit and joined him. Moments later, Gabe arrived. He seemed lost in thought and even a little troubled.

Was that because he'd felt nothing when he'd been near the painting? As the son of a powerful magician, the expectation on him to be special must have been enormous growing up. Had his family hoped and prayed that his magical ability would reveal itself in time, only to be disappointed as the years passed and it did not? Or was the pressure entirely of his own making?

Being the artless son of Lady Rycroft could have negatively affected him as he grew up with the weight of expectation on his shoulders. It was possibly still affecting him now. The hopes and dreams of family cast long shadows that weren't easy to escape.

Or so I'd heard. My mother never voiced her hopes for James or me, if indeed she had any. She wanted us to remain in the shadows where it was safe.

But she never told us what she wanted us to be safe from.

CHAPTER 14

"Cocaine?" Alex asked as we walked across the Burlington House courtyard.

"That would be my guess," Gabe said. "I suspected it when I first met him but now, I'm quite sure he has an addiction." To me, he added, "Freddie Duckworth."

I knew it wasn't uncommon for some men to become addicted to the powder after the war ended. It numbed the pain of their experience, albeit only for the brief moments while under the drug's effects.

"It's an expensive habit," Alex went on. "And he knew the Delaroche was magical."

I finally grasped what they were implying. Freddie Duckworth could be behind the theft. Selling the Delaroche on the black market would give him enough money to buy a lot of cocaine. "But he's a successful sculptor. Wouldn't he just sell some of his own pieces if he needed money?"

"Perhaps that wouldn't be enough."

We walked along Piccadilly, me heading back to the library, the men to their motor. When we reached it, however, Gabe opened the back door and indicated I should get in.

"I'll drop you off at Crooked Lane, but I want to speak to the painter of the seascape first."

"I'm not coming," Alex said. "I want to watch Lady Stanhope and Ludlow. It's possible one or both hired Tommy Allan to steal the seascape. Following them might lead us to Tommy."

"Good idea. Collect Willie and split up."

I climbed into the front passenger seat, planning to remain in the motor while Gabe spoke to the painter, but he opened the door for me when we arrived at the Chelsea address of Arthur Partridge. It seemed to be expected that I would participate in the investigation alongside him.

It was difficult not to feel pleased by his easy acceptance.

Arthur wasn't alone in his flat. There were three others with him, including Horatio, all lounging around the sitting room. A miasma of cigarette smoke hung in the air and dirty plates and mugs were scattered about on the tables. The rug could do with a good shake to remove the crumbs, but the stains wouldn't come out without a good scrub.

Arthur was a young man, barely eighteen. The reddish-blond facial hair clinging to his upper lip and chin was baby-fine and patchy, his limbs long and gangly. He was as slim as Freddie Duckworth with the telltale busy hands and jerky movements of someone under the influence of cocaine. Now that I knew the signs, I could see it in Arthur and the others. Not Horatio, however, I was pleased—and relieved—to see. The fingers of all the men were splattered with paint of various colors.

Horatio sprang up from the sofa and kissed each of my cheeks. "Sylvia, Darling! What a pleasant surprise. What are you doing here?" He indicated the book I'd carried in. I hadn't wanted to leave a valuable tome from the library in the motor. "Why have you brought along some reading material?"

I hugged it to my chest, not wanting him to see the title until Gabe had explained the situation to Arthur. "I always carry one with me."

Gabe opened a window for fresh air. "We need to speak to Mr. Partridge." When no one moved, he added, "Alone."

Arthur laughed. "Whatever you tell me will only be relayed to them the moment you leave, so they might as well stay." He indicated the sofa, but the only place left unoccupied had a brown stain. I remained standing alongside Gabe.

Arthur formed a teetering pile out of the dirty crockery while Horatio swept his hand over the table to remove the crumbs. He looked somewhat embarrassed by the state of the place. It was a wonder they didn't meet at his place. It was much nicer.

"We've just come from the Royal Academy," Gabe said. "Last night, someone tried to steal your painting, Mr. Partridge."

Arthur gasped and pressed both hands to his mouth. The other artists finally showed some interest in us.

"Tried to?" Horatio prompted.

"The attempt failed."

"You caught the thief?"

"He got away, but we have a witness who was able to describe him. It will only be a matter of time before he's caught."

Horatio glanced between each of us. "This is linked to the other theft, isn't it?"

"It's possible."

For Arthur's benefit, Gabe explained that he'd been assigned by Scotland Yard to investigate the theft of a magical painting. Arthur seemed unsurprised, however. I suspected the theft had been the talk of the art world in the last two weeks.

"We had a magician expert look at your seascape," Gabe went on. "He confirmed it's also a magical painting."

Arthur gasped again. Then he laughed. He laughed so hard, he snorted through his nose which only made him laugh more. The other painters laughed too, even Horatio.

"What's so amusing?"

"My parents," Arthur said through gasps for air. "They told me I'd amount to nothing if I didn't go to university and become a solicitor like my father." He fell back into the armchair, tears streaming down his face. It was no longer possible to tell if he was laughing or crying.

"Arthur defied them," Horatio went on, since Arthur clearly couldn't. "He insisted on becoming a painter. They threw him out of the house. And now he's going to earn a fortune. Magician-made paintings are highly sought-after. When this becomes public knowledge, the prices for his pieces will go through the roof."

One of the other painters slapped Arthur's knee, dropping ash from his cigarette on Arthur's trousers. Neither seemed to notice. "Well done, old chap. I knew there was something special about that seascape."

"We all did," Horatio added. "It was his first finished piece."

It was my turn to be surprised. "You were able to exhibit your first piece in the Royal Academy's summer exhibition? That is quite a feat."

Arthur wiped the tears from his cheeks, nodding. "I was very pleased, naturally, but I didn't know I was a magician."

"How can you not know?" I asked.

Arthur shrugged. "No one in my family is a magician, or a painter, for that matter. Well, my grandmother dabbled in oils but never exhibited. Oh!" It was the moment the pieces of a puzzle fit together. The puzzle had probably eluded him for a lifetime and now he could finally see it in all its completed glory. "She was passionate about her hobby. She used to encourage me but my parents, especially my father, hated that I loved painting. He hated that she would send me home after I visited her with canvases and pigments. She taught me how to mix paint, how to apply it, but I didn't need much instruction. It was just...instinctive." His eyes welled with tears again. He suddenly grasped Gabe's hand. "It makes so much sense now. Thank you. Thank you for telling me."

Gabe asked me for the book. "This explains paint magic a little more. Please return it to the Glass Library in Crooked Lane when you're finished."

Arthur flicked through the pages with such eagerness I grew worried he'd accidentally tear a page.

"His seascape has garnered a great deal of interest from collectors of magic art," Horatio told us. "Do you think *they* knew?"

"It's hard to say," Gabe said. "Another magician will have felt the magic, but perhaps the fact that it was judged the best piece in the exhibition was enough for it to gain recognition. Do you know many collectors of magical art, Horatio?"

"Only the one. Lady Stanhope."

Arthur pulled a face. "I know her. She's very hands-on, if you understand my meaning."

Horatio chuckled. "She's not shy in her enthusiasm for young male artists. She has launched many a career. Sunk some too, for those who've refused her advances." He drew on his cigarette then blew out the smoke through his nose and mouth as he talked. "If she knew you were a magician, she'd have been impossible to shake."

"She was here yesterday." Arthur gasped again. "Do you think she tried to steal my seascape last night?"

They all looked to Gabe. "What did she say yesterday?" he asked.

One of the artists removed a painted enamel cigarette case

from his pocket and Arthur signaled he'd like one. Horatio struck a match and lit it for him.

Arthur took a long drag and seemed to relax as he blew out the smoke. "She asked to look at my other pieces, but I refused. None are finished. I don't like to show them to anyone until they're complete. I told her to come back in a month." He puffed on the cigarette as he stared into the distance, lost in thought. "She was very nice, but insistent. She demanded she be the first to see them when they're done. She told me the reason my seascape had been moved to the best position in the exhibition was because she'd requested it and that I owed her."

"I hope you didn't promise her anything," Horatio said.

Arthur shrugged. "I had to. She wouldn't take no for an answer."

"You should have come to me for advice. I know how to deal with people who think they're the bees' knees. It requires delicate diplomacy and quite a lot of charm."

One of the other artists snorted. "We know what you mean by charm."

Horatio crossed one leg over the other and blew a smoke ring into the air. "Whatever is required, old chap. Whatever is required."

"I hope she is the thief," Arthur went on. "That way I don't have to see her again and fulfill my promise to show her the pieces in a month. I don't think I'll have finished anything by then." He joined his thumb and forefingers into a beak shape and pecked at his temple. "I just can't concentrate lately. If only I could tap into the creativity I had when I painted the seascape, it would be easy. It's still there, but I just can't *reach* it."

"Perhaps if you stopped taking cocaine you'd rediscover it," Gabe said.

The other artists glanced at one another then sank into the sofa, looking guilty. Arthur merely pressed his lips together.

"I've been trying to tell him that for some time," Horatio said with a glare for Arthur. "Maybe he'll listen to you because he certainly hasn't been listening to me."

Arthur looked down at his cigarette before drawing the smoke in with a deep breath.

"How well do you know Freddie Duckworth?" Gabe asked.

"The sculptor?" Arthur shrugged. "Not very well. Why?"

"Has he ever been here?"

"Once or twice."

Gabe touched the brim of his cap in thanks. "Don't forget to return the book to the library."

Arthur saluted him although I doubted he'd been in the army. He was too young to have fought in the war. "Yes, sir, on Crooked Lane."

We returned to the motor. I knew without having to be told that we were going to Lady Stanhope's house next. I didn't mention returning to the library to collect my bags. I enjoyed being part of this investigation. I didn't want it to end yet.

It was no surprise that Lady Stanhope lived in Mayfair, not far from Gabe's own house on Park Street. The tall, slender townhouse presented an elegant stucco façade to the street, its red door an exclamation mark within the row of black ones.

Gabe nodded at a fellow leaning against a lamp post on the other side of the street, his face obscured by a newspaper. "Alex." Once out of the motor, he didn't look in Alex's direction, so I didn't either.

An elderly butler answered Gabe's knock and informed us that Lady Stanhope had guests and could not see us.

"I work for Scotland Yard and am investigating a crime. I

don't want to intrude, but I will speak to her now. She can either come out here or we can go inside. I assume she's in the drawing room?"

The butler's lips pinched. "Wait here."

We waited in the entrance hall. On the left-hand wall was a hall table and umbrella stand, above which was a large gilt-framed mirror. Several portraits hung on the stairwell wall in which the subjects wore old fashioned clothing. While they looked to be well done, I wasn't particularly drawn to any of them like I had been to the seascape.

"Do you think any are done by magicians?" I whispered to Gabe.

"I don't know, but if I were her, I'd keep my magical paintings upstairs in the drawing room. It's harder to steal large valuables from the higher floors."

Lady Stanhope swanned downstairs dressed in a layered black skirt overlaid with panels of lace embroidered with gold thread. A black silk sash tied at the waist completed the stylish outfit. Despite the somber color of her clothes, she looked almost youthful from a distance. She kept her gaze on Gabe, completely ignoring me.

"While it is lovely to see you again, Mr. Glass, a little warning wouldn't go astray. If you'd let me know you were coming, I could have devoted more time to you."

Now I understood why she was determined to pretend I wasn't present. It was easier to flirt with Gabe.

"We're sorry to interrupt your afternoon tea," he said.

"I would invite you to join us, but I didn't think you wanted to discuss your investigation with all and sundry. You ought to be careful about who you let into your confidence." She didn't need to acknowledge me for it to be clear it was a dig at me. "Now, what can I do for you?"

"Do you collect magical art?"

"Yes."

"And you knew the Delaroche was magical?"

"Yes. You know that, Mr. Glass. It was stolen from my friend." She tilted her head to the side. "Are you insinuating that I stole it?"

"We're looking at all possibilities."

She fluttered a hand at her chest. "Good lord, you think I did! Mr. Glass, I don't see the point of stealing magical art. I want my artworks on display, not hidden away. My husband and I own two paintings done by magician artists and both are in the drawing room for everyone to admire. Whoever stole the Delaroche will have to hide it for decades until the world has forgotten about it. I honestly don't see the point."

"Where were you last night?" Gabe asked.

"Here. Why?"

"An attempt was made to steal another magician-made painting from Burlington House."

She stilled. "There is a magician-made painting in the exhibition? How extraordinary."

"You know there is. In fact, you spoke to the magician painter yesterday. You visited his home and offered to buy one of his other pieces."

"You mean Arthur Partridge? He's a very good artist, but he's not a magician. He would have said something if he were, to drive up the prices."

"He wasn't aware. But I think you were. How did you find out his seascape was magical?"

"I didn't know until you told me just now. I simply liked Mr. Partridge's style. Mr. Glass, these accusations are absurd."

"I'm just trying to establish the facts. And the fact is, you discovered the seascape was magician-made yesterday and last night someone tried to steal it."

"It wasn't me. I didn't know." She reached out and touched his forearm, her fingers skimming his sleeve. He drew away ever so slightly, but enough that she knew he was rejecting her flirtation. The muscles around her mouth twitched as she tried to control her emotions. "This is ridiculous. I'm not a thief, Mr. Glass, and your parents would be ashamed to hear you suggesting as such."

"You deny knowing the seascape was magician-made?"

"Yes! Huggins, see that Mr. Glass and his girl leave. I have to get back to my guests."

Lady Stanhope marched back up the stairs as her butler advanced out of the shadows. He couldn't have stopped Gabe from going upstairs, but Gabe had no more questions for Lady Stanhope.

He did have one for the butler, however. But it was not the question I expected. "Do you know Mr. Ludlow?"

The butler hadn't expected it either. Perhaps, like me, he thought Gabe would want to know if his mistress was indeed home last night as she claimed. Caught by surprise, his stiff exterior slipped off and he opened and closed his mouth before stammering a response. "Th—this way, sir." He indicated the door.

We left and headed down the stairs, past the second set of steep steps that led to the basement service area. Gabe's pace slowed and I thought he might head down to question the servants.

"Huggins clearly knew the name Ludlow," I said.

"He did, but he's too loyal to say anything. We'll question the other servants." He caught my hand as I stepped toward the basement stairs. "Not that way." Still holding my hand, he led me to the pavement. He finally let go, but the thrilling sensation of his touch remained, and it lingered for a long time afterward.

We drove into the rear lane behind the row of townhouses. Coach houses and garages lined one side, while doors on the other side led to service corridors at the rear of each of the townhouses. Gabe parked the Vauxhall, and we located the garage belonging to Lord Stanhope. The door was locked, however. The chauffeur must be out.

We knocked on the door to the main house and a young maid answered. She blinked up at Gabe, a blush infusing her cheeks. That was my cue to step back and let him charm her.

He smiled, earning a smile from her in return. "I'm Gabriel Glass and this is Miss Ashe. We work for Scotland Yard on magical investigations."

Her eyes widened. "Are you a detective?"

"A consultant."

"Like Sherlock Holmes," she said on a breath.

He laughed softly. "If my powers of deduction were as good as his, I'd have solved the case already. I am a fan of Conan Doyle's books."

"So am I." She leaned a shoulder against the door frame, lulled by the friendly banter. "Agatha Clegg, at your service."

"Have you worked here long, Miss Clegg?"

"Two years."

"Do you know of a fellow named Ludlow?"

She straightened. "Is he in trouble?"

"Not at all. I think he can help me clear up a few things. You know him?"

She nodded. "He used to work here. He was the cook until four months ago."

The cook? I would never have guessed that.

"Why did he leave?" Gabe asked.

"He wanted his wages increased. The mistress refused so he left in a huff, said he could get better work somewhere else. He probably could, too, on account of him being a magician."

"A magician? What kind?"

She looked at him as if it were a foolish question. "Cooking, of course. Pastries, specifically."

"Do you know if he found work in another household?"

She glanced over her shoulder to the dark corridor beyond. "The others reckon he didn't. He thought he could walk right into a better job than this one, maybe even work for one of them fancy hotels, but the mistress refused to give him a reference. Who can blame her? He said he wouldn't lower himself to working for the likes of Lady Stanhope again. Some of the names he called her! It makes me blush just thinking about them. Not that he said them to her face, mind, but with an attitude like that, who'd want him? The posh kitchens will have their pick of cooks, so a greedy old curmudgeon like him wouldn't be top of the list, magic or not."

Gabe thanked her and doffed his cap. She nibbled on her lower lip, batted her eyelashes, and gave him a smile. I even heard her sigh as we walked off. Gabe didn't seem to notice that she'd been flirting with him. Perhaps he was so used to it that flirtations no longer had any meaning.

I wondered if women flirted with him when he was with Ivy, or if it was just me. The maid would have known from the plain way I dressed that I wasn't his equal. One look at Ivy and everyone would know she was his intended. The two of them were so well matched that it was obvious.

Gabe opened the motorcar's passenger door for me. "One more stop then I'll take you back to the library. Is that all right with you?"

"Of course."

He leaned on the door instead of closing it. He gave me a smile that I'd come to think of as unique to him, a little bit secretive, a little smug, and very alluring. "You're enjoying this, aren't you?"

"Surprisingly, yes."

"Why surprising?"

"Because I didn't know I had an adventurous side. Inquisitive, yes, but usually I simply read if I want to learn something."

"You didn't interview people when you were a journalist?" He showed no sign that my past career bothered him. I still felt guilty for the way it was exposed, however. It looked like I'd been trying to hide it. I supposed I had.

"All the time, but I never enjoyed it. This is different. This has purpose. Well, a different purpose than my journalism career, that is."

"If you want to continue, we can look at having you put on as a paid consultant for Scotland Yard. That way we can work together more." He punctuated that rather dramatic statement by closing the door.

I waited as he turned the crank handle to start the engine, somewhat dazed by his suggestion. My initial thought was to smile, but it quickly faded as reality sank in. It was an absurd idea. Scotland Yard didn't need me. I had no expertise to offer. Gabe was just humoring me, charming me as he'd charmed the maid. It was easy to get sucked into his sphere when I lowered my guard.

I needed to remember to keep it up in his presence. Daisy had warned me that men who had everything handed to them in life didn't understand the realities of the world for the rest of us. In this instance, she might be right.

* * *

MR. LUDLOW LIVED in a flat located in an old building in a Soho street. At night, the area bustled with theater activity, but in the mid-afternoon, daylight showed it to be grubby with rubbish filling the gutters, and faded theater posters peeling off walls.

I'd just closed my door when a short man lounging against a red post box hissed at us.

"Willie," Gabe said, striding toward him...er...her.

She pushed up the brim of her hat with a finger, revealing her glare, directed at me. "What's she doing here?"

"Helping with the investigation," Gabe said.

"Helping how?"

"Never mind that. Have you got anything to report?"

She sniffed and dragged her gaze away from me. "He hasn't left the entire time I've been here, but I spoke to his neighbor when I arrived. She said he had a visitor early this morning. The neighbor was returning home after a night out, and it seemed real odd for a well-dressed woman to be making calls on an old man like Ludlow at that time. She didn't catch a name, but the description matches Lady Stanhope. She handed Ludlow some money."

"Did the neighbor say how it was between them? Did they argue?"

"She didn't mention it, so I reckon they didn't."

"Good work. We're going up to speak to him now." He went to walk off but turned back. "The neighbor gave that information up easily. Why?"

She rolled her eyes. "Don't worry, she wasn't tricking me. She liked me. She reckons I'm interesting."

Gabe arched his brows.

"She did! She's an actress and you know what they're like." She winked at him. "They're up for anything, and you got to admit a handsome woman with experience is mighty compelling to girls like that. We made arrangements to meet up later tonight."

"Very well, but if the information turns out to be false, I'm blaming you."

She clapped him on the shoulder. "Trust me, Gabe." She watched him walk toward the door then turned to me. "Something bothering you, Sylvia?"

I quickly shook my head. "No."

"Does me being with a woman shock you?"

"Not at all. My best friend is an artist. They're probably even more audacious than actors and, er, American cowgirls." I wasn't sure if that was a real occupation but calling her a *cowboy* didn't seem right.

"Audacious, huh?" Her lips pursed. "You ain't going to win me over with empty flattery."

"I'm not trying to win you over. There's no need."

She narrowed her gaze further but thankfully didn't say anything more.

It wasn't until I walked off that I remembered I didn't want to annoy her too much. Professor Nash said she might recall the silver magician Lady Rycroft had met years ago. He'd also suggested Cyclops might know. Later, I would ask Gabe where I could find him.

Mr. Ludlow answered Gabe's knock then immediately tried to shut the door again upon seeing us. Gabe forced it back and muscled his way into the flat. Mr. Ludlow wasn't intimidated, however. He stood his ground, chin thrust forward, and demanded to know what we wanted.

"Answers," Gabe said.

"I will speak to you but not her. I don't answer to subordinates."

"Then you *can* speak to her because Miss Ashe is not your, or anyone's, subordinate."

Mr. Ludlow made a scoffing sound. "She's a maid!"

"I'm a librarian," I snapped. "And I consult part-time for Scotland Yard alongside Mr. Glass. If you cannot accept that, then it is your problem, not mine, particularly if you refuse to answer our questions. Refusal will look very bad for you." I tried to dampen the rush of energy coursing through me lest I break out into an immature smile of triumph, but it wasn't easy. I managed to keep my reaction to a toss of my head and squaring of my shoulders.

Gabe kept a straight face. "Now that my colleague has made you aware of the importance of honesty, can you tell us where you were last night?"

Mr. Ludlow hesitated, and I thought he would refuse to answer, but then he said, "Here. Why?"

"Someone tried to steal a magical painting from Burlington House. They failed."

"I'm old, Mr. Glass. Do you think I could steal something large and heavy?"

"How do you know it was large and heavy?"

"I guessed. It must have been the seascape."

"Are you guessing the seascape because you know it's magician-made?"

"How would I know that?"

"You're a magician. You felt the magic in it."

Mr. Ludlow's throat moved with his heavy swallow. "You're mistaken. Whoever told you that is lying."

"Everyone in Lord Stanhope's household knows you're a bakery magician. It wasn't a secret. You left there in a huff and claimed you were going to find a better job elsewhere. So how did you end up as a butler working for the Royal Academy of Arts?"

"I did not leave in a huff. My departure was amicable. That's how I got the job at the Academy—Lady Stanhope arranged it. Would she do that if we parted on poor terms?"

Gabe was unfazed by Mr. Ludlow throwing the maid's evidence back at us. "She may have arranged it so that you could identify magical art at the exhibition then steal it for her. Perhaps you didn't like being used that way. Once installed as butler, you refused to do what she wanted, but then she talked you into it. This morning, she came here to pay you for your efforts."

Mr. Ludlow looked equally unconcerned by Gabe's accusations. "You said the attempt to steal the painting failed. If your theory is correct, why would she pay me for something I failed to do?"

It was a good point. Lady Stanhope also made a good point when she said she liked to display her magical artworks. I believed her. She seemed like someone who wanted people to admire her possessions. Stolen paintings would need to be hidden away.

Despite my doubts, Lady Stanhope and Mr. Ludlow were still top of my suspect list. They were certainly up to something that night I'd seen him arguing with her at Burlington House.

I voiced my doubts to Gabe as we took the elevator down to the ground floor.

"I agree on all points," he said. "While we can't see a motive, that doesn't mean there isn't one. Like you, I don't trust them."

"We didn't discover much."

"On the contrary. I discovered you're tougher than you look."

My face heated. "My temper emerges when I'm pushed too far. I shouldn't have said anything."

"You absolutely should have. Ludlow deserved it." We reached the ground floor. He opened the elevator door then the outer cage door and allowed me to step out ahead of him. "Remind me never to get on your bad side."

"I doubt you could." I brushed past him, very aware of our closeness, of his strength and height, and the way he watched me from beneath lowered lids, as if trying to hide his gaze. But I would always be aware of it on me.

Gabe drove me back to Crooked Lane. He offered to collect my luggage from the library and drive me to Daisy's flat, but I insisted it wasn't necessary. I didn't want to take up his time when he was in the midst of an investigation.

"If you can't find a decent boarding house on short notice,

you're more than welcome to stay with us again," he said. "Just until you get back on your feet, of course."

"Thank you, but I'll be fine. Daisy will help me. People have trouble saying no to her."

He laughed softly. "Try telling Alex that."

I passed through the entry into the lane just as light rain began to fall. I ducked my head into my coat collar to keep my face dry and hurried toward the library, concentrating on maintaining my balance on the slippery cobbles.

It was why I didn't see Tommy Allan until it was too late.

CHAPTER 15

ommy Allan lurched out of the shadows, blocking my path. I yelped and stepped back, but his hand whipped out and caught my wrist before I could turn and run.

"Scream and I'll strike you." The scar pulled his mouth into a gruesome, lopsided grimace. "Go on. Try it." His breath reeked of alcohol and cigarettes, and his eyes were red rimmed from exhaustion.

My insides recoiled. I wanted to vomit. I wanted to scream. I want to lash out. But I did none of those things. Despite his drunkenness, his body was tense, ready for me this time. My mother's combat lessons wouldn't save me now. Her other lessons, on the dangers of men, were also useless. I should have listened to her, should have kept alert as I walked alone through a quiet lane.

But I'd been on another plane after spending most of the afternoon in Gabe's company. My senses had been tuned to him, and the way he made me feel good about myself, and not my surroundings. My mother would have warned me not to let my guard down around Gabe, although she would have meant it as a warning about him and not other men who might be lying in wait.

"Strike me and I won't help you." I sounded braver than I felt. I wondered if Tommy could feel me trembling through his touch.

"Help me?" he sneered. "You can help me by staying away. I know you've been looking for me. I know you want to pin the theft on me."

"We only wanted to ask you some questions. If you can prove you were elsewhere—"

"It wasn't me! I didn't do it. What does an ugly, deformed soldier know about beauty and art?" He released me and wiped his mouth on his shoulder, but not before I saw it twist with emotion. "You women are all the same. You see this scar and you hear the way I talk, and you peg me into a hole I can't climb out of. Then you wonder why men like me drink all the time and lash out at you."

He was in pain, but not the physical kind. Not only had he been permanently disfigured and traumatized by war, but he'd also come home to a woman who didn't love him enough to look past his injury. He'd lost his fiancée, his home, his looks, and now his livelihood. He was also staring down the barrel of losing his freedom if he were found guilty of the theft.

No wonder he was desperate. No wonder he attacked me and not Gabe or Alex. I was a woman, and a woman had recently broken his heart and his spirit. But he needed to know violence wasn't the way out of his desperation.

I gentled my voice. "My mother used to warn me about men. Not any specific man or group of men, all of them. She would tell me none could be trusted, not a policeman, priest, or politician. The only man she said I could trust was my brother, but every other man would try to hurt me." Tommy didn't look at me, but I knew I had his attention from the way he scuffed the toe of his boot into the ground. "It took me a long time to realize she was wrong, that not every man wants to do terrible things to me. Some days I do think she might even have been right. But then I remember the employer who lets me work without looking over my shoulder, and the friend of a friend who gave me his painting, and a new acquaintance who is patient and kind and includes me in his investigation when I have no relevant skills."

"Does this story have a point?"

"What I'm trying to tell you is, I know now that not all men are the same, just as not all women are either. We are not all like your former fiancée. Some of us would give you a chance if you let us."

"You done now?"

"Not yet. Violence towards women isn't going to change their opinion of you. It's only going to reinforce it." The rain started to come down harder. We were both getting thoroughly wet. "I won't lecture you. You're intelligent enough to understand that I speak the truth."

He wiped the back of his hand across his jaw and grunted in response. No man likes to be lectured by a woman, particularly a man who doesn't have a very high opinion of us to begin with. But I gave him credit for letting me get to the end of my speech with nothing more than a grunt of defiance.

"I found your address on your employee papers in the manager's office," he said. "That's how I knew where you lived."

I nodded.

"I was angry with you," he went on. "You accused me of being involved in the theft."

"The police questioned everyone. There were many

suspects at that point. But then we discovered that you were living in the very storeroom the Delaroche was stolen from."

"So you thought me guilty because I wanted somewhere warm and dry to sleep?"

"I admit we made assumptions. But you've made them too."

Another grunt. "I didn't do it. If you want to blame someone, blame that fancy lady and the butler. I overheard them arguing on your last night working there. He was angry with her for not paying him."

"Go on."

"He told her to cough up or he'll expose her. Those were his exact words."

They'd definitely argued about money then, and this morning Lady Stanhope did "cough up." If she wasn't paying Ludlow to point out the magical paintings, what was she paying him for?

"Where were you last night?" I asked.

His head jerked up. "Why?"

"Someone tried to steal another painting."

He advanced, hands balled into fists at his sides. "It wasn't me!"

I was a fool if I thought I'd made a connection with this man. He still didn't trust me, and I certainly shouldn't trust him. I backed away. "Did someone pay you to steal it?"

He bared his teeth in a snarl. "No."

I swallowed. "Nobody thinks you are entirely to blame. It must have been a magician who identified the magic in both paintings, and we know you're not one."

Tommy stopped and I wondered if I'd been wrong, if he was a magician. My statement had certainly intrigued him, but he didn't correct me. "I was with someone all last night," was all he said. "She can vouch for me."

"You need to tell the police. They'll follow it up."

He spat onto the cobblestones. "I hate the pigs."

"Mr. Glass isn't a policeman. Come with me. We'll call on him together and you can give him the details of your alibi in person."

He wiped his hand across his mouth, stroking the end of his scar as if he was still unused to it. "So you can trap me?" He huffed a humorless laugh then shook his head. He strode off and was soon gone from sight.

I didn't bother to call after him. I headed to the library where I found the professor reading on the sofa in the ground floor nook, a cup of tea on the table beside him.

"Miss Ashe! You're all wet. Come in and get dry before you catch your death." He stoked the glowing coals in the grate to life and scooped more on top from the scuttle. "There now. Would you like a cup of tea?"

After downing a cup of tea and some cucumber sandwiches, I was nice and dry. Despite the late hour, I knew I couldn't immediately go to Daisy's and look for new accommodation. I had to see Gabe first and tell him about Tommy Allan. Some things were too important to put off. I wasn't visiting because I wanted to see him again.

So I told myself.

* * *

UNFORTUNATELY, Gabe wasn't at home. I told Bristow that I would telephone later, but the butler insisted I wait in the drawing room as he didn't expect Gabe to be long. It ended up being an hour. Bristow brought tea and scones while I waited. I would have refused, had he asked me. I wasn't going to need dinner later if I ate them on top of the sandwiches I'd just consumed at the library, but I found I couldn't turn them down. They smelled delicious.

The tray trembled in Bristow's hands, so I took it from

him with a smile and set it down on the table. He flexed his gloved fingers and gave me an apologetic look. "I'm not as steady as I used to be."

"Have you worked for the Glass family long?"

"Forty years as butler, another eight before that as footman."

No wonder he looked worn out. "There's no footman now?"

"Not at present. We lost the last one to the war."

"Oh. I'm terribly sorry for your loss."

"You misunderstand. He survived the war. He resigned from his position here four years ago when he signed up and didn't want to return once the war was over. We've been unable to replace him, despite advertising. Most of the young men who survived aren't interested in service anymore. They consider it beneath them." He sighed. "The war changed everything."

"It did indeed."

His shoulders stooped forward even more, which may have been his attempt at a bow. It was difficult to tell. As he exited the drawing room, Willie ambled in, thumbs tucked into her trouser waistband. I silently groaned. I'd rather be alone with a drunk Tommy Allan than Gabe's cousin.

She took one look at me and stepped in front of the butler as he tried to leave. She lowered her voice but didn't lower it enough. I could still hear her. "You shouldn't feed them, Bristow. It encourages them to stay."

The only sign he disliked her comment was a thinning of his lips. It wouldn't have mattered if he reproved her, however. She didn't seem to care about anyone else's opinion.

I reached for the teapot only to pull back. Now that the hostess had arrived, she ought to pour. People who lived in houses like this one were usually sticklers for the correct order of things. I didn't know if that applied to the hostesses who dressed like men and spoke with American accents, but I thought it best to err on the side of caution with Willie. That was why I bit my tongue instead of retorting that I wasn't a stray cat and wasn't staying. It was best to pretend I hadn't heard her.

Willie sprawled in one of the armchairs, her legs apart, and glared at me. She made no attempt to pour the tea, so I did it myself. Bristow had brought in four cups, and I offered her one.

She didn't respond. I took that as a refusal and set it down near her. I poured another for myself.

The sound of pouring liquid seemed as loud as a waterfall in the silent room. I tried gently placing a sugar cube into the cup and stirring it, but the *plop* and *clink* still made me wince.

I decided not to help myself to the scones and sat back with my teacup. The moment I settled, Willie leaned forward and picked up a scone. She slathered it with jam and cream then took a large bite. Dollops of cream oozed from the corners of her mouth. She licked them away with flicks of her tongue.

I tried to ignore the sound of her chewing. It wasn't easy, particularly when she glared at me again. She didn't blink, didn't look away, just watched me as if I were an annoying creature she could barely tolerate.

I searched desperately for something to say to break the ice. Fortunately, she hadn't completely frightened my mind into seizing up and I remembered something. "Professor Nash told me you might remember a silver magician that Gabe's mother met years ago. He couldn't recall her name, but perhaps you do?"

Her chewing slowed. She stared at me then her gaze dropped to her teacup. She picked it up. "I don't."

"Never mind. Perhaps Cyclops remembers her."

"He won't."

I simply smiled and let the matter go. I picked up my teacup and sipped. Dear lord, please send Gabe home now. Or, at the very least, send Bristow back in.

Unfortunately, neither event occurred, and I was left very much on my own with one of the most difficult people I'd ever met. It was time to employ some of the tactics I'd learned as a budding journalist. The profession had never quite suited me. I was shy around strangers, particularly men. I preferred research that involved reading books, not the kind where I had to interview subjects. An older journalist at the newspaper had seen my difficulty and taken me under his wing. He didn't teach me how to overcome my shyness—no one can teach that—but he showed me how I could pretend to be confident. I got quite good at it and even employed the tactics in circles outside of work. That fake confidence was how I'd met and made friends with Daisy and found employment at the Philosophical Society library.

At its core, the tactic involved asking the subjects questions about themselves. Most people liked to talk about their own lives and interests, and if I showed that I was listening, it would go a long way to getting them to warm to me.

"Was it difficult, leaving your life behind in America?"

Her only response was a narrowing of her eyes.

"Do you still have family there?"

She sipped her tea, watching me over the rim of the cup. She was closed tighter than the mayor I'd tried to interview after my newspaper accused him of corruption.

"Did you come here so Lord Rycroft could take up his position as the heir to the barony?"

"Quit the chit chat. I ain't buying it."

"Buying what?"

"You ain't interested in me any more than I'm interested in you, so quit pretending."

I looked down at the teacup in my lap. Perhaps I should leave. It would be easier. I placed the teacup and saucer on the table and rose. "I think it's best if I go."

"Aye."

"But I'd like you to know that I'm not pretending. I am interested. I've never met anyone like you before. I don't know why you've decided to dislike me, but—"

"I've got reasons."

I waited.

For a long moment, I thought the silent tactic wouldn't work, but she eventually gave him. Most people usually do. "I got good senses." She tapped the side of her nose. "And the more you stick around, the more I sense trouble brewing."

"I assure you, I won't be around after today. I'm here to pass on some information from a suspect, then I'll leave."

She snorted and shook her head.

"It's not a lie, Willie. I intend to go very soon."

"I believe you do *intend* to. But Gabe will come home and he'll be all gentlemanly and insist you stay again because it's getting late." She glanced at the clock on the mantel. "We both know you ain't going to find new accommodation now."

"I'll stay with my friend Daisy."

"Gabe will insist," she said again. With a resigned sigh, she ordered me to sit with a point of her finger at the sofa. "You want to know why I don't like you?"

I sat. "Yes."

"It ain't personal. Well, maybe it is, in a way. The thing is, Gabe ain't himself these days. He ain't been himself since the war. I want him to be like he used to be." One side of her mouth quirked with her half-smile. "He was fun. We had some wild nights, gambling and going to parties. Not when his parents were in London, mind, just when they were at the estate. They didn't know half of what Gabe, Alex and me got up to."

Cyclops had said Gabe was different now, and perhaps a better person because he'd settled down. But Willie clearly didn't think so, so I wouldn't say anything. I wanted to keep her talking while she was in the mood for sharing.

"The war affected men in different ways," she went on. "Some came back scared, a shell of the man they used to be, some wanted to drink away their sorrows, and others want to have a good time and forget. Gabe came back straight as a die. He wanted to be a good son, a good man, a good citizen. He wanted to have a *purpose*, as if he'd been saved for a reason. So he became a consultant for Scotland Yard, doesn't gamble no more, doesn't drink to excess. He gets to bed at a decent hour and accepts that one day he'll be the next Lord Rycroft. He reckons putting aside his wild past and settling down is the path to happiness. And maybe it is, for him." She pulled a face. Clearly it wasn't her idea of happiness. "That's why he got himself a fiancée. Ivy is his future. He chose her because she makes him happy." She shrugged, as if this was obvious. "She's steady and good, and she's just what he needs after years of turmoil and pressure. I like her, too, and I don't like many folk. Ivy isn't after him for his money, like all the other women were back in the day. I had a real tough time protecting Gabe from the gold diggers. But Ivy has family money. She'll be set for life, no matter who she marries. So I feel all right about letting her marry Gabe."

She might as well have called *me* a gold digger. While I ought to be offended, I found I couldn't be. She was protecting Gabe in the only way she knew how. She probably would have preferred to stand beside him on the battlefield, but women weren't allowed. She wouldn't be the first person left behind on the home front who'd found a different way to protect her loved one.

As I had done with Tommy Allan, I gentled my voice. "You're mistaken if you think I'm trying to break up their relationship. I'm not. I hardly know him. My interest in Gabe began because he could help me learn about my family's background. It continued because he involved me in the investigation. Gabe is a good man. I like him and I agree with you. He deserves to be happy. Ivy seems very nice, too. I hope they have a happy future together."

She eyed me closely. "You're a little like her."

"Oh?"

"You're not frightened off. The others scared too easy. That's why they weren't good enough. They didn't love him enough."

I picked up my teacup and sipped to hide my smug smile. I seemed to have passed some sort of test she'd set for me. I could picture the poor girls of Gabe's youth, trying to get to know him better, only to come up against his fierce cousin. A fierce cousin who spoke of love. She was full of contradictions.

Somehow, knowing the reasons for her odd behavior helped settle my nerves. Hopefully we could mend the divide between us now that my intentions were clear.

"I want to reiterate," I said. "Gabe and I are friends, nothing more."

Willie still scowled, however. It would take more than words for her to believe me.

It was an enormous relief to see Gabe and Alex walk in. It must have been written all over my face because both cast me sympathetic looks.

"I saw your bags in the hall," Gabe said. "Is something wrong?"

"I needed to pass on a piece of information."

"I hope you haven't been waiting long."

Willie thought he was speaking to her. "Too long."

Gabe poured two cups of tea, while Alex helped himself to a scone. He bit into it without bothering with jam and cream, closing his eyes and sighing deeply. "This is so good. Just what this starving man needs."

"Starving?" Willie snorted. "You ate a big lunch. You're going to be as fat as your father if you ain't careful."

"He's solid, not fat."

Gabe offered to top up my cup, but I declined. "What did you need to tell me?"

"Nothing that couldn't have waited," Willie piped up.

Considering she hadn't heard what I needed to say, she couldn't know that. But now that I'd thought it through, I realized she was right. It wasn't important. It could have waited until tomorrow. "Tommy Allan was waiting for me in Crooked Lane."

Gabe swore under his breath. "I should have come with you."

"We just talked. He told me he has an alibi for last night."

"Ha!" Willie barked. "You can't believe pig swill like that."

"Did he give you the details?" Gabe asked.

I shook my head. "He claimed he was with a woman. He also told me he overheard Ludlow demand that Lady Stanhope pay him. 'Cough up' was the phrase he used."

Gabe nodded thoughtfully. "It seems more and more likely that Ludlow was telling Lady Stanhope which paintings were magical, for a fee. That puts her squarely in the mix for the theft of the Delaroche and the attempted theft of the Arthur Partridge seascape. Alex, Willie, can you report on their movements this afternoon?"

They each gave an account of the comings and goings of

Lady Stanhope and Ludlow. Both were brief and provided no more clues.

When she finished her account, Willie added, "Now that Sylvia's given her information, she should get going. Didn't you say your friend was waiting for you, Sylvia?"

"Yes, she is." I rose. "Thank you for your hospitality, Willie. I enjoyed our chat."

All three sets of eyes narrowed.

Then Alex laughed. "You're a joker."

Gabe smiled. "Stay for dinner, Sylvia. In fact, you should stay the night. I can't have you roaming around in the dark looking for a lodging house that might have a vacancy. Not with Tommy Allan still on the loose."

"I can sleep at Daisy's."

"It's too cramped for two. Stay here. You can have your old bedroom." He made it sound like I was a regular lodger.

The thought must have occurred to Willie too. She looked angry, but a quelling glare from Gabe had her snapping her mouth closed. She must respect him a lot to keep her opinion to herself. I doubted she was someone who did that for just anyone.

"It's the least we can do," Alex said with a childish smirk of satisfaction aimed at Willie. "You've been a great help in this investigation, Sylvia. And I'd wager Daisy's breakfasts aren't half as good as ours. Mrs. Ling puts on a delicious spread."

Willie opened her mouth again, but shut it once more upon another quelling glare, this time from Alex.

Gabe tugged on the bell pull to summon Bristow then asked him to inform Mrs. Bristow that I would be staying the night.

"We made the assumption that Miss Ashe would require the spare room again, sir. Mrs. Bristow has already made it up. I'll take up Miss Ashe's luggage now."

"No need. I'll do it."

As Bristow gave a nod, he caught sight of Willie glaring at him. His features hardly moved, but somehow all his wrinkles formed what could almost be called a smile. Willie muttered something under her breath.

Gabe invited me to leave the drawing room ahead of him. I waited while he fetched my bags from the entrance hall and together we headed upstairs. "I don't let Bristow carry anything heavier than a tray anymore. He hates admitting it, but he's getting on in years and can't do the things he used to."

"He must be nearing retirement age."

His eyes widened and he glanced around. "Don't mention that to him, or to Mrs. Bristow. Neither of them will entertain the thought of stopping. They've refused, even though there's a cottage set aside for them on the estate. Mrs. Bristow has a maid to help her, but Bristow needs a footman."

"He told me you've had trouble finding one."

"We'll keep looking."

He deposited my bags inside the bedroom and was about to leave when he spotted a small blue gauze pouch tied with a white ribbon on the pillow. A card was attached. "What's that?"

I picked it up and sniffed. "Rose petals." I read the card. "It's from Mrs. Bristow, welcoming me back. How lovely. She's very sweet. Last night, she left a warming pan in the bed. It was very thoughtful of her.

"Odd. She doesn't do that for anyone else."

He informed me that dinner would be at eight then left, closing the door behind him. I wondered if he was going to telephone Ivy to tell her I was staying overnight again.

At eight, I headed to the dining room, familiar with the layout of the house now. The meal was a casual affair with just the residents sitting down to eat. Ivy didn't join us and her name wasn't mentioned all night.

Once dinner was over, Willie announced she was heading out. "The SSO are playing at a club in Kingly Street tonight."

"SSO?" I asked.

"Southern Syncopated Orchestra," Willie said with barely disguised impatience. "It's a jazz band."

"I like the SSO," Alex said.

"Come with me."

He hesitated, most likely on my account.

"Don't worry about me," I said. "You should go."

"Would you like to go too, Sylvia?" Gabe asked.

Willie looked like she wanted to throttle him. She didn't want to socialize with me.

I put her out of her misery. "I'll be quite all right here with my book."

After a little more discussion, Gabe decided to stay home while Alex would go with Willie to the club. They departed at ten-thirty, which Gabe assured me was an early hour. Sometimes the music and dancing didn't get into full swing until two or three AM.

Although I had my own books to re-read, Gabe offered to show me his library. I tried to contain my excitement but the sight of so many books packed into the shelves elicited a small gasp. I turned slowly and gazed up at the shelves, my skin prickling with the knowledge and possibility contained within the pages. There were shelves on all the walls, except where there was a fireplace and windows, all filled with books of varying sizes. On closer inspection, I realized they were also on various topics.

"Are any about magic?" I asked.

Gabe joined me and removed a book with a blue cover from a shelf. "No. The Glass Library has all of those. These are books collected by my grandfather during his travels. He traveled widely." He showed me the book. "This is one of his journals, written before he met my grandmother in America. It covers the time he spent in Egypt."

The book wasn't just an account of each day, although it did include that. It contained sketches of the places and people he encountered, tickets to shows he'd seen, or a leaf from an interesting native plant. A photograph of him standing beside a camel looked remarkably like Gabe.

"The men in your family all look alike." I closed the book. "May I borrow this to read?"

"Of course. You do realize that means you'll need to return it, which in turn means you'll have to come back here." He leaned a shoulder against the bookshelf and gave me a crooked smile. "I overheard you assure Willie you won't need to return after tonight."

"Ah. Yes. She seemed to need the assurance."

His smile vanished. "Don't let her scare you."

"She doesn't. I know she's merely trying to protect you."

"She's the one who needs protecting, usually from herself. She still thinks she's twenty years old and bullet proof." His gaze shifted to a folded newspaper on the central table. "Did she accuse you of spying on me to gather information for an article?"

"Not this time. Perhaps she believed me this morning when I denied it."

He remained silent but didn't look convinced.

"Do you believe me, Gabe?"

He offered a reassuring smile. "Of course."

"Good," I murmured.

"Why 'good?'"

I pretended to study the journal's blue cover to avoid looking him in the eye. I lifted a shoulder in a shrug. "Because I don't want you to think poorly of me."

He reached out, as if to touch my shoulder, but diverted

his hand and rested it on the bookshelf instead. His finger caressed one of the spines. I didn't dare look at his face and instead concentrated on the journal in my hand. "I can't," he said quietly. "I mean, I don't think poorly of you. Quite the opposite." He cleared his throat and lowered his arm to his side. He took a small step back, away from me.

"I'm glad we had this discussion then." It was said lightly, as if his words had not made my heart thud wildly. "I think I'll retire. Goodnight, Gabe." I stepped around him only to pause and look up at a high shelf. One of the books had caught my eye. "What's that one about? The one with the faded green spine with the decorative border?"

It was too high for me, and even Gabe had to stand on his toes to retrieve it. He didn't need to be so close to me to do so, however. I could have moved away, too.

But I did not. I liked being near him.

He pulled the book off the shelf and handed it to me but did not immediately let go. We faced each other over the top of it, neither of us looking away to break the spell that enveloped us. I was drawn to him, sucked into the depths of his sea-green eyes, overwhelmed by his masculinity and good looks, and something baser that I couldn't explain. Having the undivided attention of this man was a heady, dizzying experience.

Gabe suddenly drew in a sharp breath and stepped away. We both let go of the book at the same time. I caught it before it fell on the floor and hugged it to my chest.

"Good catch," he said.

"Goodnight, Gabe."

"Goodnight, Sylvia."

I hurried out of the library with both books. I didn't even know what the green one was about. It didn't matter. The topic was irrelevant. The book was irrelevant. I'd only asked him to retrieve it because it meant he'd have to stand close to me to do so and that had led to the moment of madness. It hadn't been a conscious decision to ask him to get it, but what else could have led me to do so?

Gabe was not a free man, and I was an utter fool for staying here again. It was tantamount to throwing myself at him. My mother would have been horrified. I simply felt ashamed.

CHAPTER 16

I couldn't sleep so read the book with the green cover. It was about birds native to North America, written sixty years ago. It was surprisingly interesting. I fell asleep a little before dawn, the open book on my chest, and woke to the distant sound of the telephone ringing. It was almost eight. For me, that was late.

I quickly dressed and went downstairs to find Gabe returning to the dining room for breakfast. He looked grave.

"Cyclops just telephoned," he said. "He was called out to Wapping a few hours ago. A body was found floating in the river. It's been identified as Tommy Allan."

I sat heavily on one of the chairs, not quite able to believe it. Poor Tommy. "Does Cyclops know what happened?"

He poured coffee from the pot at the sideboard and handed a cup to me. I clutched it in both hands but didn't sip. "There were signs of a fight as well as a laceration on the back of the head which was probably the fatal blow. Cyclops will know more after the autopsy."

I shivered.

"I'm sorry," he murmured. "That was a little too much information."

"It's all right. But it just occurred to me that I was one of the last people to see him alive."

"It's a sobering thought." He sat at the table opposite me. He'd already started breakfast, but it was unfinished. He pushed the plate away, his appetite gone. "Did he say anything to you yesterday? Anything that might suggest who he was going to see last night, or where he was going?"

I tried to recreate the conversation in my head. Tommy told me he'd been with a woman on the night of the attempted theft, but he'd not given any details about her. Nor had he mentioned anyone else.

But he had given me a small clue in his reaction to something *I* said to him. "I mentioned the fact that a magician had identified both paintings as being magician-made, someone who wasn't necessarily an art magician but could be talented in another discipline. His expression changed and he left in a hurry."

Gabe sat forward. "You think he realized who that magician is?"

"It's very likely." My gaze connected with his and we both spoke the name at the same time. "Ludlow."

Gabe pulled his plate close again and picked up his knife and fork. "We'll pay him a visit after breakfast."

I wasn't sure if he was referring to me accompanying him or Alex. He didn't elaborate until after we'd finished eating.

"We'll meet in the entrance hall in fifteen minutes. Will that give you enough time?"

"You want me to go with you?"

"Of course. This is as much your investigation now as mine. Besides, if I've learned anything over the years, it's to not interrogate suspects alone."

"And you don't want to wake Alex."

He gave a sly grin. "According to Bristow, Alex didn't come home last night. Nor did Willie." He seemed unconcerned. Perhaps it happened frequently.

Fifteen minutes later, we were motoring to Ludlow's flat. I was very aware of my conviction to stay away from Gabe, but I conceded that this was different. This was part of the investigation and wasn't about staying in his house.

Ludlow did not welcome us, but he didn't try to close the door in our faces this time. He knew he couldn't possibly keep Gabe out. He didn't invite us in either, however, and we had to question him while standing in the communal corridor.

"Where were you last night?" Gabe began.

"Why?" Ludlow shot back. He sounded nervous, but that could have been because he was once again under interrogation. He knew our presence meant we hadn't believed him yesterday.

"Just answer the question."

"I went out for a bite to eat at about seven. I returned at ten-to-nine. The staff at the Crown and Thorn will remember me. One of the neighbors saw me come home." He indicated the door to the flat opposite.

"And after nine? Did anyone see you?"

Mr. Ludlow hesitated, then shook his head. "I was here alone."

"When was the last time you saw Tommy Allan?"

"Who?"

"You know who he is. One of the packers employed by the Royal Academy of Arts. We mentioned him to you yesterday."

Mr. Ludlow's face turned ashen, making the age spots in his cheeks stand out more.

"If you don't answer the question, I'll have to ask you to accompany me to Scotland Yard." I wasn't sure how Gabe was going to manage that. Tie Ludlow up and bundle him into the Vauxhall?

Then I realized it was probably merely a tactic to frighten Mr. Ludlow into speaking. It worked.

"I don't know who that man is. I've never met him, although I think I know the fellow you're talking about. I saw him watching Lady Stanhope and me in the gallery when we were...talking." Mr. Ludlow's throat moved with his heavy swallow. "Miss Ashe, you believe me, don't you? We were colleagues, once. You know I'm a man of my word." He must be panicking if he was appealing to me.

"I know you to be a lot of things," I said. "But trustworthy is not among them. Snobbery and rudeness seem to be more your thing."

"I *am* trustworthy! I'm sorry if I ever treated you poorly. It's just the way of things, as an employer to an employee." His wide eyes turned to Gabe. "You know how it is, Mr. Glass."

Gabe gave him a flat glare. "No."

Mr. Ludlow dragged a hand through his thin hair. "Listen." He kept his voice low. "I admit that I identified the seascape as being magical for Lady Stanhope. I felt the magic in it the moment I got near it. When you saw us arguing, Miss Ashe, I was demanding she give me what she promised in exchange for my advice. She was refusing to at that point, as she said I'd not told her something she hadn't worked out herself. She'd gathered from the throng attracted to the painting that it was magician-made. That night in the gallery, I threatened to inform the newspapers what she was doing if she didn't pay."

"And what is she doing?"

"Hiring me to identify magical paintings before the artists themselves knew. She'd swoop in, offer the market value to buy it or one of the artist's other works, then, when the magician became aware of their talent, the price would rise and she'd have a valuable painting on her hands. My involvement in her scheme began and ended with identifying the magic paintings."

"How many paintings had you identified for her before the seascape?"

"None. That was the first time. I think she'd thought of the scheme after the theft of the Delaroche. It occurred to her that no one, including the original artist, had known for certain that it was magician-made until another magician identified the magic in it. She saw the potential, if she could only buy the paintings early, and that required a magician to identify which ones contained magic." He tapped his chest. "She knew I was a magician. She promised me a glowing reference if I helped her during the exhibition as well as a small payment. After it was over, I was going to look for work as a chef."

"Why didn't you tell us any of this yesterday?" Gabe asked.

Mr. Ludlow released a shaky breath and visibly relaxed. "I wanted that reference. I *needed* it. I only have a few years left in me. I want to fulfil my lifelong dream of working in the grand kitchen of a luxury hotel, but the managers don't hire people they can't trust. A good reference is vital." Now that he sensed Gabe believed him, his old confidence returned. Or, rather, his arrogance. "I haven't done anything illegal."

"You've hindered an investigation by not answering our questions honestly when they were first asked."

Mr. Ludlow went to close the door, but Gabe put up his hand to stop it.

"Tell me. Has Lady Stanhope given you that reference yet?"

"She paid me the money but has yet to give me the reference. Why?"

Gabe merely smiled. He tugged on the brim of his cap. "Good day, Mr. Ludlow." We walked off toward the elevator.

"Don't tell her I said anything! Mr. Glass! I'm begging you not to mention we had this conversation."

The elevator was all the way down on the ground floor and would take an age to reach us. "I'd rather take the stairs," I said.

We headed down the staircase.

"Miss Ashe! Miss Ashe, please, make him see reason." Mr. Ludlow leaned over the railing, shouting down the stairwell as we retreated. "I'll write an excellent reference for you if you can convince him not to speak to her. You'll be able to get any type of employment in domestic service that you want." His voice echoed around the stairwell, strong at first, then fading to nothing.

We closed the door to the building, ending his pathetic plea.

Gabe opened the passenger door of the motorcar, but his mind was clearly not on the task. He barely opened it wide enough for me to slide onto the seat. "He didn't know the Delaroche was painted on magical canvas, not with magical paint," I said. "Nor does Lady Stanhope, I'd wager. They think Delaroche was a magician, like Arthur Partridge."

With the motor's door still open, Gabe tapped a finger on the edge of the windshield. A small frown dented his brow.

"Gabe?"

He shook himself. "Sorry. I was thinking. We know Ludlow is a magician and have been assuming he was the only one. But other magicians could have seen the Delaroche and the seascape and recognized the magic in them."

"But we assumed Ludlow is guilty because Tommy Allan worked it out. I told him yesterday that a magician is involved in the theft. He knew Ludlow was a magician, so... here we are." I nodded at the building.

Gabe's eyes flashed with triumph. "What if Tommy knew *another* magician, someone who is not Ludlow?"

I tried to think it through. "It would have to be a magician connected to the art world. Someone Tommy knows saw both paintings. That limits it to another employee or an artist who delivered their work to Burlington House. Tommy had nothing to do with the public. That's still a lot of people, Gabe."

"But it narrows the field. Who shall we question first? Artists or employees?"

"Artists," I said. "Specifically, someone we know is a magician."

"Freddie Duckworth, the sculptor. Very well."

By the time Gabe cranked the car engine to life and took his seat behind the steering wheel, I'd changed my mind, however.

"Wait," I said as he pulled a lever that made the motorcar's gears clunk. "I think we should go to Burlington House. Tommy admitted he snuck into Mr. Bolton's office to find my address. What if he saw something there that indicated Mr. Bolton is a magician of some description?"

"Or the assistant, perhaps, if the employee files are kept in the outer office. I know a way we can find out before we confront them." He turned the motorcar into the traffic and sped off.

I had to clamp my hand to my hat to stop it flying away. It was difficult to talk over the noise of the engine, so I was left to wonder where we were heading. It appeared to be back to Mayfair.

The journey allowed me to think about the few occasions I'd been in Mr. Bolton's office. What evidence was there that he or Mr. Driscoll were magicians? What could Tommy Allan possibly have seen when he'd snuck in?

And then it occurred to me.

Gabe had also been thinking on the drive. The moment he switched off the engine outside his Park Street townhouse, he turned to me. "The assistant was acting oddly about being sick. Did you notice that? Could he have been well all along and lying about his illness?"

"He was acting oddly, but I can't think why or how it relates to this."

He sighed. "True. Wait here. I'll be back in a few moments." He went to open his door, but I caught his arm.

"Gabe. I think it's Mr. Bolton. I think he's a magician, most likely rubber."

"Rubber?"

"He had a lot of stamps in a box. They were all neatly arranged, lovingly almost. He seemed proud of them."

"That sounds like a magician infatuated with his craft." He smiled. "Hopefully I can confirm your hunch." Again, he asked me to wait.

I watched him go, taking the front steps two at a time. Bristow opened the door just as Gabe reached it. He gave Gabe a bemused look as he rushed past then peered outside.

I waved. He came down the steps to join me. "Would you like to come inside, Miss Ashe?"

"I'll wait here, thank you. Gabe said he won't be long." I was about to ask him why he thought Gabe was being so secretive about this visit but decided against it. It wasn't fair to ask a servant to tattle on his employer.

True to his word, Gabe returned only a few minutes later. He cranked the car engine, climbed into the seat beside me, and smiled broadly. "You were right. Bolton is a rubber magician."

"You seem certain."

"I am." He drove off before I could speak, but I wasn't sure I would have asked him to elaborate anyway. Our friendship wasn't strong enough for me to be more forthright.

If he wanted me to know how he confirmed Mr. Bolton was a rubber magician, he would have told me.

The exhibition at Burlington House was quiet. It had been open to the public for almost two weeks and being a Sunday morning when many were attending church meant the crowds were low. I worried that we wouldn't find Mr. Bolton there, but he was in his office, attending to some paperwork. There was no sign of Mr. Driscoll, his assistant.

Mr. Bolton blinked up at us in surprise. Something in our expressions must have alerted him to our reason for being there, because his hand closed over his pointing stick. He did not raise it, however. He was going to try to bluff his way out first.

"Good morning, Mr. Glass, Miss Ashe. This is a surprise. Have you come to tell me you found the wretched Tommy Allan?"

"He was found dead this morning," Gabe said.

Mr. Bolton's face blanched. His lips moved, but no sound came out.

Gabe indicated the filing cabinet to one side of the room. "Are employee files kept in there?"

Mr. Bolton blinked furiously as he tried to catch up with the rapidly moving conversation. "Yes. Why?"

"When did you start working here?"

"A year before war broke out." He indicated a photograph hanging on the wall, showing six soldiers with their arms around each other and Mr. Bolton in an officer's uniform standing to one side. "I repeat: why?"

"Did you work for your family's rubber manufacturing business before that?"

Mr. Bolton remained silent.

Gabe rounded the desk and pulled open the top drawer. Mr. Bolton raised his stick and whipped it down to strike Gabe's hand, but Gabe snatched it out of his grip.

Mr. Bolton shot to his feet. "This is outrageous! You can't come in here and rifle through my belongings!"

Gabe removed the box of stamps from the drawer and flipped open the lid. There were at least eight stamps inside, all with polished wooden handles and rubber bases. Several were spotless, as if they hadn't been used or had been recently cleaned.

Gabe pulled one out, but Mr. Bolton snatched it off him, returned it to the box and closed the lid. He hugged the box to his chest. "Get out," he growled. "You have no authority here."

"You made that yourself," Gabe said. "You made all of them, probably before the war. For whatever reason, you no longer work in your family's rubber factory, but you kept some pieces. Holding them, cleaning them, using them, satisfies your compulsion, the itch you must scratch from time to time. For you, the rubber pieces you keep near are in the form of stamps, which your family of rubber magicians manufactures."

Mr. Bolton's grip on the box tightened.

Gabe continued. "Being a magician, you were able to identify magician-made paintings. You stole one with the intention of selling it on the black market. You attempted to steal another by an as-yet unknown magician painter, but the attempt failed."

"I did nothing of the sort!" His pitch rose and a bead of sweat slid down his temple. I was no expert at interrogation, but he looked guilty to me.

Gabe clearly thought so too. "Sylvia, please use the telephone on Mr. Driscoll's desk to call Scotland Yard. Tell them to send men to take Mr. Bolton into custody for the theft of the Delaroche, the attempted theft of the Partridge seascape, and the murder of Tommy Allan."

Mr. Bolton stumbled into the chair, his jaw slack and his shoulders stooped.

It felt like an interminably long wait for the police to arrive as we had to listen to Mr. Bolton alternately deny the crimes in between stretches of morose silence. Gone was the direct and commanding man who'd employed me. I'd liked him. I'd respected him as a manager and as a person. In comparison, the fellow slumped at the desk resembled a puppet without strings.

Cyclops arrived with four constables to oversee the arrest. He listened as Gabe explained our theory. When laid bare, it became clear the evidence was thin. It might not be enough for a conviction.

Cyclops didn't point that out, however. After Mr. Bolton was escorted from the office, he clapped Gabe on the shoulder. "Good work. Hopefully he'll confess after a few hours stewing in the cells."

"And if he doesn't?" Gabe asked.

"We might find something in his house to link him to the theft and murder." He smiled at me. "What did you think of your first arrest, Sylvia?"

"It was quite a thrill, although Gabe did all the work. I was merely a bystander."

"I'm sure you've been a great help to Gabe or he wouldn't have involved you. Where's Alex?"

Gabe checked his wristwatch. "He might be home by now."

Cyclops sighed. "I wish he'd settle down."

"He will, in his own time."

"His mother worries. We both do."

"There's no need. He's with Willie."

Cyclops's gaze drilled into Gabe.

Gabe put up his hands in surrender. "Sorry, I just heard how that sounded. I'll keep an eye on him, I promise."

Cyclops picked up the box of rubber stamps then went to follow his men out of the office, but Gabe called after him.

"Can you ask Bolton about the attempted kidnapping on me? I want to know if he was involved."

Cyclops nodded and left.

Gabe and I followed behind and headed back to the motorcar, parked on Piccadilly. Neither of us spoke. I felt somewhat low after the excitement of the confrontation, and perhaps Gabe did too. For me, it was because the investigation was over. My part was finished. The arrest ended my involvement, and I had no more reasons to see Gabe.

I'd come to enjoy our time together. My spirits lifted upon seeing him. Conversation wasn't required for me to feel comfortable in his company. I liked simply sitting alongside him in the motorcar.

It was probably just as well we wouldn't see each other again if I felt that way.

Whether Gabe was quiet for the same reason or because he worried there was not enough evidence against Mr. Bolton, I couldn't tell. We drove back to Park Street where we were met by a sleepy Alex. Apparently, Willie had gone straight to bed upon their return just after we left this morning, but Alex stayed up. Gabe explained what had happened. Alex groaned when he mentioned his father came to take Mr. Bolton away.

"I'm going to get a lecture next time I see him."

"Probably," Gabe said cheerfully.

Alex wiped a hand over his face. "I need another coffee. Anyone else?"

I declined. "I'll take my leave now. I want to spend the rest of the day looking for a place to stay."

Gabe drew in a breath as if he was about to say something but stopped. He simply nodded. "I'll help with your bags." He asked Bristow to have Dodson bring around the Hudson to drive me home, then we headed upstairs.

My luggage was waiting for me just inside the bedroom, a small posy of sweet peas and jonquils sitting on top of the hat box. The attached note card was written in Mrs. Bristow's now-familiar hand. "We hope your stay was comfortable," it read. "You are very welcome to call on us at any time. The residents of 16 Park Street have enjoyed your company and will miss you." It was signed Mr. and Mrs. B.

I smiled. She was most thoughtful.

Gabe frowned as I tucked the note into my bag and picked up the posy and hat box. "What do I have to do to receive the same treatment? The most Mrs. Bristow's given me is a needle and thread to sew a button back on my jacket myself."

"Was that after a night out with Willie and Alex?"

He flashed a lopsided grin in answer.

He had more people who cared about him than he realized. His parents might have resided at their country estate while Gabe lived a wild lifestyle in London, but he had Willie looking out for him, as well as Cyclops and Catherine, and Mr. and Mrs. Bristow seemed to have taken on the role of parents too. They'd all made sure Gabe didn't come to any harm because of his wayward lifestyle and that he continued to grow into a man who was down to earth, kind, and someone they could all be proud of.

I blinked away tears as I headed downstairs, not quite sure why Gabe's good fortune made me tearful in the first place. While I waited for Dodson, I asked Bristow if I could say goodbye to his wife.

He led me through a door that was difficult to see in the shadows of the staircase, down a narrow flight of stairs, to the basement service area. I thanked the housekeeper, cook, and maid for their hospitality, praising Mrs. Ling for her delicious food. She shook my hand, smiling, and told me she would like to make me a specialty from her home country of China one day.

"I would be honored." I didn't tell her I wasn't coming back. She seemed so happy with my response that I didn't want to disappoint her.

By the time I returned to the entrance hall, the motorcar had arrived. The engine of the Hudson rumbled like distant thunder, and Dodson stood by the rear passenger door, waiting for me.

Gabe, who'd sported a tight smile on his face when I returned from the basement service area, shook my hand as if we'd just completed a business transaction. I suppose we were colleagues, after working together for the last few days, in a way. Still, it felt odd. But how else could he farewell me? A kiss on the cheek seemed too familiar, a bow too formal. So a handshake it was, and not a lingering one either. Indeed, he suddenly seemed eager for me to go. He picked up my bags and carried them down the front steps. He strapped them to the luggage rack at the back of the Hudson while I slipped into the rear seat. Dodson closed the door and once the luggage was secured, we drove off.

Gabe simply waved at me from the pavement. I waved too and then faced forward. There was no point in looking back. No point at all. That way lay melancholy. I'd had too much of it in recent years. It was time to look forward to what came next. Only forward.

CHAPTER 17

*D*aisy and I spent Sunday afternoon looking for a lodging house. We gave up at dusk. Those that did have rooms available did not like the fact I had no reference from my previous lodging house matron nor one from my last employer. My employment at the Glass Library wasn't long enough to qualify. Without references, the reputable lodging houses wouldn't take me. I didn't want to try the disreputable ones. Even Daisy turned her nose up at those, and she was far more intrepid than me.

She insisted I stay with her until I found something more permanent. "I'll enjoy the company," she told me over dinner at a cheap Italian restaurant around the corner from her flat. "When I lived with my family, all I wanted to do was get away from them so I could spread my wings and live life as a free bird. But after a few months, I miss them. Well, not them so much as the noise they made, the chatter, laughter and even the arguments and lectures. Living alone is so...lonely."

"Perhaps you need to get out more. It must be hard living *and* working in your flat."

Her eyes lit up. "Shall we go to a club? I heard of a new

one that plays ragtime and jazz." She did a little jig in her seat, as if she could hear the music.

I wondered if it was the club on Kingly Street where Willie and Alex had gone last night. Thoughts of them inevitably led to thoughts of Gabe, and I didn't want to be reminded of him. "I think I'll stay in, but you should go."

She leveled her gaze with mine. "Have you ever been to a nightclub, Sylvia?"

"I've been to pubs and dance halls. Nightclubs are just a combination of the two, aren't they?"

She rolled her eyes. "They are not. Perhaps there weren't many where you used to live, but they're popping up all over London these days. You simply must come with me one evening. We'll have a marvelous time, drinking cocktails and dancing the night away."

"I will go with you but not tonight."

"That's settled then." She gave me an innocent look but spoiled it with a wink. "It's like being with a man. You simply have to experience a club at least once in your life."

It was my turn to roll my eyes. "Both experiences will have to wait. I have to work tomorrow."

"If you get tired, you can nap in one of those lovely armchairs. Professor Nash won't mind. He seems very sweet."

"He is which is why I won't take advantage of him."

"I don't want to go out alone." She pouted then filled her mouth with a forkful of lasagna.

"Why not take Horatio?"

She pulled a face. When she finished her mouthful, she said, "Men won't ask me to dance with him hovering. They'll think we're together."

"Would you like to be together?"

"You are not serious." Her tone was flat.

"I suppose not."

After more deliberation, she decided not to go to the club. I suspected she was somewhat frustrated when I declared I wanted to go to bed early, however. After a poor night's sleep the night before, I was too tired to stay up late. Daisy insisted I take half of the bed while she slipped under the covers on the other side. She kept the light beside her on while she read, and I decided to read a few pages too. It wasn't until I had the green book from Gabe's library in hand that I realized my error. I would have to return to his house, after all. I needed to give the book back.

Perhaps I would send it by post or take it to the service door. Whatever method I chose, I knew avoiding him was the right course of action.

* * *

MY RESOLVE TO avoid Gabe was completely ruined the following morning when I arrived at the Glass Library to see him chatting to Professor Nash at the front desk. I paused on the threshold and merely blinked stupidly at him as I tried to sort through my scrambled thoughts. I wanted to see him. I was glad to see him. And yet I was not at the same time. It didn't make sense.

He'd been perching on the edge of the desk, and he now stood to greet me. "May I take your coat?" He helped me out of it and hung it on the stand by the door.

"Is this about the book?" I asked.

"What book?"

"The one I borrowed from you."

"No. Keep it. I don't mind. This is about the investigation. I wanted to tell you how the interrogation went last night. Cyclops telephoned me this morning." He released a heavy sigh. "It's not good. Bolton didn't confess. He denied involvement in everything—the thefts and the murder, as well as my attempted kidnapping. Not that I'm convinced he was involved in that, but there's a possibility it was linked to this case so the question had to be asked."

"Did a search of his house find any evidence?"

He shook his head. "Cyclops said they'll have to let him go if they don't find more definitive proof soon." He sat on the edge of the desk again and his thumb tapped out a rapid rhythm on his thigh. He frowned in thought. "There was one thing Bolton did take pains to mention and that is to point out he is merely employed by the Royal Academy as an administrator, not because he has any art experience. He claims to have no connection to the art world, magician-made or otherwise."

Professor Nash had been listening in and he now cleared his throat and leaned forward. "Excuse me for interrupting, but I've studied criminal behavior. It's a hobby of mine." He pushed his glasses up his nose. "If the only deviation from his denials was to point out that he has no connections to the art world. That means it's probably significant."

Gabe nodded. "Cyclops and I agree. We think he's guilty but didn't act alone. His partner has the art connections. Whether Bolton was merely the identifier of the magic art, like Mr. Ludlow was for Lady Stanhope in their scheme, or he was the mastermind remains to be seen."

"The puppet master," I murmured.

"Precisely. Whether he was or wasn't the one pulling the strings."

"I don't think he was. He looked quite deflated when he realized we'd guessed he was a magician. At the time, he reminded me of a puppet whose strings had been released. He was adrift. He didn't know what to say without someone guiding him. I think he was merely the accomplice in this crime, not the leader."

We fell into silence, considering who the puppet master could be.

Professor Nash spoke up first. "Cyclops should put more pressure on Mr. Bolton. If he applied enough pressure, he could make him confess. Mr. Bolton won't know he's actually a kind-hearted soul, so Cyclops should use that to his advantage."

Gabe and I both stared at him. He smiled back, quite chuffed with himself.

"I think Cyclops prefers to use non-violent ways of getting answers," Gabe said.

The professor merely shrugged. "It will take longer, but so be it. I commend him for his morals. So…" He removed his glasses and wiped them with his handkerchief. "Who are your other suspects? Which ones knew Bolton?"

"An employee is my guess," Gabe said. "While Bolton would have met the artists, he would have had more dealings with the staff." He turned to me, eyes bright. "The person he dealt with the most was his assistant, Driscoll."

I smiled, unable to contain it. "Mr. Driscoll was lying to us about his illness, I'm sure of it."

"What does that have to do with the theft?" Professor Nash asked.

"I don't know, but we're going to find out," Gabe said. "May I borrow Sylvia for a while?"

"Of course."

I didn't insist on staying. I wanted to go with Gabe. I wanted to see the investigation through. If my manager didn't mind, who was I to argue?

* * *

WE FOUND Mr. Driscoll standing at Mr. Bolton's desk in the manager's office, papers spread out before him. He picked one up, scanned it, and tossed it away. It slid off the desk onto the floor. Mr. Driscoll rifled through the others, creating a bigger mess.

Gabe cleared his throat and the assistant looked up. "What is it? Oh. It's you two." He straightened with a self-conscious glance at the paperwork. He shuffled some of them together into a pile.

"Leave the documents," Gabe ordered.

Mr. Driscoll's fingers recoiled as if Gabe had rapped him across the knuckles. "The police have already been here, going through his things. I don't know what you expect to find."

"We're not here to look at documents. We want a word with you."

I gathered up some of the papers. They were financial statements and receipts. Mr. Driscoll made no attempt to stop me. He focused on Gabe, not me. If he was searching for evidence that could incriminate him to destroy it, it wasn't amongst these papers.

Gabe indicated the paperwork. "Are you looking for something in particular?"

Mr. Driscoll released a heavy sigh. "The board want to know how much the exhibition has made so far. They want it today! They know Mr. Bolton has been arrested. They know I'm on my own here. I asked for an extra day's grace and they won't give it to me. They're furious with him for bringing the Royal Academy into disrepute, but that doesn't mean I should be punished!"

I handed him the papers I'd gathered. "I took your place here when you were feeling unwell."

His gaze lowered. A sign of guilt perhaps?

"You weren't really sick, were you?"

He touched his collar. "I had a sore throat."

"This is the first mention of a sore throat. Last time, you

claimed you had a cough."

Mr. Driscoll tugged on his collar and eyed the exit.

Gabe moved to block it. "Why did you stay away when you weren't ill?"

Mr. Driscoll swallowed heavily.

"Why are you lying to us? What are you hiding?"

"Nothing," he squeaked.

"We don't believe you. You're involved in the theft somehow. Either explain it to us here or go to Scotland Yard and explain it to them. I doubt they'll ask as nicely."

"All right! I give in. I'll tell you." Mr. Driscoll pushed a hand through his great wave of fringe, forcing it off kilter. "Close the door."

Gabe did as requested then approached the desk. We faced off the assistant on the other side.

Mr. Driscoll drew in a deep breath and let it out slowly. "I had nothing to do with the theft. But you're right. I wasn't ill. Someone paid me to take a few days off." He shrugged. "It was money for doing nothing. How could I refuse?"

"Who paid you?" Gabe asked.

"I don't know."

"I don't believe you."

"It's true!" Mr. Driscoll's gaze flicked back and forth between us. "He sent me a note to meet him in Green Park where he'd pay me. It was dark and he wore a hooded cloak. I didn't see his face."

"You seem to know it was a man."

He nodded. "It was. He didn't try to disguise his voice. He wasn't tall or fat, just regular sized."

"It wasn't Mr. Bolton?"

"No. I'd recognize his voice."

Gabe's thumb tapped against his thigh.

The longer the silence dragged on, the more Mr. Driscoll fidgeted with the papers. "You have to believe me! I was paid not to be here. I don't know what that has to do with your theft. The Delaroche was stolen before my absence, and the attempt on the seascape was after my return. Nothing untoward happened during my absence, so how is it relevant?"

It didn't make sense to me either. I'd been employed in his stead, so if something was due to happen then, had my sudden employment thwarted it? Had my presence hindered Mr. Bolton's plans? If so, why employ me? Why not simply tell me to go away, that he didn't need a temporary assistant?

Gabe's thumb suddenly stilled. He turned to me. From the look on his face, I knew his thoughts followed the same path as mine. And he'd jumped to the most obvious conclusion.

My mouth went dry. "It wasn't me. I didn't pay Mr. Driscoll to be sick. I'd never met him or Mr. Bolton." The words tumbled over themselves in my eagerness to deny it. At that moment, it wasn't the fear of arrest that forced my denial. It was the fear that Gabe thought me guilty.

He gently grasped my arms and dipped his head to look me in the eyes. "I know it wasn't you, Sylvia. I know you're innocent in all this."

Mr. Driscoll folded his arms over his chest, looking relieved that no one had continued to accuse him. "How do you know?"

Gabe pointed to the photograph on the wall, the one showing Mr. Bolton in uniform beside six soldiers with their arms around one another. I took it down and studied the faces. I didn't recognize any of them. I read the names written on the bottom, but they weren't familiar.

"I don't understand. Is one of these men Mr. Bolton's accomplice?"

Gabe pointed to a word at the end of the caption. "Passchendaele."

"The Battle of Passchendaele was in 1917, wasn't it? We

lost so many men there." Gabe had been there too. I remembered him saying as much. But *where* had I heard him say it?

"Sylvia, who got you the job here?"

"Mr. Bolton."

"Not who employed you. Who suggested you apply?"

My heart plunged. *Oh God.* "Horatio." He'd painted a scene from the Battle of Passchendaele on the wood panel partition in his flat.

Gabe nodded grimly. "I'm sure if we checked the military records, we'll find Bolton was Horatio's sergeant. They probably got to know one another well in the trenches."

"And they found a way to combine their respective talents and make some money upon their return to civilian life," I added, thinking it through as I spoke. "Mr. Bolton could identify magic and he was already working here at the Academy, most likely guaranteed the position of manager upon his return from the war. And Horatio knew the art world inside and out. He had the connections with the black market, where a stolen painting could be auctioned off in secret to the highest bidder without the authorities ever finding out."

Gabe nodded along, agreeing with everything.

"What I don't understand," I went on, "is what role I played in all of this? Why did I have to take Mr. Driscoll's position here?"

"We'll ask Horatio that after he's arrested." Gabe handed the photograph to a rather stunned Mr. Driscoll. "Thank you for your time. You were most helpful. May I use your telephone?"

Gabe telephoned Cyclops at Scotland Yard and told him to meet us at Horatio's flat. From the glance Gabe gave me as he listened, I gathered Cyclops was telling him I shouldn't be included.

"Thank you for your advice," Gabe said. He hung up the

receiver. "He doesn't think you should go. I tend to agree. Horatio could get violent when he realizes he's cornered."

"Don't take me back to the library," I said as we left Burlington House. "It's out of your way. Take me to Daisy's. Her flat isn't far from Horatio's so you won't lose much time."

Despite the Monday traffic, Gabe's speedy driving got us to Bloomsbury in a short time. I asked him to keep me informed before I alighted. I knocked on Daisy's door, unable to contain my excitement. Blood coursed through my veins. I could hardly stand still. If this was how it felt to defeat a criminal, I could understand the appeal of becoming a policeman or a consultant detective.

My mood dampened when Daisy opened the door. I was about to tell my friend that her friend was a thief and a liar. I needed to remember that lives were about to be shattered. There was a very real possibility she might hate me for my role in uncovering Horatio's crime.

"You don't have to knock, silly," she said. "You live here now."

"Daisy, I have something very serious to tell you."

"Is it about the scarf?" She pointed to the orange and red silk scarf wrapped around her head and tied at the side, the ends draped across her left shoulder. "I saw a model in the latest edition of *Femina* who wore a scarf this way and we decided to try it."

My blood chilled. "We?"

She walked ahead of me to the sitting room. I stopped dead.

Horatio sat on the sofa, legs stretched out in front of him and crossed at the ankles. He smiled brightly but it quickly vanished. He must have guessed that I knew by the look on my face.

"Are you all right, Syl?" Daisy asked. "You've gone pale.

Come in. Sit down and I'll make you a cup of tea. Is that why you came home early? You're not feeling well?"

She tried to usher me further into the room, but I resisted. I didn't want to get anywhere near Horatio. He'd recovered from his surprise and now his eyes darkened. Gone was the affable man, replaced by a desperate one. Desperate and dangerous.

He sprang to his feet and rushed toward us, grabbing the bronze sculpture of the basset hound off a table as he passed. He raised it to strike.

Daisy screamed and threw her arms over her head. I dodged out of the way, slamming into the wall. The edges of my vision blurred and the room tilted.

Footsteps pounded up the staircase outside. "Sylvia!" It was Gabe.

But he would arrive too late. Going by the sound of his voice, he was too far away to reach me before Horatio struck. He towered over me, the veins in his neck standing out, his face red and growing redder. He wasn't a big man, but he was big enough and the statue looked solid.

I focused on it, preparing to dodge out of its way again at the last moment when it was too late to change the angle of his swing. It was another thing my mother taught me—use the larger attacker's momentum against him.

But I didn't need to move. Gabe was suddenly there, the statue in his hand after he'd wrenched it from Horatio's grip. Horatio stood there, arm still raised, blinking stupidly up at his empty hand.

Then he tried to flee.

Gabe shoved the statue into Horatio's stomach, winding him. Horatio bent over, gasping and coughing. Gabe caught his wrist, twisted it behind his back and pushed him forward into the wall. I scrambled to Daisy's side. We clutched each other.

Gabe breathed just as heavily as Horatio but without the wheeze. He must have sprinted up the stairs to arrive in time. It was a Herculean effort. He'd sounded too far away when he called my name. "May I borrow your scarf, Daisy?" he asked between breaths.

Daisy's fingers shook too much to manage the knot, so I helped her and handed the scarf to Gabe. He tied Horatio's wrists together behind his back.

"I noticed a telephone in the foyer," Gabe said. "Daisy, would you mind telephoning the local constabulary."

I wasn't sure she'd be capable. She was speechless as she stared wide-eyed at Horatio. But she nodded and raced out the door.

Gabe sucked another gulp of air into his lungs. He seemed to be regaining his breath, albeit slowly. It reminded me of one other time I'd seen him like this, drawing air in as if he'd been the one winded, not the assailant. It had happened in the kidnapping attempt, when he'd freed himself and captured the thug who'd tried to push him into the vehicle. He hadn't exerted as much energy that time and he'd regained his regular breathing pattern faster. Then, as now, he'd suddenly and unexpectedly turned the tables.

How?

CHAPTER 18

I had no time to ponder Gabe's extraordinary efforts because Horatio had recovered enough to talk and Gabe was keen for answers.

"Why did you involve Sylvia in your scheme?"

I wasn't sure if it was the best first question, but it was certainly the one I wanted to know the answer to the most.

So did Gabe, if the rough way he grasped Horatio and spun him around to face us was any indication. When Horatio didn't answer, Gabe shoved him back into the wall. Horatio winced and coughed again.

Gabe let him go. "Bolton has already confessed to the theft and implicated you. He's blaming you for Tommy Allan's murder." It was a bluff, but a very good one.

Horatio believe him. "It wasn't me! It was him!"

"If you want us to believe you, you have to explain. Start at the beginning. Why did you involve Sylvia in your scheme?"

"She was the go-between. She delivered messages from me to Bolton. Two, to be precise."

"How?" I asked. "You gave me no messages to pass along."

"You didn't notice. They were in your coat pocket."

I'd left my coat at the library. It was the only one I owned. I'd worn it each evening to and from Burlington House because the weather was cool. I'd removed it in Mr. Bolton's office and left it there before setting about my work for the evening. Indeed, he had hung it up for me on one occasion. The other time, he'd slipped back into his office to retrieve his stick. He must have fished the note out of the pocket then.

"The first time you slipped it into my pocket at Daisy's you made a point of asking me if it was my only coat." We'd laughed about how poor I was, unable to afford another winter coat. "The second time, you called on me at the lodging house before I went to work. You pretended to gift me the painting so you could handle my coat."

"I wasn't pretending. I did gift it to you."

"I can't believe I didn't notice a piece of paper," I muttered.

"Bolton and I didn't want to be seen together too many times," Horatio went on. "We didn't want people to know we were well acquainted."

"From Passchendaele," Gabe said.

"He was my sergeant. That's when we devised the scheme, but it didn't come to fruition until this year. Our interaction has been extremely limited. On our last meeting, I told him I'd send him a new employee and he was to check her coat pockets for messages."

"You paid Driscoll to be ill for a few days," Gabe said. "Then you had Sylvia fired as a waitress and suggested she apply for the job as assistant to the manager, knowing she'd get it because Bolton would be expecting her."

"I didn't get her fired. In fact, waitressing was the first plan. I hadn't thought about removing Driscoll from the scene at that point. I knew the exhibition needed temporary wait staff, so when I heard Daisy and Sylvia wanted to meet you, I suggested they apply, knowing my influence would help. They were hired but were fired on the first day before I had the opportunity to write a note for Bolton. I had to find an alternative method and that's when I thought about paying off Driscoll and sending Sylvia in as a replacement. It was a much better idea anyway. Easier for him."

That was why Mr. Bolton hadn't looked very closely at my references. I was going to be hired no matter how good or bad they were.

"Who decided to steal the Delaroche?" Gabe asked.

"I did. I knew the owner—we were lovers. I saw the painting in her drawing room. She boasted about it being done by a painter whom no one knew was a magician. When I heard it was going into the exhibition, I told Bolton. We decided it would be our first piece. After it was delivered to Burlington House, he saw it and confirmed it was magician made, then removed it from its frame and hid it behind another until he heard from me. That's where Sylvia and her coat pocket comes in. My note told Bolton where to leave it for me to collect. I then passed it on to the buyer, a fellow I know who collects magical art."

"You'll be giving that name to the police," Gabe said.

"I can't do that. He'll retaliate."

"He'll retaliate anyway when he finds out the *canvas* was magical, not the paint. I assume that will lower the price."

His guess hit the mark. Horatio swore.

"And the second note in Sylvia's pocket?"

Horatio sighed, all the fight gone out of him. "It was where and when to meet so I could pay Bolton his half."

"What about the second painting, the seascape by Arthur Partridge? You tried to steal that too but failed."

Horatio lowered his head and nodded. "Bolton should never have tried with the police there."

"He was in the middle of taking it when he was caught," Gabe went on. "He had to think of something to point suspicion elsewhere. So he pretended to have caught Tommy Allan in the act and frightened him off just before the constable arrived. But Tommy Allan was never there. Bolton was alone the entire time."

"He got greedy. He wanted to take the seascape too."

"He accused an innocent man," I snapped. "Tommy Allan was no saint, but he didn't deserve to die for your crime."

"His death had nothing to do with me! I didn't find out about it until afterwards. Bolton called on me in the middle of the night, hysterical, telling me I had to help him. He said he received an anonymous note demanding he pay a sum of money or the police will be informed that he identified magic paintings and stole them. The note was unsigned but had a meeting time and place. Bolton went. It was down at the docks. The packer revealed himself. Bolton was angry and got into a confrontation with the fellow. He pushed him. Allan fell and hit his head before tumbling into the water."

"He might still have been alive at that point," Gabe said.

Horatio merely shrugged one shoulder. "It's not my fault. You can't blame me for his death."

"A little over two weeks ago, someone tried to kidnap me outside Burlington House. Was that you?"

"No. Why would I try to kidnap you? I didn't even know you then."

Daisy returned with two policemen. They were about to escort Horatio downstairs when she stopped them. "May I have my scarf back please?"

One of the constables untied the scarf and the other immediately clapped his handcuffs around Horatio's wrists.

Daisy accepted the scarf, smiling charmingly at the constable. "One more thing before you take him away." She slapped Horatio across the cheek, leaving behind a red mark in the shape of her hand. "Rot in prison, you pig."

The constables marched Horatio away, his eyes watering.

Another two bobbies replaced them, as well as Cyclops. He informed us that he'd telephoned Scotland Yard once he realized Horatio wasn't at home and they'd told him about Daisy's call.

Gabe repeated Horatio's confession, and afterwards, Cyclops left too.

Daisy closed the door but remained staring at it, her back to us. Her shoulders trembled, and I heard a sniff. I put my arms around her waist from behind and she leaned into me.

"I can't believe I trusted him," she said. "I let him into my home. I talked about fashion and art with him!" That seemed to be high on her barometer of betrayal.

I hugged her tightly. "He had us all duped. As awful as he turned out to be, I do think he liked you as a friend. He didn't use you." I tugged on the scarf she held. "He liked discussing fashion with you too."

Daisy suddenly turned, her eyes bright with tears but also excitement. "His flat will become vacant now. You should move in, Sylvia."

"The rent will be too high."

"Not once I start a campaign that a thief and murderer lived there. I'll tell the letting agency and neighbors, the nearby restaurant staff and shopkeepers..." She clasped my hands. "When they have trouble leasing it, you'll apply with a low offer."

I laughed, relieved she wasn't mourning the loss of her friendship. "It won't work."

"I can be very convincing."

"Besides, Horatio might not be the murderer."

She waved off the concern. "No one knows that." She took

my hand. "Come along, sit down. You too, Gabe. We all deserve a cup of tea."

Gabe and I sat on the sofa while she made the tea in the kitchen. I was still a little shaken from the experience, but my nerves were settling down again.

"Are you sure you're all right?" he asked.

I nodded. "I'm unharmed."

"You'll need to give a statement to Cyclops, but if you're not up to it today, it can wait."

I didn't particularly want to relive it, but it might be better to get it over with sooner rather than later, so I didn't forget the details. But no matter how much I thought about it, there was one detail I couldn't pin down. Everything happened so fast...that was the point, as well as the problem. "Gabe, how did you know to come up after you dropped me off outside?"

"I didn't. Not really. I just thought there was a slim chance that Horatio wasn't at home and was here instead. It was only a small chance, but a chance nevertheless. It would worry me if I left without checking. I hadn't got far so I turned around, parked, and came up."

"You heard Daisy's scream."

"Was that who it was?"

"You responded, but you seemed too far away to reach us on time. Your voice was distant, as if you were on the ground floor."

He merely lifted a shoulder in a shrug. "I took the stairs three at a time."

That explained the breathlessness when he arrived. But even so...he'd been too far away to reach me after he called out and before Horatio struck. He'd arrived in what felt like a fraction of a second.

He seemed to understand my confusion because he said, "One's perception of time alters during a crisis. For some it speeds up, for others it slows down."

He'd lived through enough crises to know.

Daisy returned and deposited a tray on the table. Instead of pouring the tea immediately, she picked up the bronze dog statue from where Gabe had set it on the floor after hitting Horatio with it. She clutched it to her chest. "Sylvia had it in hand, you know. She was about to dodge out of the way as he brought this down, then trip him over, snatch it off him and hit him over the head with it."

"Was I?" I said with a laugh. "I'm not sure I could have done all of that, although I certainly planned to dart out of the way before he cracked my skull."

She placed the statue of the dog back in its original position on the side table and patted its head as if it were a dutiful pet. "It's what I would have done." We shared a smile. It was the second confrontation where she'd screamed instead of fighting back.

After we finished our tea, Gabe drove me to the library. He parked the motor and walked me down Crooked Lane to the library's door. Although Tommy Allan was dead, and Horatio and Mr. Bolton were in prison, he still worried.

"Besides, Albert Scarrow the journalist could confront you," he pointed out when I told him I didn't need an escort.

"Speaking of journalists, do you think your kidnapping attempt is related to the article?"

"It seems an extreme way to obtain an interview."

"I don't mean the journalists are trying to kidnap you. I mean..." I sighed. "I don't know what I mean. But the timing is curious. The article about you saving the boy at the Isle of Wight appeared in the newspaper then the following day someone tried to bundle you into their motorcar."

He tucked his hands into his pockets and stared grimly ahead.

"It's just very coincidental," I went on. "Do you think

there's a connection with how you get out of trouble so easily and quickly?"

"No."

"But—"

"No, Sylvia. There's no connection. It's just a coincidence, and I'm sure it was simply a case of mistaken identity."

Which was it? Coincidence or mistaken identity? I bit the inside of my lip to stop my retort.

He opened the library door for me but did not enter. "Thanks for your help, not just today, but throughout the investigation. Take care." It was formal, and he didn't smile. He didn't even look at me. My inquiry into the kidnapping attempt annoyed him.

It likely spelled the end of our friendship, if that's what our relationship could be called. If it could be so easily ended, then perhaps it wasn't strong in the first place. I'd probably over-emphasized it in my own head.

It was for the best. I'd begun to develop feelings for him, feelings beyond friendship. But he was engaged to be married. He was not free. It was better to end all contact with him here and now rather than let those feelings grow any more than they had. The formality of our parting was safe and wise. It was the way it had to be.

We shook hands before he turned and walked away down Crooked Lane, his broad shoulders squared, his strides determined. He did not look back.

* * *

Daisy declared the early evening required cocktails. I agreed. It had been quite a day. My nerves were still jangling after experiencing every possible emotion. Working in the library for the entire afternoon had been the soothing balm I'd needed, allowing me to digest the day's events without dwelling on them. It helped to talk them over with Professor Nash too. He was level-headed and insightful. I did not mention my theory about Gabe's attempted kidnapping, however. The more I thought about it, the more ridiculous it seemed.

He was probably right. It was simply a case of mistaken identity, otherwise there would have been another attempt.

Daisy handed me a martini. "Chin up, Old Girl. I know you lost the man, but you caught a murderer and a thief." She winked. "And the man won't be lost to you forever."

I gave her a stern look. "He's getting married, Daisy."

"If I were you, I'd fight for him. Men like him don't come along every day."

"I'm perfectly happy as I am. I don't need a man in my life."

"Hear, hear." She clinked her glass with mine then sipped. "But you shouldn't let a good one walk out of your life. Not when you clearly like him. Don't let your fear get in the way of your happiness."

I spluttered. "What fear?"

"Your fear of getting too close to men." She blinked owlishly at me. When I shrugged in question, she added, "You're not scared of men, but you are scared of letting them get to know you. Gabe is the first you've allowed to get close since you've been in London."

"That's not true," I mumbled.

She barreled on as if I hadn't spoken. "It's understandable, considering your background. You had no father, and you moved a lot, so you never had many friends, and certainly no male ones."

It was true. My brother James had been the only male in my life.

"But you shouldn't let that fear dictate to you or you'll be lonely for the rest of your life. And I think I know you well enough to know you want to marry and have children, one day."

I did, but only if the right man came along.

I took a long sip of my cocktail, not wanting to consider how perfect Gabe would be as a husband and father. I hardly knew him. My emotions were still too raw after the day I'd had, that was my problem. I'd feel differently about him tomorrow.

"If you want him, you should fight for him," she said again. "I've seen the way he looks at you, and I think you're capable of winning his heart."

I quickly shook my head, wanting to shake off her words before they settled into my mind, and my heart. "He's engaged to a very nice woman."

"I don't think you're backing away from him because he's engaged. You're backing away because he's a man and he was getting close, and that terrifies you."

I drained my glass and held it out to her. "I need another cocktail, and you need to stop talking."

She took the glass with a smug smile. "I'm good at understanding people and giving advice. Perhaps I should be a psychotic."

"I think you mean psychologist, and they require a university education."

She pouted. "So that profession is off the table too. This morning I was considering acting, but I failed rather miserably in acting confident when Horatio attacked."

"You were under pressure. Why do you want to change profession, anyway? I thought you were an artist?"

She sighed as she pushed herself to her feet. "I'm not very good at painting. Horatio was just humoring me. Speaking of which, what are you going to do with the painting he gave you?"

"I don't know. I don't want it. Throw it away?"

"Don't do that. I think you should sell it. He's about to become notorious. It might increase the value of his art."

It was a marvelous idea. I could ask Freddie Duckworth or Arthur Partridge if they knew a buyer who'd want a painting done by an infamous art thief.

When Daisy handed me another cocktail, I saluted her with the glass. "You really are good at giving advice. I promise I will try to overcome my fear of letting men get close to me."

"Good. Because tonight we're going to a club."

I pulled a face. "Not tonight. I'm exhausted. Today has been a long day."

She rolled her eyes, shook her head, and gave me a genuine smile.

* * *

ACCORDING TO PROFESSOR NASH, a key component of being a librarian at the Glass Library involved knowing the content contained within the pages of the books. Having personally purchased and collected many of the books himself over the years, he was already quite familiar with them. If a patron asked him about cotton magic, for example, he knew the topic was touched upon in texts on other magics such as painting canvases and clothing. He wanted me to develop the same knowledge, over time, and suggested the best place to start was to read at least part of every book, beginning with the general ones before moving on to specialized topics.

It was going to take a lifetime to read all of them. Even just the introductions or first chapters would take years. Even so, I wasn't averse to sitting and reading. I collected an armful of books and sat at the desk in the ground floor nook. With Professor Nash's card system beside me, I could also check the books had been accurately catalogued.

The job was a dream come true for this bibliophile.

I was engrossed in learning about ceramic magic when someone cleared their throat. I looked up from the amphora painted with images of naked, athletic men to Gabe. Blushing, I quickly closed the book but not before he saw the focus of my attention.

Being a gentleman, he didn't acknowledge my blush. He held up a paper bag. "Doughnut?"

I glanced past him but couldn't see the professor.

"He's eating his at the front desk." Gabe opened the bag in front of me. "Peace offering."

"You didn't have to. There's no argument between us so no need of a peace offering."

He winced. "Actually, I have something to confess. I lied to you."

"Oh?"

"When you asked me if I knew a silver magician, I said I didn't. That part isn't a lie." He put down the bag and perched on the edge of the desk. "The lie was that I could have found out if one existed. I just…didn't." He watched me carefully, monitoring me for signs of what I was thinking.

"Does this have anything to do with how you found out Mr. Bolton was a rubber magician?"

His lips twitched in a tentative smile. "Not much gets past you. You're right. I have access to a…vast store of knowledge about magician lineages." The hesitation was telling; he didn't want to give away too much.

I understood that and respected it. Some things must remain a secret. "Your family are the keepers of this knowledge?"

He nodded. "And some others."

Again, he didn't elaborate. Whether the knowledge was written down or in someone's head, I couldn't be certain. When he'd left me in the motor to check Mr. Bolton's family name, he could have been telephoning someone or looking up a list stored in the house. Either made sense.

"When you first asked me about your family being silver magicians, I didn't want you to know that I could find out. I didn't know if I could trust you. Now I do."

Hearing that was more uplifting than it ought to have been. "I trust you too." It was said automatically, without thinking, but it came from the very depths of me. I trusted him implicitly.

He smiled. "Thank you. That means a lot to me." He lowered his gaze, as if he could no longer bear to look at me because too much was exchanged between us through glances alone. At least, that's how it felt for me. "There are no magician families named Ashe, by the way. Not in any magical discipline."

"Oh. Never mind. It was a wild theory anyway."

"There are other branches in your family, and if you don't know their names and origins, it's impossible to be sure. But there is one silversmith magician. Or there was. Marianne Folgate. Does the name mean anything to you?"

"Professor Nash mentioned someone named Marianne, but I don't know any Mariannes or Folgates."

"My parents met her in 1891, here in London. She was young, aged about eighteen or nineteen. They don't know anything else about her, whether she's alive or dead, or whether she married and had children. I'm sorry I can't give you more than that."

"It's all right. Thank you for looking into it, but I'm quite sure I'm not a silver magician. I feel no affinity for silverware."

He frowned down at the paper bag, bulging with our doughnuts. "Are you sure you're not a magician of some description?"

Of all the things he could have said to me today, that was

perhaps the most surprising. It took me several moments to recover and even then I remained speechless. I merely shrugged.

"It's just that you recognized how special the seascape was."

"Many people did, magicians and general public alike. It was beautiful."

"You also spotted the stolen canvas hidden behind the village painting. That wouldn't have been easy to see. Perhaps you were attracted to it because its magic called to yours."

"The corner had come loose. I simply happened to look over at the right time. It was more luck than anything."

He shrugged and picked up the bag. "Take one or I'll be forced to eat both, and when Willie asks me why I'm too full to eat dinner, I'll have to confess that I ate two doughnuts. She'll tell me I'm putting on weight. Next thing I know, Mrs. Ling is removing desserts and sauces from the menu. You'll be saving the entire household from bland diets if you eat your share."

I laughed. "You're very convincing."

"It's because you know I'm not joking. That's precisely what Willie would do."

I reached into the bag and as I scooped out a doughnut, I touched Gabe's hand. With a layer of paper between us, it shouldn't have meant anything. It shouldn't have sent a jolt through me, warming me from head to toe.

But it did.

I glanced up to see if he'd felt it too. Our gazes met, and I knew he had.

Neither of us moved. Both of us sat there, frozen, unsure how to proceed or what to say. With every passing thud of my heart, the intensity deepened, throbbing in time to my pulse.

Professor Nash wandered in, licking his fingers. I snatched my doughnut out of the bag. "That was the best doughnut I've ever had. Where did you get it?"

Gabe removed his doughnut too and scrunched up the empty bag. "A magician baker on—"

"Don't tell me!" The professor put up both his hands, warding Gabe off. "I've changed my mind. I don't want to know. If I know then I'll want to buy a treat every day, and Willie will soon be admonishing me." He patted his stomach.

I bit into the cinnamon goodness. He was right. It was deliciously light, and somehow retained some warmth. I savored every mouthful until not a speck of sugar was left. "There needs to be a spell that a magician baker can put on their food that will stop you putting on weight, no matter how much of it you eat."

Gabe tossed the balled-up paper bag into the rubbish bin. "The magician baker who knows that spell will make a fortune."

The professor rubbed his jaw and turned to the bookshelves. "I'm going to re-read the tomes on food magic. Sylvia, you should help me. If there's so much as a hint of such a spell, we'll find it."

I stood to follow him as Gabe laughed softly. "I told you working here wouldn't be a doddle."

"Not a doddle," I said. "But it's going to be fun if every day is like this."

He grinned. "If it makes you this happy, then I'm glad I was the reason you were fired from your other job."

"You weren't the sole reason."

"When friends ask, I'm going to tell them my version."

I laughed. I liked that he wanted to talk about me to his friends. I wasn't sure what it meant for the future, but at that moment, the future looked brighter and clearer than it had in a long time. The fog that had enveloped me ever since my brother's and mother's deaths had finally lifted.

Available from 7th March 2023:
THE MEDICI MANUSCRIPT
The 2nd Glass Library novel

A MESSAGE FROM THE AUTHOR

I hope you enjoyed reading THE LIBRARIAN OF CROOKED LANE as much as I enjoyed writing it. As an independent author, getting the word out about my book is vital to its success, so if you liked this book please consider telling your friends and writing a review at the store where you purchased it. If you would like to be contacted when I release a new book, subscribe to my newsletter at http://cjarcher.com/contact-cj/newsletter/. You will only be contacted when I have a new book out.

ALSO BY C.J. ARCHER

SERIES WITH 2 OR MORE BOOKS

The Glass Library

Cleopatra Fox Mysteries

After The Rift

Glass and Steele

The Ministry of Curiosities Series

The Emily Chambers Spirit Medium Trilogy

The 1st Freak House Trilogy

The 2nd Freak House Trilogy

The 3rd Freak House Trilogy

The Assassins Guild Series

Lord Hawkesbury's Players Series

Witch Born

SINGLE TITLES NOT IN A SERIES

Courting His Countess

Surrender

Redemption

The Mercenary's Price

ABOUT THE AUTHOR

C.J. Archer has loved history and books for as long as she can remember and feels fortunate that she found a way to combine the two. She spent her early childhood in the dramatic beauty of outback Queensland, Australia, but now lives in suburban Melbourne with her husband, two children and a mischievous black & white cat named Coco.

Subscribe to C.J.'s newsletter through her website to be notified when she releases a new book, as well as get access to exclusive content and subscriber-only giveaways. Her website also contains up to date details on all her books: http://cjarcher.com

Follow her on social media to get the latest updates on her books:

facebook.com/CJArcherAuthorPage
twitter.com/cj_archer
instagram.com/authorcjarcher